Immortal Clash

Immortal Trilogy, Book 2

James McNally

Prologue

As the girl ran through the night in the New Mexican desert, she wiped at the dried blood on her face. It wasn't her blood. Though exhausted beyond words, she couldn't rest. Not yet. Hunger made her weak, and the cold air chilled the sweat on her skin, causing a shiver to run through her body.

She was thirsty.

In the distance, a wolf howled, and the girl stopped with a gasp. The sound seemed too close. They would be there soon, and then she would die like the others. She moaned and continued forward, running to who knew where?

Remembering the carnage in the banquet hall caused her to cry, but she stubbornly rubbed away the tears. She had precious little body moisture, and crying was using up resources she couldn't afford to lose.

But still, the memories came back to her.

One minute the room was full of people, talking and laughing. Only moments later, the wolves came, killing everyone, just killing them. Why would wolves do that? She would have to grieve for her friends another time, not now. Not while her own life was still in danger. Those wolves were after her now, and she had no way to protect herself.

Heavy breathing nearby startled her. Emotionally and physically exhausted, she knew she should run, but she could go no further. Instead, she dropped into the sand and waited to die.

Cringing in a fetal ball with her head cradled in her arms, she felt the warmth of breath on her neck. The girl lifted her head, and a gasp hitched in her throat. She peered into the depths of the wolf's eyes that were eerily human in shape and color. Human brown eyes that looked back at her from the head of a wolf. When the girl released the breath she had been holding, unconsciousness devoured her before the wolf could.

***

Two raven-black wolves circled the lifeless girl, sniffing the body, and nudging her with their muzzles. When she did not respond, the wolves transformed into their naked human forms. Werewolves could not afford the luxury of modesty. The male, Gardner, stood over the girl with his mother, Maggie standing beside him.

Although Gardner and Maggie had been tracking the girl, they were not the wolves from the banquet hall from which she was fleeing. They spotted the girl running from the hacienda and followed, not to harm but to protect her. The boy and his mother were determined to protect the innocent and had been tracking the vicious pack of werewolves long before the girl's involvement. This particular group of monsters, Maggie believed, was the same pack that had infected her friend Dylan forty-one years ago. Dylan had survived his attack but at a price. One of the wolves bit Dylan, transforming him into a werewolf. Dylan's attack had happened in Yellowstone National Park. Maggie met Dylan twenty-two years after the Yellowstone attack and became a werewolf when bitten as she attempted to contain him during his change. Although Dylan could never control his wolf side, Maggie managed her beast with an ability called astral projection. Maggie was clairvoyant, but that was not the only ability she possessed. Maggie could project her consciousness out into the world during periods when her body was at rest. It was this ability—astral projection—that allowed Maggie to control her wolf. She used astral projection to watch over her wolf and even communicate with it. Maggie could stop the wolf from attacking innocent people. She learned more about being a werewolf in one night than Dylan had learned in twenty-two years. She helped Dylan control his werewolf.

Gardner had been a baby when Maggie turned, but when he reached the age of eighteen, she bit him intentionally, believing it was the only way to protect her son from the violence that followed them like a plague.

Gardner turned into a werewolf, and she helped him control the wolf.

Before Maggie met Dylan, her clan of vampires, Antony, David, and a boy vampire named Randal, had been hunting a vampire known as the Houseguest Killer (so dubbed by the media). After Maggie met Dylan, he joined the fight; and although they ultimately destroyed the Houseguest, Dylan died during the battle. Maggie vowed to finish what Dylan started and hunt down the perpetrators of the unsolved — unpunished — crime that had ended the lives of Dylan's friends. Maggie and Dylan had been planning the mission together when he had been alive, but he had died before giving Maggie enough information to track down the werewolves. Maggie was undeterred. She used her clairvoyance to track their violence. Maggie's journey began at the campsite of the attack. From there, she hunted the werewolves back to their den in New Mexico. Gardner had been almost nineteen when she turned him into a wolf. She did it, in part, because she needed his help, but there was also a selfish part of her that didn't want to watch her son grow old and die. She gave him immortality whether he liked it or not.

It turned out he did. And he was an invaluable ally.

Maggie had one more trick in her mystical arsenal. She knew when other preternatural beings were nearby because they gave off colors. It was a smoky light only she could see, and she called them auras. Vampires were always black, and werewolves gave off a brown haze. Humans had auras as well that changed depending on the purity of the soul. The glow of innocent children was nearly snow-white in appearance, and at the other end of the spectrum were murderers and rapists — whose auras had a blood-red hue.

Antony, the leader and the oldest of the group, insisted on killing the vilest humans. It was a matter of necessity that vampires drank human blood. These vampires hunted killers and rapist, and other sex offenders who the police could not seem to catch. This system of selection ensured Antony and David never put innocent lives at risk. Maggie proved the validity of their system. She had been marked for death by Antony and David, but when she turned out to be innocent of the crime of killing her child, they spared her life. She joined them because she believed in what they were doing, and she had abilities that could help them.

Randal came next. Before the Houseguest killed his human family and turned Randal into a child vampire, he had been an innocent twelve-year-old boy. David, Gardner's father, was human at the time and had been mortally wounded by the houseguest.

Antony turned David into a vampire to save his life, even though it went against his most fervent directive to never create another vampire. Antony had lost a friend in the past, not by watching him grow old, but by first turning him into a vampire and then watching him turn evil. Bane had been Antony's first time turning another vampire but ultimately had to be destroyed. Antony vowed never to make that mistake again. He broke that vow when he knew that losing David to death would be far higher than losing him to a dark path.

And possibly, deep down, Antony knew David would never drink innocent blood.

Dylan joined the group after Antony hunted him and determined that Dylan's evil deeds were his werewolf's and not a conscious decision.

Now, forty years had passed since the attack in Yellowstone, and the killer pack was in Maggie's sights.

Obsessed with the idea of infiltrating the pack, Maggie laid the groundwork for joining the crew. Aware of the danger this posed to her and Gardner, Maggie believed the benefits outweighed the risks. David objected to her plan, but she was obstinate and refused to give up the idea. Even David's reasonable arguments could not deter her from this path. And Gardner refused to let his mother do it alone. David agreed to discuss it again when they returned to Antony and the rest of the group back in Philadelphia.

"I should have known this wasn't going to be a normal family outing." David joined his son and Maggie standing over the still form.

He held out a pile of clothes, and the two naked people changed, pros at the art of the quick change.

"Who is she?" David asked.

"I don't know yet," Gardner said and kneeled to wipe some of the blood from her face. He could see no wounds and discerned the blood wasn't hers. Gardner had been looking for a bite wound but saw none. Gardner then lifted her as gently as he could and carried her back to the Zephyr.

The Zephyr was their mansion on wheels owned by Antony and dozens of other vehicles and properties worldwide. Having lived thousands of years, Antony was wealthy beyond imagination and seemed to possess never-ending supplies of "toys," as David called them.

"Does that other pack of werewolves know where we are?" David asked.

Maggie used her ability to astral project and sent her consciousness to the hacienda. She saw no evidence the wolves had given chase, so she returned to her body.

"No," she said. "I don't think so."

Maggie stayed with the girl as she lay sleeping in the queen-sized bed. Gardner and David retreated to the front of the cabin. David hopped into the driver's seat and drove the RV to their campground in the nearby town of Folsom.

As the Zephyr headed west toward town, and passed by a large rock formation, kicking up dust, a dark form stepped from behind the rocks and watched as the vehicle's rear lights faded into the distance.

Part One: Alex

Chapter One

The girl woke slowly, her vision coming into focus as if emerging from a fog. Her prone body swayed gently. *I'm on a boat.* When she managed to pull herself across the huge bed and look out the window, she saw no water, only the moonlit New Mexican desert. She was in some kind of large, well-furnished vehicle. She glanced down at the pink silk pajamas covering her body, then touched her face. The blood was gone, and her hair was clean. Someone had taken care of her.

She turned away from the window and spotted the boy sitting in a recliner next to the bed. He looked to be about her age, eighteen, or maybe a little older. He slept with his head resting on the arm of the chair, and his legs hung over the other side. *He looks so uncomfortable.* Her head tilted to the side, examining him. A slight snore emanated from him, and a line of drool pooled on the fabric under his face. He let out a chuffing sigh that reminded her of a napping dog. She stifled a giggle with her hands over her mouth. She expected to wake the boy, but he only snorted and continued sleeping.

She felt nothing threatening about him. She sensed a protectiveness about him that led her to believe he was there to guard her. He wore a tee-shirt and sweats and only a pair of clean white socks on his feet. When she refocused on his face, she saw he was now awake and looking back at her. He bolted up in his seat and wiped away the drool. He bowed his head slightly and turned away from her. She smirked. *He's trying to hide his blushing. How cute.*

"Mom," he said in a hoarse whisper. "She's awake."

The girl turned to the doorway and watched the woman approach from the front of the vehicle. The woman stopped at the entrance to the bedroom. She was smiling pleasantly. "How are you feeling, honey?"

13

"Fine," the girl said. "Comfortable. Thank you for cleaning me up." Her eyes flicked from the woman to the boy and back again to the woman.

"That would be me," the woman said. "My name is Maggie, my son Gardner, and the driver is his dad, David."

"My name is Alex." She corrected herself. "Alexandria Robinson, but my friends call me Alex." The girl suddenly looked stricken. "My friends." Her voice trailed off, and tears puddled under her eyelashes. "My friends are dead." The words caused the tears to roll down her cheeks, and she cried silently.

Maggie motioned for Gardner to leave. After the boy walked out, the woman sat down on the bed next to her. Maggie gently eased Alex's head onto her shoulder. She stroked Alex's hair, staying quiet and allowing her to grieve. When Alex's sobs tapered off, Maggie dried the girl's eyes with a tissue.

"Come join me and check out the rest of the RV."

Alex's eyes still burned from crying, but she thought she was ready to meet the rest of the people who had rescued her.

Maggie and Alex exited the room and sat down at the kitchen table just as David pulled into the campsite and the vehicle rocked to a stop. David and Gardner joined them at the table.

"Hi there," David said. Alex offered him just a hint of a smile. "If you're hungry, there are all kinds of goodies in the fridge."

"I'm fine, thank you."

"It's mostly all vegetables. Gardner does the shopping, and he's a vegetarian. But I think there is some lunch meat in there."

"She said she's not hungry, Dad. Give it a rest," Gardner said.

Alex turned to Gardner. "You have vegetables? I'll nibble."

Gardner didn't hesitate. He jumped up and rushed to the fridge, pulling out a silver tray with every vegetable imaginable cut up in an attractive display. Gardner peeled off the hard-plastic top and held the plate out to her, balanced like a professional server. She scanned the arrangement.

"It's so beautiful," she said. "I'm afraid to touch it and mess it up. Who is your caterer?"

"I did it." Gardner's jaw squared.

Alex felt the pride radiating from him. She smiled and forced away another giggle as his face reddened again, but this time he didn't turn his gaze.

"You have a good eye for color," she said. "This is amazing." She finally chose a baby carrot. Gardner set the tray on the table and chose a carrot for himself.

"I'm having trouble believing the two of you are Gardner's parents. You both don't look old enough to be the parents of an eighteen-year-old." Alex placed a hand to her mouth to prevent bits of food from flying out as she spoke.

Maggie smiled. "We are older than we look."

She didn't explain, and Alex didn't ask.

When the carrot was gone and her mouth was devoid of any stray pieces, Alex leaned forward in her chair. The three rescuers turned to look at her. "How in the world were you there when I needed you?"

"We were..." Maggie looked down and then looked back into Alex's eyes. "We were in the neighborhood for other reasons. But before we go into that, would you be willing to tell us what happened to you back at the hacienda?

Alex sat back and turned away.

"If you can't, I'll understand..."

She sat up again. "I'll tell you. I want to—need to—tell someone." Her eyes fell away from the group for a second as her memories swirled in her head. She turned and looked at Maggie. "I watched my friends die back there." She turned

15

to look at Gardner. He didn't turn away from her gaze. "I don't ever want to forget what I happened to them. My friends deserve to be remembered." She peered at David last, and his sympathetic face gave her the strength to continue.

As she began, her loud yet low voice echoed in the small space of the cabin.

Alex's Story

Amie won the contest. What kind I don't know, and she wouldn't tell. She just kept saying, "It's the ultimate." But she was most excited that she was allowed to bring two friends with her. Of course, Tom, her boyfriend, was her first choice. She decided I would be the second.

"Now, are you ready to hear what the prize is?" she asked when I had finished packing my bag and were in Tom's car, heading to her house.

"Yes," I said. "Please." I laughed.

"We are spending the weekend as guests in one of the most beautiful Spanish haciendas I've ever seen."

"We're going to Spain?" Tom's car veered slightly as his head swiveled to look at Amie in the passenger seat.

"Eyes on the road," I said from the back seat when my head whipped back and forth, giving me a kink in my neck.

Amie ignored me and continued talking. "I'm not sure where it is yet, but there's a pool and all kinds of other fun activities."

She handed me the brochure, and I could see she wasn't kidding. It looked like paradise, and yet nowhere on the flyer did it provide a location.

"It's the ultimate camping trip. At the end of the weekend, there is an amazing feast in a banquet hall that'll put any other banquets you've attended to shame."

"Hey, I'm just excited to be going somewhere besides the mall," Tom said. "Huzzah."

Amie and I shared a look and laughed.

That was Wednesday night, and the following day we were picked up by a big white bus with the words Night Wolf Cruise Lines written on the side. The driver was a blonde guy with a ponytail. He was chewing gum and smiling as we approached.

"No Cell phones," he said and held out a box full of phones.

We didn't argue or complain. We handed over the cells without a word.

As I stepped into the bus's cold, dark interior, I could tell this was no mass-produced thing. People were sitting in reclining bucket seats that looked more like recliners than ordinary vehicle seats. Chandeliers were giving off soft purple light.

There were already six people on the bus, and by the seating arrangement, we were just one group of three winners. On the right side of the bus, toward the back, was a man in a cowboy hat with two pretty girls sitting with him.

As we stepped into view, he looked up and smiled. "Two more lovely ladies to join us. Gonna be a good time, a perfect time." He pointed to the three boys in the other seats. "Thought it was going to be a sausage fest in this tin can."

I ignored him and took an empty seat farthest from him.

Tom was mesmerized by the beauties next to the Texan, and Amie had to punch him in the arm to get him to stop staring.

The three guys looked to be around 18 to 22. They wore similar dress shirts buttoned right up to their throats. These boys only casually glanced at us as we took our seats. The boys were quiet and kept to themselves, but the guy in the cowboy hat was boisterous, laughing and hollering, making his girls giggle and squeal. We ignored them, but it was apparent they didn't want to be missed.

The ride from Ohio to the hacienda was comfortable. The air conditioning was blowing, and the air was cold. After about an hour on the road, I couldn't hold it anymore, and I decided I would have to use the bathroom at the back of the bus. As I worked my way back, I passed the guy in the hat, and he grabbed my hand.

"Always room for one more in my posse," he said.

I smiled, yanked my hand away, and kept going.

"Suit yourself, Sweetheart," he said. After I walked a few steps away, he added: "you know, you'd be a might prettier if you fixed yourself up. Put on a little make-up."

One of the girls with the cowboy raised a hand to catch my attention, also speaking with a Texan accent. "Don't listen to him, Sweetie. You're one of them natural beauties."

The bathroom smelled fresh and looked amazing as well, but I heard the liquid sloshing around in the stainless-steel toilet, and my stomach lurched. Dark blue liquid sloshed about inside the bowl. I tried to hover without touching the seat, but the wavering bus made it challenging to aim. Once or twice my bare butt brushed the cold steel. Public bathrooms were terrible enough, but vehicle toilets — even one as nice as this — left me feeling skeeved out. Thank goodness there was a working sink with soap.

I walked out of the bathroom and started back to my seat. I guess the girls with Cowboy were getting bored. One of them was messing with the hair of the boy with glasses. She took the glasses off his face and held them out at arm's length. He snatched them back and awkwardly struggled to place them back on his face. The girl unbuttoned the top two buttons on his shirt. I had to cut between them as I passed, and the boy was audibly relieved for the distraction. He took the opportunity to button his shirt back up. The two boys with him were of no help. They wouldn't even look at him.

"You're a cute kid," the woman said after I passed. She resumed the task of undressing him. "You should lose the glasses and show a little skin."

18

"Leave the boy alone, Alice," Cowboy said. "Get back here."

I sat down and managed to relax for the rest of the ride.

Upon arrival at our destination, we learned that we were in New Mexico. The ride had taken twenty hours, and we arrived around four in the morning on Friday, but still, the temperature was in the high 80's. I found it strange that the driver never changed. The same driver took us the entire way without stopping or rest. Was that even humanly possible? I think that's when I first began to get suspicious of our hosts. I didn't know why I didn't trust them, so I didn't say anything.

The road to the Hacienda, County Route 31, amounted to nothing more than just a tamped down sand trail in the middle of nowhere, but the place was nothing less than spectacular. We passed through the front gates and pulled up in front of a beautiful terra cotta and stucco building that filled me with awe. The front doors opened into the foyer, and we gaped at marble statues of several naked men and women. It wasn't until later that I realized the figures were of our illustrious hosts under better scrutiny.

To the left was a kitchen the size of a school gymnasium. We toured the house and found the kitchen, and the diversity of food made my mouth water. Our hosts gave us a snack, and everyone sat with their groups as they ate.

Once everyone had finished eating, our guide, a pretty dark-haired woman with alabaster skin, took us to a staircase. The ornately carved woodwork of the handrail caused me to trace the lines with my finger, and I fell behind.

I ran to catch up to the others and was out of breath when I made it up the three flights to the living quarters. Our bags waited outside the doors to our rooms, and we unpacked. When I met up with Tom and Amie in the hallway, I noted their swimsuits. I returned to my room and donned my suit.

The first thing to catch our eye as we approached the pool was the beautifully carved stone fountain of a fish in the swimming pool's center. Crystal clear water flowed over the spout and trickled like a light spring rain from the fish's mouth into the pool. It was the most fantastic thing I had ever seen, and I couldn't wait to swim under the spray.

Terra cotta bricks, the color of dried blood, served as the deck around the pool. Tiny palm trees grew from the soil in white stone pots scattered around the courtyard. Further back, past the swimming pool, a row of arches led to another area of the compound that we had yet to explore.

"This is the ultimate," Amie said in a whisper.

"I have to get into that pool." Tom ran forward and did a cannonball into the water. A massive splash rose three feet into the air. A wave washed over the side of the pool, making the bricks look even more like blood when wet. Amie and I joined him.

We swam for a while then climbed out of the pool. A pretty Hispanic woman offered us towels on which to dry ourselves. From the open roof, sunshine covered us as we relaxed in lawn chairs. When the cowboy and his girls arrived at the pool, we decided we had had enough sun and explored our surroundings. We headed toward the arches. I worried about getting lost and suggested we head back. Tom called me a chicken, but Amie agreed with me, so we returned to our rooms.

Amie and I shared a room. The women with the cowboy shared the room next to ours. The three boys had insisted on sharing a room, and down the hall, across from the two Texan women, Tom and Cowboy bunked. However, these arrangements would turn out to be pointless since the only group to stick to this plan was the three boys. Tom came into our room with us, and the two groupies bunked with Cowboy. Each room had two queen-sized beds in them, so this wasn't that big a deal. As long as Tom and Amie were quiet about it, I didn't care what they did in the other bed.

I took a shower but ended up taking a bath, and it was a bath made in heaven. The large tub was an open marble pool set into the floor. I filled it with water as hot as I could stand and then added bath oils and fruity scented soap. I soaked in it for an hour. I didn't get out until I was wrinkly and felt thoroughly cleaned off the day's dust and grime. The room was empty when I exited the bathroom. I put on a sundress and headed to the pool. Everyone was there—even the three boys.

"Come back in," Tom said.

"I'm fine for now," I said. "Maybe later."

"Night Swim. Good idea." Tom returned to his game of splashing Amie, making her squeal and laugh.

I had napped on the bus, but I didn't feel rested, and the bath made me sleepy, so I laid in one of the lawn chairs and watched the others play. Cowboy had his hat on, but he was shirtless. A thick mat of black hair covered his chest. The two girls wore skimpy bikinis, and the three boys clustered together wearing tee shirts. The boy that the cowboy had harassed on the bus had removed his glasses. In my head, I declared him leader because the other two never seemed to do anything until they consulted with him first.

The sound of the laughter and the cool breeze blowing across the courtyard all conspired to make me fall asleep. I woke up sometime later when Amie was drying herself off. The others were off to adventures unknown, I supposed.

The Hispanic woman returned to inform us that dinner awaited.

Amie and I headed back to the room and dressed for dinner. Tom was not there, thankfully. He had had enough sense to keep his belongings in his place. I guess he was there getting dressed. Amie put on a pair of pink sweats and a tank top. I wore a pair of shorts and a baggy shirt. We met Tom coming out of his room, and we headed down to the dining hall together.

The dining hall consisted of two tables. Our nameplates denoted where we were to sit. Tom was seated between Amie and me. The boys lined up to our left and Cowboy, and his girls sat to the right of us. The second table had three men and two women sitting at it. The two tables offered just enough room for servers to move between them, and both were covered with a white silk tablecloth and decorated with red candles and flower arrangements. Servants poured drinks, and then the blond man with a ponytail stood. I recognized him as the bus driver.

"Welcome, friends." His voice was deep and straightforward, but I noted a touch of sarcasm in the word 'friends.'

I huffed, annoyed by the condemnation in his voice. Amie gave me a look. Was I the only one to hear his disapproval?

"My name is Roman. When my sister, Bethany...," he indicated the raven-haired woman to his right. "...brought us the idea to start this contest—I have to say—I was skeptical. Who would want to win a trip out into the desert? But when thousands upon thousands of entries started to pile in, I had to admit that she might have been on to something. Bethany, please stand and introduce yourself."

The woman stood to polite applause from our group.

"Good evening," she said with a smile, then cleared her throat. "I'm Bethany. I hope that your stay in our humble little abode is a pleasant one. I expect tomorrow will be even better. The activities we have planned, well, let's say if you're bored, then you just don't know how to have fun." Bethany laughed at the lame joke. "I love this opportunity to share my home with you. Congratulations on being part of a lucky few. Feel free to explore and make yourselves at home. Mi casa es su casa. You are free to go anywhere you wish." She started to sit but stopped and looked around at us. "Just don't walk in on someone getting dressed." She laughed again and sat down.

Roman stood again. "At this time, I would like to introduce you to the rest of the group. To my left are Herman and Rose."

To his left sat a very handsome brown-haired man with striking gray eyes. Next to him was a pale-complexioned girl with long red hair. Her green eyes did not reflect the smile plastered on her face like a mask. This one looked shifty to me, and I didn't trust her right from the start. Her eyes said: I have a secret. I kept my gaze on her even after Roman had moved on to introduce the others.

"Now to my right is Bethany, whom you have already met, and next to her is Vince. Vince is our newest member."

Vince stood and bowed.

"We have one more member to introduce before we eat."

At this point, the doors on both sides of the room opened, and servers started pouring in. They were Hispanic women in white outfits. They moved quickly to place food on the tables in front of us. They moved with an efficiency that seemed almost unnatural. With the meals plated, the servers hurried back out, and the most distinguished – and dare I say handsome--older woman entered the room. She was old, no doubt about that, with her gray hair tied up in a bun on the top of her head and her aged, creased skin, but she was by no means frail. She was dressed in black, walked with a stiff back, and tight, militant steps. She took her place between Bethany and Roman but did not sit down. When she spoke, her words were as tight as the bun on her head.

"Good evening, my honored guests." She glanced at each of us in turn. "My name is Minerva, the matriarch of this little group. Before we dig in, I want to share with you a little background about why you are here. Many years ago, my husband died. That is to say...murdered. This act of violence happened during a trip he and my children had taken to the Yellowstone National Park. My grief had been profound. Recently, our beloved Bethany came to me with a proposal. She asked me to put aside my grief and invite people to come here, into our home, and take part in a little soiree. She suggested a celebration of his life rather than perpetual mourning. At first, I wanted no part of this; but then I began to think about Arthur, my husband, what he would want. I concluded he would insist that I celebrate his life. He enjoyed life too much to let his memory fade away in such a morbid and depressing manner. In the end, it was the natural thing to do, so we went with Bethany's plan to host a contest free of charge and throw the winners a party: the reason you have come to be here today. May Arthur look upon us from wherever his soul has gone and rejoice."

There was soft reluctant applause, and Minerva smiled at us. The skin around her eyes formed deep wrinkles, and her irises seemed to turn black. She clapped as well.

Her hands dropped to her sides as the applause died down. "Now, without further ado, let's eat." '

She sat.

When the group at the head table lifted the lid on their trays, we did the same.

I stared in disbelief at what we uncovered. We saw buttery, roasted potatoes, grilled vegetables, and salads. I am a vegetarian, so these were the dishes I chose. But there was also a whole roasted pig with a baked apple in its mouth (Cowboy took the apple out of its mouth and ate it. The girls squealed). There were lamb chops and rotisserie chicken and grilled corn on the cob, something I'd never had that before. The food was delicious, and we all stuffed ourselves, even the skinny groupies with Cowboy gobbled up tons of food.

After dinner, the three groups hung out in the lounge area. The only takers were Cowboy and his crew. We returned to our room, as did the three boys. When Tom and Amie started fooling around, they made plans to go to his room while Cowboy was out, but I told them to stay, and I would go for a walk. I felt too wound up to sleep anyway.

I strolled lazily through the main building and studied its architecture, even though I had no idea if this place was the Mediterranean style or Colonial Revival. I just thought it was pretty and wanted to see more. I ended up in a dark room and—I thought—empty. It wasn't. I walked deeper into the room and heard: "You're not in here by yourself, you know."

I jumped at the voice, a husky, deep, almost hypnotic tone.

"Who's there?" I asked. A shadowy movement to my left caught my eye. As my vision adjusted to the darkness, I was able to make out the boy I had deemed the leader of the three-boy group sitting in a recliner. I stood in front of the chair across from him. "Mind if I sit here?"

He motioned with one hand that it was okay.

"Do you usually hang out in the dark?"

"Do you?" he said.

I ignored him. "What's your name?"

"'Chuck," he said. "Charles Bolen, but call me Chuck." Then he added, "If you want to, I mean."

"'I'll call you Chuck. My name's Alex." We formally said 'hi' to each other and then fell into silence for a while.

Chuck started to say something but stopped.

"Did you win the contest?" I asked. "Or are you a guest?"

"Yeah," he said. "I won. Did you?"

"No, my friend Amie did."

"I wasn't allowed to tell my friends where we were going. Were you allowed to know?"

"No," I said. "We were kept out of the loop as well."

"I think it's strange that no one knows where we are, and we aren't allowed to have our cellphones. We could disappear, and no one would know what happened to us."

I felt a chill pass through me because I had been thinking the same thing. Why did I agree to come here?

Even in the darkness, the fear and anxiety on my face made Chuck smile.

"I'm sure someone knows we're here—authorities or someone. There must be proof somewhere of this contest, right?"

"Would you mind going for a walk with me?" I was suddenly uncomfortable sitting in the dark.

He nodded, and we walked through the halls, passing by empty rooms. We entered a courtyard and passed by the windows of vacant buildings. There were no locks anywhere. We could walk out the door at any time, which reassured me because if our hosts held us against our will, surely there would be better security. The windows would have bars and the doors locked, wouldn't they?

We passed by the pool, and I suddenly wanted to go for a swim. I would strip off all my clothes and immerse myself in the cold water so that I could free myself of this searing wave of panic that surged through me. I didn't, of course, and we kept walking.

We entered another building, and in a short time, we were standing in front of the double doors leading to the banquet room. I stared at them. They were the doors to our freedom because, after the banquet, we would be on our way home, and all this nonsense about being trapped would be over. I reached for the left door handle, but Chuck stayed my hand.

"We shouldn't," he said.

"Why?" I asked. He thought for a moment, then dropped his hand away. I opened the door.

The banquet room was cool and dark. I felt around on the wall until I found a light switch. It was a dimmer dial, and I turned it up to make the room as bright as possible. We looked around the room in awe. The vaulted ceilings seemed to rise above us into the heavens, and curved rafters looked like the rib cage of a giant animal: a dragon, perhaps. A thick, enormous table ran down the center of the room.

The room itself was devoid of any decorative paraphernalia, but the architecture alone made it look magnificent.

Feeling a draft near my legs, I looked down at a vent with a grill set into the wall. Looking around, I saw several more on each wall. I knelt and, with my hand against the grate, felt the air blowing.

When Chuck finished admiring the room, he looked at what I was doing. Although I hadn't asked, he explained the vents.

"This room is in the center of the main building. Look around. There are no windows. Those vents, I'll bet you, lead directly to the outside. That's why you feel airflow. Without those vents, this room would be stuffy and dry. Might just as well be a closet."

As I stood to take a last look around, a door on the other side of the room opened, and the host known as Vince entered. He spotted us and walked toward us.

"What are you doing?" he asked, trying—and failing—to sound pleasant.

"Exploring." I'm not sure why, but I stepped in front of Chuck.

"Explore somewhere else, or better yet, go to bed. You're not supposed to be in here."

"Bethany said we were free to go anywhere." I took a step toward him. "And if we aren't allowed in here, you should lock the doors."

After a moment of hesitation, he said, "whatever, just get out."

Something in his voice left no room for discussion.

We left. Chuck walked me back to my room. He stayed at his door until I entered the room. As I slowly closed the door, I could still see him. He didn't open his door until I was inside my room, and the door was closed. Only after he heard the click of my latch fall into place did I hear his door close. I leaned against the door, smiling.

My smile faded as I stepped into the room and realized there was more than just Amie in her bed. Although the room was dark, the moon glow from the window lit enough of it to let me that Tom was lying next to her. Their prone bodies covered with a thin silk sheet outlined every curve so well I could see their nakedness. Sighing, I stripped down to my panties and bra and climbed into my bed. Sleep came to me that first night, but it was fitful and sporadic. I had nightmares.

I woke before Tom and Amie, so I was the first to get showered and dressed. I went out looking for Chuck. I went to the pool, but he wasn't there. It was still early, so I relaxed by the pool and waited for others. I didn't see Chuck until breakfast. Although they didn't assign seats this time, Chuck sat with his two friends, and I sat with mine. I started thinking I would shake things up a little. I wanted to start seeing a little intermingling of the groups, so I decided to sit with Chuck and his group at lunchtime. Amie — and Tom, too — were welcome to come, but I had little faith they would make that move.

Bethany's plan to blow our minds with a great time included a series of competitions, complete with prizes to be won. The teams were random for each game. The first was a relay race that included an obstacle course. My teammates for the competition included Chuck's taller friend and one of the cowgirls, as I had begun to call them. Amie's team included Chuck and the Cowboy himself. I ran against Amie and the cowgirl on Tom's side, made it through the relay first, and then handed off to Chuck's boy. And wow, he was fast. His competition was the Cowboy, which was no competition at all. The last one to finish the race was Tom. To his credit, though, the girl in his group was a total head case. Several times she had to be told where to run. Her idea of running was a quick scuttle. I was embarrassed for her.

The next competition was a swimming race, which was a brilliant move as everyone was all sweaty and gross from running. The water felt good. This time I teamed up with Tom and Chuck. I am not a great swimmer, so Tom and Chuck had to carry that race.

Amie and I were on the same team with Cowboy for the scavenger hunt, but we broke for lunch first. As planned, I sat next to Chuck. His friends refused to look at me. Amie looked at me as though I had betrayed her. Tom didn't care. Chuck let me know he was happy I was sitting next to him, which made the awkwardness easier to take.

We resumed the scavenger hunt. As Amie and I walked the stone path between the main hall and a smaller building looking for our most elusive 'treasure'—something purple— I noticed a narrow pathway between two buildings that was gated. I was curious to know what was beyond that gate. Amie pulled me away before I could enter it and see what was on the other side.

While we hunted for our secret treasures, I thought about that gated alleyway. But after we had managed to find almost everything on our list, the purple object still eluded us. Amie had given up and gone off in search of Tom. I found myself going back toward the gated alleyway. I tried the latch, and it opened. Looking around for any witnesses and seeing none, I continued. The two buildings' gabled roofs forming this alley touched and made a kind of ceiling above my head. After a hundred yards or so, the aisle ended, and I found myself standing in the most beautiful garden I had ever seen. At one end of this hidden enclosure was a myriad of colorful flowers. Closer to me was a vegetable garden. I could see all kinds of vegetables growing in rows.

The backs of other buildings surrounded the enclosure. Other than dropping down from one of the buildings' roofs, there seemed to be no other way into this area except the way I had come. I walked the path through the plants to the center and stared in awe at the brightly colored stones of a koi pond. I watched as several of the fish skittered lazily through the crystal-clear water. They were as multicolored as the stones and hard to spot except when moving. I watched the koi for several minutes before noticing the pedestal jutting from a stone base on the other side of the small pond. I walked around the water and looked over the plaque bolted to the stand.

In Loving Memory

Arthur

I turned around and scanned the multitude of plants growing in the dark soil, which was not sand but some other fertile type of dirt brought in for the sole purpose of fertilizing this garden. There were tomatoes and peppers and cucumbers ripening on their stems. Further on, I saw pumpkin and corn plants still not even close to producing fruit.

I examined a ripened pepper and considered plucking it off the bush and eating it when I heard: "I see you found my secret garden."

Startled, I let the pepper go and stood. Minerva approached from the opening to the alley. She was holding a wicker basket in her right hand, and from it, jutted a white pair of gardening gloves and pruning shears.

"I'm sorry, I..." I struggled for words, my face heating up.

"Hush, child." She gave a dismissive wave of her free hand. "You are perfectly welcome here. You can help me. I'm picking flowers for the banquet. I think I'll use roses to create the centerpieces. But first..." She took my arm and led me toward a patch of purple flowers. She picked one and placed it in my hair.

"It's an Ecuador Princess...for the treasure hunt. This garden is the only place to find anything purple, so you're sure to win." She laughed heartily.

We moved on to the roses, and she donned the gloves. She used the pruning shears to clip about a dozen flowers with long stems. "The trick is to cut them at an angle, so the water can be sucked up through the stem easier, extending their life."

When she finished, she turned to face me. "Now, let us pick a few vegetables for salads. You were eating vegetables from this very garden at dinner last night."

"They were delicious," I said.

"I noticed you didn't touch any meat." Her head was tilted down so that she was peering at me through her upper eyelashes.

"I'm a vegetarian." I chewed at my lower lip.

"You should have told us we could make meals that cater to your specific dietary requirements."

"The food was amazing." I had suddenly grown distracted by the cluster of roses sticking out of her basket. Red roses. "I was stuffed when I left the table."

"I'm glad," she said and smiled. She must have seen that my eyes were on the flowers in her basket because she took one, used some kind of stripping tool to remove the thorns, and handed it to me. She then turned to the vegetable plants and walked away.

When she had collected all the vegetables, including some herbs growing in a small pot among the other plants, she led me back through the alley and out the gate to the central courtyard.

We parted ways. Minerva walked toward the kitchen, and I headed to the main hall to turn in my purple flower for the scavenger hunt, then decided I wanted to go for a leisurely swim. Amie and Tom were already in the water making out. I told them PDA's were annoying and gross. They pulled away from each other, and Amie splashed me. Tom cheered for me as I made my way into the water. I was finally starting to relax. I swam over and hovered under the water, cascading off the lip of the fountain fish. It felt good to be cold and wet.

At dinnertime, as I had at the previous meal, I sat with Chuck. His two friends sat away from us, and Amie and

31

Tom sat at the other end of the table. I told Chuck about the secret garden and the koi pond. He said he wanted to see it.

"I'll show you when we have free time."

Dinner arrived, and what a feast it was. I ate a salad made from the ingredients picked from the garden. Minerva winked at me as I ate. I smiled and nodded my approval.

Bethany passed out the awards for the competitions after everyone had finished their meal. The scavenger hunt winners were Amie, Cowboy, and I, thanks to that purple flower. The prize for winning was a pass for each of us to the Albuquerque Zoo.

After dinner, we all split up into our groups. The three in Cowboy's group went their own way, as Tom and Amie did their thing. Chuck and I went for a walk. I invited his two friends, but they declined and went back to their room. I distinctly got the impression they were not happy with Chuck spending so much time with me.

"Tomorrow's the last day," Chuck said as we wandered through the compound. He sounded unsure of something.

"You still think we're not leaving here," I asked.

"I know we're not," he said. I stopped and grabbed his arm. He continued. "A girl is talking to me. I know this is the end. I'm probably dead already and just don't know it yet." He looked over carefully to gauge my reaction to his comment. I smiled, and he relaxed, content that his joke had not fizzled.

"How long did it take you to wiggle that one out?" I asked.

"A long time." He exaggerated the word 'long.'

I suddenly had the urge to take his hand but refrained. I wanted to see if he would take mine. When he didn't, we continued in silence.

I decided I had to break the silence and end the tension. "Your friends don't like me, do they?"

"They don't trust you." He twisted his hands into knots. "I mean, they need to get to know you. I've been friends

32

with them since childhood. Billy is the tall guy. When he gets nervous, he stops making sense. Girls make him nervous, so he doesn't talk to them if he can help it. Paul is the other one. He will speak his mind, and I'm worried he'll offend you, so I tell him to keep his distance. They think you'll hurt me if that makes any sense."

"It does," I said. "And for the record, I'm hard to offend. Tell your friends to stop worrying about petty things and get to know me. I want to meet them."

As if brokering a business deal, Chuck nodded. "I'll arrange a meeting."

I laughed at how he said it, and I could tell he wasn't sure why I was laughing, but he laughed, too. Without thinking, I reached out and hugged him. At first, he stiffened, then relaxed. As I pulled away, our cheeks brushed together. I wanted to turn my head and see if our lips would meet in a kiss but thought moving too fast might scare him away. I wasn't that kind of girl, anyway.

We grew quiet again for a time, but it wasn't an uncomfortable silence, just a peaceful one. We walked like that for a while. Chuck turned and was about to say something but stopped. I stood, waiting, but neither spoke when we heard voices beyond a nearby open door. We stared at each other, frozen, listening. Two of the voices belonged to Minerva and Bethany. There was a third voice — a man — that I didn't recognize.

Bethany: "Everything is ready for tomorrow's feast."

Minerva said, "Good, good. I want everything to be perfect. No mistakes. Who has that big man with the hat?"

The unknown male: "He's mine."

Minerva again: "I have some concerns about this group. There have been too many questions. I'm not sure if I trust that this was a successful campaign. Maybe we should call it off. Send everyone home early."

Bethany, sounding annoyed: "the campaign has been flawless. Your concerns are unfounded."

Minerva: "what about the reports that there have been figures spotted outside the compound, snooping around?"

The male voice said, "just a pair of lone wolves. They are maybe looking to join a pack. That is not related to this campaign. We can deal with that after."

At this point, Chuck pulled me away from the conversation. I didn't understand anything they were saying. Chuck looked as though he had just heard the voices of ghosts, however. He was visibly shaken by what he had heard.

"We shouldn't have heard that," he said.

"Why?" I asked. "What did you get from that conversation?"

"Nothing good." He didn't elaborate.

We returned to our rooms. My sleep was fitful and troubled, but we were going home the next day, so I wasn't too surprised. I usually have trouble sleeping before a long trip. Still, I couldn't shake the unease Chuck's agitation caused in me.

I woke late and missed breakfast, then fiddled around until lunch. I sat with Amie and Tom near the pool after I tried and failed to find Chuck. At lunch, I sat with Amie and Tom, discouraged and a little heartbroken when Chuck didn't show. Was he avoiding me?

After lunch, I returned to the room to pack. We placed our bags outside the doors to our facilities as per instructions Bethany had given us at lunch. Chuck still hadn't made an appearance by this time, and I couldn't help but try and rationalize his behavior. Were his friends pressuring him to ignore me? They believed I was setting Chuck up to be hurt, and I understood their fear, but it was unfounded. I knew that if they got to know me, they would see I was nothing to be feared.

My concern turned to anger, so I decided I had to talk to Chuck before heading out. When I finally spotted him sneaking into his room, I cornered him and forced him to speak to me. He seemed distracted. "Why have you been avoiding me?"

He ignored the fact that he had been avoiding me, or so I thought. Instead of answering that question, he asked one of his own.

"Why are we leaving so late?"

I cringed. At first, I figured Chuck was trying to change the subject, but something in his face looked so scared it caused me to forget what I had confronted him about in the first place. I shook my head questioningly, but he wasn't even looking at me. He swiveled his head as if trapped and looking for an escape.

"What's going on?" I asked.

Chuck's scared and darting eyes only met my confusion.

He seemed to look at me for the first time when he spoke again, clearly addressing me this time. "The banquet is at seven. We'll be on the road by nine or so. Why? Why not just wait until morning? What's the rush?"

"'It's a long trip. Our hosts want to get us home. What does it matter? We'll sleep on the bus tonight instead of tomorrow night. I, for one, am happy about that. This place is excellent, but I want to go home." I was annoyed he was making such a big deal out of this.

He didn't say anything. He just stared at me with that lost look in his eyes. This look told me he had given up. He was a person who had been sentenced to death and had run out of appeals. When he could no longer take my questioning gaze, he dropped his head and walked away.

As we entered the banquet hall through the large double doors beyond the arches, we were ushered to our seats by the Hispanic servants. As with the banquet, this final feast was had our names telling us where to sit. On our plates was a black cloth I thought was a napkin, but when I picked it up and looked at it more closely, I realized it was something else. I looked down the length of the table at Chuck. He was lifting the black cloth with two fingers, holding it out as though it was contaminated. I scanned the room, but no one else seemed the least bit concerned about the black cloth folded on their plates.

Our hosts entered the room through the door at the other end of the hall. I watched as Bethany strode past us to the double doors and closed them with a resounding boom that caused all random conversations to stop. She smiled, clearly pleased by the startled faces sitting around the table. She returned to her place at the other end of the table. I didn't have a good view of our hosts, and I leaned forward to see past Amie and the rest. Our hosts seemed to be in a huddle, discussing something to which we could not hear. Minerva took a seat at the table's head with Bethany and Rose to her left and Roman, Vince, and Herman. There was a good four or five feet of the table between their group and ours. When their conversation ended, Bethany pushed her chair back with an ear-splitting scrape of wood on stone and stood. She strolled toward our end of the table and paced the area behind us.

She spoke loudly. "Good evening to you all. If you look at your plate, you'll see a black cloth. This cloth is a blindfold. We ask that you put these on at this time. We have a special event planned, but before we get started, we wish to have your cooperation." She walked around and helped people put their blindfolds in place. I watched as Chuck put on his blindfold, moving like a robot performing a menial task. I then put on my blindfold, purposely leaving it loose. Bethany didn't check it.

The room had grown preternaturally quiet. I could feel the tension coming from the other guests like a wave of heat. The anxiety caused a lump to form in my throat that I couldn't seem to swallow away. I wished they had at least poured us drinks first.

The events that followed happened so quickly I have trouble remembering what order they occurred, so I'll recall it in the order the facts come to me.

My blindfold slipped further off my eyes. I turned my head and saw Amie sitting next to me with a nervous smile on her face. The smile quickly faded as the room filled first with growls and then with screams. Amie slammed into me from the side, sending me sprawling onto the floor. I reached out to grab something to stop my fall but only managed to snag a fork. I took it with me and scampered up against the wall. I ripped my blindfold off completely.

All around me, people were rushing to escape their seats as the attack commenced. I watched a ginger wolf pounce and pushed Amie to the floor. The wolf tore out her throat. Someone ran past the wolf, and it took off in pursuit.

I crawled over to Amie. Through my tears and the blood that had gotten into my eyes, I saw Amie's dead eyes staring up at the ceiling. Blood still oozed from the terrible gash in her neck. I shook with terror and rage as I looked around for something to strike. If I was going to die, I was going to die fighting.

I spotted Tom lying in a puddle of his blood. A yellow wolf was gnawing at his torso, breaking through his ribcage with powerful jaws. All fight drained out of me at that moment, and my despair threatened to cripple me.

Cowboy ran toward the door at the other end of the room, but a wolf took him from behind. The force of the attack caused his hat to fly away from him. I heard the gruesome crack of his skull hitting the hard stone floor. Blood oozed from his fractured skull, and I could tell he was dead by the slack way his body moved when the black wolf tore at his back—like a bear ripping into a deer carcass.

Tears streamed down my face in rivulets, mixing with the blood, and I could taste it on my lips. I backed up until the wall stopped me, and I dropped to the floor, exhausted.

A severed arm skittered across the floor in front of me as I struggled not to scream.

To my left, the door was blocked by the ginger wolf, eating the blonde girl.

I looked up and saw Chuck's face appear at the edge of the table. His glasses were gone. There was blood on his face. His eyes seemed more alert than I had remembered seeing them in the past few days.

He spoke. "They lead outside."

I shook my head in desperation. "I don't understand."

Chuck didn't say anything more. He simply averted his eyes to a fixed point in front of him. I followed his gaze to the spot on the wall: the vent.

He reminded me of the vents in the wall, and there was one right next to me. I looked down at my hand and saw the fork still clutched in my fist. I used it to pry the grating from the wall and crawled inside. There was enough room for me, but Chuck was too big. He wouldn't be able to fit his broad shoulders through the small opening. Inside the vent, I turned around so that my head poked out of the hole. I motioned for him to follow, to at least try to escape. He shook his head and motioned for me to go.

I couldn't leave him behind. I tried again to convince him to follow me, but a silver wolf leaped onto his back. I gasped and ducked inside the vent. I heard tearing, wet cloth, maybe. Blood splashed to the floor in a wave, and I used my fist to stifle a scream.

Then I heard a cracking sound like a drumstick ripped from a turkey carcass. Chuck's head dropped to the floor, and I had to swallow the scream with the vomit that rose in my throat. I crawled away after that. I could feel a breeze blowing against my face, and I followed it. I don't know how long it took me to get out of the vent, but as soon as I located the cover leading to the outside, I kicked it off and ran. I didn't know where I was running to, only that I had to get as far away from that house as possible.

"I ran until I collapsed from exhaustion. A wolf was on me when I passed out. I don't know how I survived being that close to a wolf without being killed. Was it there when you found me?"

Maggie and Gardner exchanged a glance.

"That wolf was no danger to you," Maggie said.

Alex blinked, confused.

"Alex, Honey, I have something to tell you. I need you to listen because everything you know about the world is going to change."

"First, understand is that those six people back at the hacienda were werewolves. Can you accept that?"

"If you'd asked me less than a week ago, I would have thought you were crazy." Alex's voice dropped to a whisper as she continued. "But I was peeking. I saw them change. I believe you."

"Good because it's not over yet. For the next bit of information, you need to stay calm and understand that what you are about to hear doesn't change the fact that we are here to help you. We three are no danger to you. Do you believe me?"

Alex nodded hesitantly.

"I need to hear you say the words, Sweetie." Maggie tilted her head slightly.

"Yes." Alex gave a stern nod. "I believe you."

"Ok, good. Now we have established that there are werewolves in the world. There are other preternatural beings as well."

"Such as vampires," David said.

Alex turned and looked at him. He was smiling, and she noticed his fangs, which she hadn't seen when she first met him.

"You?" A shudder passed through her.

David nodded. "But I won't hurt you."

She nodded and tried to offer him a smile in return.

"And neither will we," Gardner said from behind his mother.

"Are you vampires too?" she asked.

"No," Maggie said softly. "We are werewolves."

Gardner's hand rested on her shoulder, and Maggie reached up to touch it. "Gardner was the wolf in the desert."

Alex peered up at Gardner. "My guardian werewolf."

"I'm impressed at how well you're taking this," Maggie said. "Though, I was where you are at one time. I took the news in much the same way."

Alex leaned forward. "When you know, you know. It's as simple as that."

Maggie smiled and reached out to caress Alex's cheek.

"While we are on the subject," David said to Maggie. "There's something you never explained, and I never understood."

She gave him a questioning look.

"On that first night when the wolf bit you, your wound healed almost immediately. How did you do that?"

Maggie shrugged. "I guess you change right away. The poison works that fast."

"Poison?" David said.

"Yes," Maggie said. "Don't think of the werewolf infection as a disease that would take days or even weeks to incubate. It's more like a poison — think: snakebite — and the poison can spread in a matter of minutes."

"I see." David offered an enlightening nod.

Maggie turned back to Alex. "You will have more time to learn everything we know, but for now, let's stick to the events of last night. We were in the desert tracking the group that killed your friends. We, too, have a history with them — in a matter of speaking. We have other friends who can help us take them down. Now that we know where they are, we can destroy them."

"They know about you," Alex said.

"What?" asked David.

"They know about the two of you," she corrected, pointing to Maggie and Gardner. "When Chuck and I overheard their conversation, they were talking about the two of you."

"Yes, they probably were," Maggie said. "But you also said they thought we were looking to join their pack. We can use that to our advantage."

"Well, one thing's for sure," David said. "We certainly can't stick around here much longer. We should start heading back to PA at first light."

"No," Maggie said. "We're staying."

"Why?" Gardner and David asked at the same time.

"Because I still want to get inside that compound."

Chapter Two

As Randal drained the last of the blood from the murderer lying beneath him, he sat up and wiped the dribble of gore off his chin. Wasting no time, he reached into his belt and pulled his Tanto blade from its sheath, using it to decapitate the corpse. He disposed of the corpse in the Schuylkill Canal and waited until the body parts sank into the muck before moving on.

He strolled along the road back to town at a human pace, kicking at rocks and raising clouds of dust around his canvas sneakers. He turned a corner and peered down the street at the burned-out structure where he and his mother, father, and sister had called home. Randal had walked that dirt path from the park many times. Randal spent the last several years trying to forget his dead family, wishing only to look toward the future because the past was just too horrible to relive for eternity.

The city should have demolished the house years ago, but after the tragedy that had befallen Randal's family, the neighborhood slowly disintegrated, and the street abandoned. No one had bothered to destroy the house since no one wished to rebuild. Randal looked to his left and right, then entered the structure.

In his mind, he could hear the echoes of all the fun, pain, and boredom he felt when he'd been a member of that house. All that ended the night the Houseguest Killer burst through the front door. Cindy, his father, and mother were all dead, his mortal world gone. What had taken its place was a never-ending nightmare life that he despised. Randal's anger intensified the longer he stood over the ruined relics of his lost humanity, and Randal could not shake off the rage, no matter how hard he tried. Unable to trust himself, he left the house through the front door without looking back. Randal often felt like a ticking bomb, ready to destroy everything around him. He had considered on more than one occasion leaving the group before he had the opportunity to hurt them. But where would he go? Maggie, David, Gardner, Antony--they were his family now. He loved them and appreciated what they had done for him. They rescued him from the creator who meant to torture and humiliated him. He couldn't leave them and would never disappoint them. Well, not intentionally.

But the anger was still in him, and if he didn't learn to control it, he would eventually do something he would regret. Randal thought perhaps the rage stemmed from the Dark Father. But recently, he discovered a grimmer truth about himself.

Thinking that his creator, the one he called the Dark Father, was the source of his troubles, Randal had confronted the father alone. It had been a foolish move. Dark Father and his minions surrounded Randal. Outnumbered and alone, Randal's distress led Maggie and the others to the mansion. They came to save Randal and destroyed the Dark Father in the process.

But not without casualties.

Dylan had been killed in the fight to free Randal. Dylan had been the newest member of the group, and although Randal had not known him that well, Maggie was quite fond of him. Maggie had lost someone she cared about because of Randal's foolish actions. Did she blame him? Perhaps, but it didn't matter because Randal blamed himself. And there it was: Randal hated himself for what he had done to the group.

He glanced around and found himself circling the park once again near his old house. He had gone the entire circumference of the park when the woman finally came into view. She stepped away from the trees and walked toward him. If he had not gotten lost in his thoughts, he might have seen her sooner.

As she grew closer, he realized she was a vampire. The five men hiding in the shadows of the pines were also vampires. The woman approached Randal without fear. He didn't retreat and instead waited for her to cross the distance between them. The woman was strangely familiar.

"Who are you?" Randal asked as she stopped directly in front of him.

"You don't remember me, honey?" she asked. Randal looked into her blue eyes. He studied her black hair. She looked so much like his dead mother that he thought he was looking at a ghost.

"Who are you?" Randal said again.

The woman dropped her head sadly. "I remember the night you attacked very well." She looked into his eyes. "You called me your mother then came at me and drained me, left me to die. I turned immortal and knew nothing of what I was, what I needed to know. You left me to fend for myself. Instinctively, I knew to get to safety before sunrise. My need for blood drives me to take victims randomly, but I didn't understand that I was making more of our kind. Not at first, anyway. I had quite a group of followers at one time, gone now, destroyed by the sun. I now know to destroy the bodies of my victims before they turn. I only have the five now. I'm sure you've seen them, hiding in the bushes. They're a moronic bunch, but they're loyal. And we take care of each other. We hunt in the low-rent district where there are fewer worries over the missing, but I return to this park every night in hopes of seeing you again."

Randal stared at her for a moment, then looked around. "It happened right over there, near the benches."

"You remember."

"Yes," Randal said.

"I saw you again several nights ago. You've been back here often. Why is that, I wonder? Were you looking for me as well?"

Randal didn't respond.

The woman sighed. "No worries. We found each other now."

"What do you want from me? Revenge? An apology? I was a fledgling myself when I turned you. I never meant to make you immortal. I didn't know I could pass on..." He almost said, 'the curse.'

The woman laughed. "Don't be sorry for giving me eternal life."

She stepped closer, and he took that as a threat. He hissed, showing his fangs. She backed off, her hands raised in a display of trust.

"I don't want to harm you. I've been watching you. I see that you take murderers and rapists for your victims. The world is full of bodies ripe for the picking, and you limit yourself to killers. Why is that?"

"You should know that if you continue to kill innocent victims, my family will destroy you."

"You're threatening me? I come here with the most honorable intentions, to ask you to lead us--to teach us--and you want to kill us?"

Randal's eyes widened. "That's not what I meant. It's just that they hunt killers of the innocent, and if you kill innocent people, they will know, and they'll come after you."

"That's exactly why I want you to join us. Leave here with us and teach us how to live among the living. This place holds nothing but bad memories for you. Why do you torture yourself? We could be your family. after all, you made us."

"I am happy where I am."

"I don't believe you."

"I'm leaving now, and if your flunkies try to stop me…."

The woman barked a laugh that cut Randal off. "We won't stop you."

He took a step backward, never taking his eyes off the woman.

"We'll do what you say and not kill innocent people, so don't unleash your ferocious family on us. If you decide to change your mind, though, I'll be right here. Come back to me at any time. The offer still stands."

Randal didn't respond. He stared at the woman for a moment longer, then sped away in a crackle of wind and sound, returning to an empty house. Antony must still be out hunting, he surmised.

Then David, Maggie, and Gardner had gone off in search of a murderous pack of werewolves without inviting Randal along, but he didn't want to go anyway, not really. Killing werewolves didn't sound like a good time to him. To be honest, he didn't understand why they should be so concerned with other immortals in the first place. The woman he'd met in the park and her minions came to mind. He thought that maybe he held a certain amount of responsibility to her. She was his creation, and her actions reflected on him. It came to him suddenly that he didn't even know her name. She said they had been killing indiscriminately. Maggie would sense that when she returned. Randal needed to intervene. It would be bad enough when they learned he had accidentally created another immortal but then discovered he had allowed them just to run around killing innocent people.

Maggie would be furious.

Randal had confided something to Maggie that he hadn't dared reveal to the others. He had told her of his views on killing innocent people. Randal explained that he sometimes felt the urge to explore other options. Maggie expressed openness to understand this desire to seek new and—dare Randal to say—innocent blood, though she warned against it. Till now, he had been able to curb his appetite to strike out against people who were not acceptable targets by his family's standards.

Antony's code forbade killing any people who had not committed heinous crimes, murder, rape, and the like. Randal dreaded the possibility of making an error in judgment that might lead to them executing him. Would they? Gardner and Maggie would plead his case and try to prevent it, but he didn't know where David fell on this sliding scale of death. And as for Antony? Well, Antony already threatened to kill him.

When Randal first came into the group, Antony had every intention of "euthanizing" Randal. Antony explained that child vampires couldn't control their baser urges. It was after Maggie swore on her life that she would keep Randal on the narrow path.

Randal had the urges to kill the innocent, just as Antony predicted, but it wasn't the fear of dying at Antony's hand that had kept him on that "narrow path." Instead, Maggie's approval stayed his actions.

The third floor of the mansion consisted of three rooms and was inhabited solely by Randal and Gardner. The stairs to the third floor opened up to a hall that ran the length of the house. Three doors lined the hallway. The first door led to Gardner's room. The third door led to Randal's room, which Antony reinforced with steel shutters to allow no light in, but Randal only retreated there to sleep. He spent more time in Gardner's bedroom or in the second room, which housed a 55-inch flat-screen TV, a PlayStation 4 console, and a pool table. On the wall was a dartboard with the darts still placed from a game Randal and Gardner had shared just before Gardner left for his trip. Randal climbed the stairs, entered Gardner's room, lay on Gardner's bed, and sniffed the pillow. Gardner's scent was a mixture of Axe body spray and wet dog, and Randal loved this smell, missing Gardner immensely.

Randal had been only twelve and four feet nine inches tall when the psychotic vampire, Dark Father, had turned him. He had watched Gardner grow from an infant into a pre-teen. As it would turn out, Randal could live a thousand years, and still, his mind would stay that of a 12-year-old child. He could learn, but he couldn't mature. When Gardner had hit the age of twelve, Randal found him to be the perfect companion, the ideal age to be turned immortal. But Gardner continued to grow. Randal had considered, very briefly, biting Gardner, but he knew the repercussions of such an act would have been devastating. He had no choice but to let Gardner mature into adolescence. And in the end, it was the right thing to do. Had he turned Gardner at twelve, no one would have wanted him in the house anymore, including Gardner. As it turned out, Gardner and Randal grew to be even closer as Gardner aged.

Randal stood and exited the room, headed back downstairs. He was bored, and the woman was a constant thought in his head. Should Randal tell the others about her? Could he? He felt it would be best not to say anything about her just yet. Randal might go to her again, just to get a better understanding of who she was. If she killed innocents and the others came across her, would he help to destroy her? He, too, had the urge to kill innocents and wondered if helping to kill those immortals who murder made him a hypocrite.

Randal's head spun with the ideas running through it, and he couldn't sit still any longer. With plenty of time before sunrise, Randal stepped out the front door and into the night. He only required one victim to sate the hunger, but lately, he had been craving a second. He didn't need this victim for sustenance but to satiate a need to hunt. Randal had been doing this for weeks now. He believed that if he could handle a third before gluttony saddled him, he would try it. Randal thought it appropriate to take a victim, just as Antony and David did. If possible, he'd condition himself to handle that third infusion.

Randal sped off in search of a victim.

Chapter Three

Antony stepped through the tall gray building's sliding glass door and headed to the elevators at the other end of the lobby. He punched the button with the number five lit up, rode the elevator to that floor, and then stepped into the hall on that floor. Antony peered down the hall to his left. Past visits told him that entrance led to the sleeping quarters of the inhabitants at the nursing home. He watched an elderly gentleman shuffle up the hall toward him in a robe and slippers. The man's hair was in disarray.

Antony continued toward the lounge until a short Italian woman wrapped her skinny arms around his waist, smiling a toothless grin. She pulled away and laid her palm gently on his stomach, mumbling something he could not understand in a language that probably didn't exist, except in her addled mind. He guided the frail body aside and continued, walking through the lounge to the row of chairs near the windows. The object of his visit sat in the third chair from the left.

A nurse's aide hovered over the senior sitting in the chair, looking more like a bird of prey than a nurturing caretaker. "How are you enjoying the view, Gladys?" The aide snorted and turned back to the dark square of a window behind her. The aide then held a cup of pudding just out of the woman's reach. Antony frowned at the aide's behavior.

"How long have you worked here, darling?" the old woman asked in a slight French accent.

"I've worked here for three months now, Gladys. Don't you remember me?" The aide spoke slowly, as if to a child.

"Yes," the old woman said. "I do remember you. Your name is Lisa."

The aide's smirk faded.

"If I may ask, could you please remember my name? Lisa. It's Grace, not Gladys, my dear, Grace. If I can remember your name at my age, the least you can do is learn mine. Now please, Lisa, hand over my pudding and get out of the damn way so I can enjoy whatever view I wish to see."

With a harrumph, the aide pushed the pudding into Grace's gnarled hands.

Antony laughed as the aide shambled away, grumbling. Grace smiled and commenced spooning chocolate pudding into her denture-filled maw.

"This is the Grace I know and love."

The woman looked up as a shadow passed over her. She saw Antony, recognized him, and set her pudding aside.

"Antoine," she exclaimed in her French accent. "I've missed you."

Antony knelt beside her chair and hugged her. He kissed her gently on the mouth, tasting her chocolate lips. "How have you been?"

"How do you think? I'm 97." She smiled at him. He squeezed her hand gently.

"I think you are just fine. I'm sorry I have not been here to see you sooner."

"You're right on time, I should say," she said. "I'm still alive, aren't I? If I'm not dead, then you're not late."

Antony smiled at this, remembering the first time he had spoken similar words to her. Did she say this in remembrance, or was it just a coincidence? He liked to believe the former was true.

"You are going to be around for a very long time. I demand it."

"You demand it, do you? Well then, I shall stay for a while longer."

"Would you like to go for a walk?" Antony asked.

"I would, my distinguished and handsome friend. I need to show you off to the other crones around here."

Antony pulled a wheelchair over to her from the corner and helped her into it. He wheeled Grace to the elevator, and they rode it down to the lobby. Antony pushed her into the crisp night air, and they followed the lighted path through the garden. He listened to her stories, commenting when necessary, and delighted in her presence. Some days Grace was not this lucid. On those days, he did not take her for walks. Antony, instead, sat with her and helped her with anything she required. She did not know who he was, and on her coherent days, she would have no memory of those other visits.

When their circuit of the grounds was complete, Antony wheeled her back to the chair where he had found her.

The aide, who had not known her name earlier, approached as Antony finished placing her back in the recliner. Antony could see by the glassy stare that Grace was slipping into that fog of senility.

"Did you have a nice walk with your grandson?" the aide asked.

Grace followed the voice to look into the face of the approaching aide.

"He's not my grandson," Grace said with splendid superiority. "He is my fiancé. We're to marry in the spring."

"That's nice, Grace," the aide said.

Antony frowned at the aide's condescending tone, but at least she called her by the correct name.

"Yes, he's immortal. Isn't he handsome? I was in my twenties when we first met. He hasn't aged a day. I could have been immortal too, but I wasn't able to convince my sweet Antoine to bless me with his gift."

As Antony walked away, he heard the aide say, "Time for bed, Gladys." The incorrect name was grating to Antony's ears, and he considered returning to the aide, throttling her and demanding she repeat the correct word over and over: "It is Grace, Grace, Grace."

But he knew his intervention would not matter. The aide was saying the incorrect name on purpose. He loathed the aide and thought he would have trouble protecting her if someone attacked her.

"Time for bed," Grace muttered as Antony entered the elevator. "Will my poppa be coming in to kiss me goodnight?"

"I'm sure he will," said the aide in a single breath.

The door mercifully closed on the insensitive aide, and the cab dropped to the lobby. He hurried out of the building, afraid of doing something to the aide he might regret. Moving quickly through the night, Antony returned to the house, entered the living room, and glanced at Randal as the boy sat in the recliner flipping through the channels on the large, flat-screen TV. The boy's eyes flicked briefly from the glowing screen to Antony and then back again.

Antony assumed Randal was moping because he had not gone with the others. Antony left him to his self-commiseration and retired to his room. He opened the French doors to his closet and pulled a shoebox from the top shelf. Antony flipped through the faded photographs of Grace and himself in the days of her youth. Had he done the right thing allowing her to live a mortal life? Of course, he had. Antony would soon have to part with her. Grace had been one of the most beautiful women he had ever seen. She was, still. In the years of her youth, she had witnessed Antony feed, learning what he was, and they had become very close. So close that he had come close to making her his first vampire companion since Bane. In the end, he had left her mortality intact. Even now, as he fought through his doubts, he was sure it had done the right thing. She married, had children, and grandchildren, and then great-grandchildren. He had watched over her, protecting her for all those years they had been apart. Only after she had entered the nursing home did he dare to make contact with her again.

In those first days, Grace had been a French immigrant in Virginia. He had spotted her standing in a pavilion at the center of a garden park. He stared at her beautiful face, captivated by her smile, so intoxicating that he had to stop and drink it in.

"You're staring, sir," she had said to him.

"I am sorry," he said and lowered his eyes.

"In France, it is customary for the gentleman to introduce himself before speaking to a woman."

"I am sorry," he said again. "My name is Antony Grayson."

"Antoine," she said, pronouncing his name in French. "My name is Grace Beaulieu."

"I am pleased to meet you." He bowed politely.

"I am pleased to meet you, Antoine," she said. "Will you walk with me?"

"I will."

He hooked his arm in hers, and they walked along the path that wound around the park. Antony stole a glance at Grace on occasion, and although she never turned in his direction, she knew when he was looking and smiled.

Finally, Antony spoke. "What brings such a lovely young lady out into the night walking alone? It is not safe."

"I have trouble sleeping. I walk the park paths to try and get some fresh air. Sometimes it works to help me sleep, and sometimes it doesn't. Why are you out so late?"

"I am a creature of the night," he said. "I sleep during the day and walk at night. I have done this way for a very long time."

"Interesting," Grace said. "Does this mean I'll see more of you if I continue to walk at night?"

"I would say yes." Antony smiled.

Grace smiled. "Good."

They spent the rest of that night walking the park and talking. He learned much and more about her life as a farmer's daughter in France and her family's flight from the war-torn country. They had escaped during World War 2's *drôle de Guerre* period. As they continued to meet on many more nights together, Antony spoke of his past and only removed the events' time, lest he would reveal his actual age. Every night he would feed quickly then look for her in the park. She was always there, patiently waiting.

On the night she was not there, Antony thought that perhaps she had grown bored of their time together. Disappointed, he turned to leave. His preternatural hearing picked up a whisper of the brush in the trees to his left. He moved closer to find the source of the disturbance. There was no wind, no natural reason for the sound. After many seconds of hearing nothing more, he decided to leave. But even as he turned to walk away, he heard the sound again: a muffled rustle of something moving through foliage.

Antony burst through the trees toward the sound. The scuffling was louder and faster now, more frantic and no longer masking the sound. Antony came to a small clearing where he saw Grace pinned beneath an immigrant worker in dirty work clothes, threatening Grace, whispering demands to her in French. Her eyes were wild with fear, and she did not see Antony.

He flew at the man and ripped him off, Grace. The man was pulled off his feet and tossed like a ragdoll to the opposite side of the clearing. Antony then raced to where the man had landed and, without realizing what he was doing, bit into the man's carotid artery and drained him.

With eyes still red from the blood lust, he glanced over where Grace still lay in the grass. She stared at him, shivering and clutching her torn blouse to her breasts.

"You are safe now," Antony said.

He took a step toward her, but Grace scrambled to her feet and ran away. Antony closed his eyes and cursed his decision to allow her to see what he had done. When he opened his eyes again, he turned back to the corpse and disappeared in a crackle of movement with the body in tow.

Antony destroyed the corpse and disposed of it. He returned where he and Grace typically met, but she wasn't there. Did Antony genuinely expect her to be? No, he supposed not. Antony suspected that his time with Grace had ended. Still, he continued to return to the spot for weeks. Grace did not come back. What if she told the authorities of what she had seen? Should he move now? It was not wise to stay in an area where his secret was no longer secure. He knew to leave was the right thing to do, but still, he could not go. He could not leave without knowing what had happened to her. He stood at the pavilion where they had first met, and he looked out over the park. He searched the star-dappled night sky for answers, but none came to him. His attention broke when he heard someone approaching from behind. He turned and saw Grace standing there.

"I'm sorry I'm late, Antoine," she said.

"I have not gone yet, so I would say you were right on time."

"I had to build up my courage to return here," she said. "I used to think this place was safe, but now I'm not so sure."

"I would never harm you," Antony said. He tried to step closer to her but was afraid of how she would react.

"It's not you, Antione. You saved me. I'm afraid of the men whose intentions are not so noble. I've never been afraid of you."

"But you ran away when you saw what...saw what I am."

Grace smiled. "I ran, my dear Antione, out of embarrassment."

Antony went to her then. He embraced her, and they kissed. They continued to meet at the park many years after that night, but Antony explained he could never be anything more than a friend.

She hugged him. "That's all I need."

On the night they parted ways forever, Grace ran to Antony and threw herself into his arms.

"I'm to go away. Daddy is moving us away. Antoine, I do not wish to go." Tears streamed down her face. "Turn me, Antoine. Make me like you, and we can run off together."

Antony smiled, but inside, his heart sank. "I cannot do that, Grace."

Tearfully, Grace ran away. She did not return, and Antony did not seek her out. He found her years later and read about her marriage in the papers. Antony kept track of her over the years but never approached her. One time about a year before he met David, Antony did let Grace see him. She was aging well and was still as lovely as that first night. Grace met his gaze, and he watched as the woman worked out how this stranger fit into her life. When recognition dawned, she smiled at him. A tear slipped from her eye. She wiped her eyes and asked her husband to excuse her for a moment. She walked over to where Antony stood.

Antony bowed slightly and, remembering that a proper gentleman greeted a lady by name, said, "Good evening, Grace."

"Good evening, Antoine."

"You look well. You look *happy*."

"I am. I was so hoping I would see you again so I could thank you," Grace said.

"Thank me?"

"For doing the right thing by me," she said. "For letting me live my life. I would not have made a very good immortal. I needed to be allowed to have my family. I missed you terribly over the years, but my family was a comfort."

"I will never forget you, Grace," Antony said.

"I should think not." She glared at him. The stern looked faded to a smile. "Nor I, you."

Antony continued to watch over her and was there in the shadows when her husband died. He was there when her children could no longer care for her and placed her in the nursing home. Antony did not approach her again until she began arguing with an aide one day in the nursing home. He stepped in on her behalf, and, although she did not recognize him on that day, he had been able to calm her down. In future visits, she would sometimes remember him, who he was and what he was. On visits when she did not seem to know him, she still accepted him. That was good enough for him.

Antony returned his keepsakes to the box and placed the box back in the closet.

Chapter Four

Maggie returned to her body with a gasp and sat up abruptly in the white plush chair. She glanced around at the worried faces in front of her. Once adjusted to her surroundings and was sure of where she was and who was with her, Maggie relaxed.

"Where is Alex?" Maggie sat up quickly when she did not see the girl.

"Resting in the bedroom." Gardner moved closer to his mother. "Why? What's wrong?"

"The banquet hall." She swallowed hard. "It was awful. I saw half-eaten corpses and body parts all over the room. The place was awash in blood." Maggie clapped a hand over her mouth and fought back the flood of tears threatening to come. When she had gained control, she continued. "I can't believe Alex survived that. I blinked from the banquet hall to a parlor of some kind. I heard voices and thought they had spotted me. They hadn't, so I blinked around a corner. I listened for as long as I could but was too out in the open and feared they would see me, so I blinked back here."

"What were they saying?" Gardner asked.

"They know Alex got away. They're planning to get her back. I heard enough to know that if Alex had gone to the police, she would be dead now."

"The police are helping them?"

Maggie shook her head. "No, I don't think so. Nothing that conspiratorial, but I do think they have a spy on the force."

"Thank goodness she didn't go to the police then," David said.

"Mother thinks that…"

"Mother?" asked Gardner.

Maggie smiled. "That's what they call the old woman. Mother thinks that Alex is out in the world, wandering alone and distrustful of strangers. They are looking for her, but they are also waiting for the authorities to pick her up. If she ended up in the police station, they would know, and they would swoop in and get her."

All three looked back at the sleeping girl.

"Then you're saying they don't know about us and don't know we have her."

Maggie nodded. "Yes."

"What do we do? How do we stop them?" Gardner asked.

"Listening to them gave me an idea," Maggie said.

"What's the plan?" David scowled. "I'm sure it's going to put you in danger, and I already don't like it."

"I hope you don't plan on using Alex as bait."

Maggie didn't dignify Gardner's complaint with an answer.

"They already know we are stalking their land. They have an escapee they want back. They aren't above receiving outside help. I say we walk right up to the door and knock, ask to join their pack."

Maggie studied their shocked faces.

Finally, David broke the silence. "When do you plan to put this plan into effect?"

She didn't say a word. Maggie began to disrobe.

"Now?" Gardner's voice echoed through the small cabin. "Am I coming with you?"

"No, you stay here for now. I'll be back."

She exited the Zephyr and transformed into the wolf and sprinted across the distance, skirting the town and headed into the desert, back to the hacienda. Once outside the gate, she howled to draw the attention of the group inside. Even Minerva came to the entrance. The blond man and the black-haired beauty, Bethany, accompanied her.

Maggie transformed back to her human form and stood at the gate. "I have your girl."

Maggie focused on Minerva. Something was off about the older woman—something to do with her aura—but

Maggie couldn't quite make out what it was and didn't have time to worry about it at that moment. If they didn't kill her on the spot, she would work it out later.

"You have our girl?" Minerva said.

"Yes, and if you want her back, you must agree to allow my son and me to join your pack."

"Not on your life, bitch," Bethany said, but Minerva quieted her.

"Why would you want to join us?" Minerva asked.

"We are finding it difficult to live on our own. We've run into a bit of trouble and are vulnerable. I'm afraid my son is very naughty. We have seen your methods, and I must say I'm quite impressed. We want in on that action."

"We will need time to consider this," Minerva said. "Where can we find you?"

"You can't. We will return in two weeks if the girl lasts that long. You see, my son has taken a liking to her. I've had to stop him from eating her twice already."

"You left him alone with her now? Poor girl," Roman said. "She's probably going to be a bowel movement by morning."

Maggie turned to him. "I'm not that stupid. We have a human handler who is there to see that no harm comes to her until we deliver her to you."

"We merely want her dead. We could just let you kill her."

"True, but she told us a fascinating story. If you don't let us join your pack, we might take her home to her family. Before long, everyone will know what happened here."

Minerva's eyes went wide. "Insolence. I won't stand for it. No one threatens me."

Maggie flinched but hoped no one had noticed.

Minerva controlled her anger by taking a breath, brushing at her sleeves. "Come back in two weeks, and we will offer you a trial period." She blinked. "Now go, before I change my mind and kill you where you stand."

Chapter Five

By the time Maggie returned, the sun had risen, and David sealed himself safely away inside the steel chamber under the table.

"Were you followed?" Gardner asked as Maggie jumped into the driver's seat.

"No, I took an indirect route and doubled back several times. I even blinked back to the compound. They didn't even try to follow me."

"What does that mean?"

"It either means they trust me to keep my word, or they don't see us as any kind of credible threat. Either way, I think we're okay. I bought some time to prepare. We're heading home and returning in two weeks.

Gardner and Alex took a seat on the plush white sofa in the living quarters of the cabin.

As Maggie started up the RV, Alex asked, "I'm sure you'll be helping her make the long drive."

"No, she's got this. Werewolves have extraordinary endurance. She can make the drive to Philadelphia on her own without stopping. That's also how the driver of the bus had been able to make the extremely long ride without stopping."

"Should I go back to Ohio? My parents..." Alex wasn't able to complete her thought.

"No," Gardner said, maybe a little too harshly. He continued in a softer tone. "Going back to Ohio now would only put them in danger. They have to go on thinking you are one of the missing. It sounds harsh, but if they knew the truth now, the pack might come after them. Once we have this situation under control, you can return to them."

Alex nodded.

As the miles rocketed past them outside the Zephyr, Gardner decided it was time to tell Alex what she would find at the house. "You are going to meet two more vampires." He gaged her reaction. When she didn't seem shocked or frightened, he continued. "Antony is ancient. He doesn't look it, but he is. The Vampire who created Randal also killed my father around the same time. Antony had no choice but to turn Dad into a blood-drinking fiend."

"Randal is the child vampire?" Alex asked.

Gardner nodded. "He's unique in that he is physically a twelve-year-old boy. He was a child when he turned and hasn't aged since. And although Randal can seem very childlike in many ways, treating him like one is a big mistake. Do you understand what I'm saying?"

Alex nodded the affirmative. "Don't tease the monsters, got it."

"He's not so bad. Randal is my best friend. I've known him since my infancy to be a small child. I felt bad about leaving him behind. I miss him so much right now."

"Did it upset you that I called him a monster? I didn't mean—"

Gardner laughed. "Don't worry. We have a thick skin when it comes to what we call ourselves."

"Still, it was a joke in bad taste, and I apologize."

Night had fallen when they pulled up in front of the house, and David emerged from the steel cabinet. He smiled at Alex, who seemed unnerved by his sudden appearance.

"You'll get used to it," he said.

Maggie and David entered the house first. Randal looked up from the magazine lying across his lap. When Gardner came into the house, Randal ran to him and hugged him. Gardner hugged him back briskly and then pulled away. "We have a visitor," Gardner said.

As Alex passed timidly into the house, Randal backed away.

"Who is this?" he asked.

"This is Alex," Gardner said. "We rescued her."

"When is she leaving?" Randal asked.

"She isn't going anywhere," Maggie said. "She has information about the group of werewolves we're hunting."

Randal walked up and sniffed her. She flinched but didn't back away.

"She's human," Randal said. "When we're done with her, can we eat her?"

"He's joking," Gardner said and pulled Randal away from Alex by his shoulders.

"No, I'm not," Randal mumbled as he walked away.

Gardner led Alex to the living room. Antony entered and introduced himself to Alex.

She stared at him, opened her mouth to speak, then closed it again. She gulped hard as if trying to swallow a whole piece of hard candy. "You're the old vampire. I mean, they told me you've been around a long time. I didn't mean to—" She covered her face with her hands. "I'm sorry. I don't know how to behave around someone who's been around as long as you." Her hands shook visibly.

Antony laughed. "You do not have to treat me any differently just because I am 'old.' Think of me as one of the guys."

Alex dropped her hands away. "I'll try."

Gardner stood next to Alex. "She's concerned about her parents. What if we went to them and brought them here?"

"No." Alex's words came out too quickly. "I mean, I want them as far from this as possible." She looked around at the group, abashed. "My parents would never be able to handle knowing the truth. I wouldn't want to put you in a position to lie to them about who you are. I think my father would have a heart attack if he knew there were vampires and werewolves in the world. Even if he didn't believe us, he's bound to see something he could un-see, if you know what I mean."

Gardner shook his head. "I think they'd be safer here with us."

"No," Maggie said. "Alex is right. We should keep them out of this for as long as possible." She turned to Alex. "Once we have this situation under control, we can take you home."

Alex nodded.

Chapter Six

David had been tracking a certain prey before they left for New Mexico, and he thought there might be just enough time to finish what he started before they returned to the task of ousting the werewolf clan. He woke on that first night back in his bed, showered and dressed in his usual khakis and a silk shirt. David crept through the house, running into no one on his way out the door. He hunted, taking his first two victims quickly. His third victim that night would require a little more work.

Although he suspected the man of rape, David had not yet seen him in action. According to the code, his intended victim couldn't be guilty of wanting to rape someone. The rape would have to have already happened. This situation would pose a problem without Maggie's sight. A vampire's ability to taste his victim's memories was only helpful if the vampire already knew of the crime. If David drained the prey only to learn he had not committed a crime, Antony would be disappointed in him. Antony had sired a vampire named Bane, who indiscriminately killed. He had nearly allowed David to die a human death rather than turn David and create another killer offspring.

In the end, Antony had trusted David enough to make another vampire, and David would never betray that trust. All of David's victims had to be guilty.

As a human, David had escaped a terrible life with a maniacal stepfather by becoming a male prostitute. He had been discovered by his stepfather and nearly killed, but it was then that Antony came to David's rescue, killing the stepfather and taking David as a young prodigy.

The motel rooms in which David had sold his body to despicable older men had burned down, but there were plenty more, and David was back in that old neighborhood. He spotted his prey as the man left a motel room. David recalled his own experiences in such motel rooms and trembled with rage.

When the man had gone out of sight, David entered the room and saw the young girl huddled on the bed. She was crying. She flinched when David approached.

"You have to talk to Jacob, mister. I don't just take people off the street."

The girl was only thirteen, fourteen at best.

"Get dressed," David said. He threw the girl's clothes on the bed. "You're going home."

"No, I'm not. I'm..."

"You're going home." David's eyes turned red. He didn't know if he could hold back the hunger for much longer, but for the girl's sake, he'd have to last a while longer. He had strong willpower when it came to his desire; he could control it longer than most, even longer than Antony, but would have to test that control tonight.

The girl saw the change in David's eyes and got dressed. David placed several one-hundred-dollar bills in her hand, and she stared down at them.

"Jacob's gonna want this haul turned in right away."

"The money's not for Jacob." David glared at the girl, knowing she could see the blood hunger in his eyes. The girl didn't argue.

David drove her to the bus station and didn't leave until the girl was on the bus and it was on the move, heading back to her parents. When the bus drew out of sight, David turned away, ready to finish with his prey.

There had been no fear of losing sight of the man because David knew his prey's routine. The man would first get something to eat. He would eat and drink, and get drunk and then return home to his wife. David knew where the man lived and would meet up with him there.

David walked around the house, but the man wasn't home yet. David saw the man's wife sitting in the living room, glance at the clock, then stood and paced, continually looking back at the clock.

Does she know what her husband is doing?

David's rage intensified. No, he couldn't jump to that conclusion. The woman possibly knew her husband is cheating, but that didn't mean she knew with whom he cheated.

Time grew short, and David needed to feed soon. David's eyes swam with hunger as a red glaze covered his vision. He fought the urge to break into the house and take the woman. He thought he had just about lost the battle when at last, the man's station wagon pulled into the driveway. David followed the man from the shadows, unseen. When David peered into the window, he saw the man fixing a drink.

The wife had gone upstairs. "Are you coming to bed?" the woman shouted down to her husband.

"In a minute," the man shouted. "Keep your granny panties on."

David had seen enough to know that this man was a violator of women and had no doubt of his guilt. The man finished his drink, staggered to the security pad next to the back door, and set the alarm. Then the man stumbled up the stairs to what David could only believe was a loveless bed.

David went to his car and pulled the heavy black plastic bag from the trunk. He threw it over his shoulder and carried it back to the house with him. He returned to the back door and twisted the knob until the mechanisms inside broke apart. There was no deadbolt on this door, but that would not have posed a problem either. David stepped through the threshold and turned to the security pad. David's preternatural sight allowed him to see the body heat the man's fingers left on the keypad. The buttons lit up in sequence like a memory game, showing him the correct pattern. David deactivated the security alarm and stalked to the stairs. Even as a human, David was a master at moving in complete silence. As a vampire, the silence was even more profound. As the man and the woman slept, David entered their room. He moved silently, without disturbing a shadow. He stood over the man, studying him. The man's mouth hung slightly open, and a droning snore escaped him. The man fell asleep quickly, and David laid the thick plastic bag out on the floor. Then he turned back to the man.

As David cupped his hand over the man's mouth, he woke, startled. His eyes bulged with fear. David climbed onto the bed, straddling the man. The woman stirred but didn't wake up. David leaned over and whispered into the man's ear.

"Your time on this earth has come to an end." David's eyes glowed like embers in the night.

The man tried to struggle free, but David held him tight. He worked futilely for several seconds. Then David leaned down and ripped a gaping hole in the man's neck with his fangs. Perfectly round puncture wounds were for the movies. David sealed his mouth over the slashes and allowed the blood to course down his throat. The blood pumped fiercely at first, but as the heart slowed, David needed to suck out the blood when the muscle was no longer strong enough to do the job. David tasted memories of many girls — none over the age of fifteen — that this man had defiled. When the heart stopped, so did the memories. David's third transfusion was complete.

David sat up and removed a dagger from its hip sheath. Before beheading the man, David turned to the woman and shook her awake. As the woman opened her eyes, she stared out at David in shock and disbelief. She used a hand to stifle a scream.

The woman's dry lips parted. "You're supposed to be dead."

"I am dead, Mother," David said. "And so is husband number two that I've killed. Pick a good man next time, or I'll be back."

David allowed her to watch as he decapitated the corpse. He tossed the head into the open body bag. David turned to his mother again. "I've left behind no blood and no evidence that I've been here. Tell people he left you. Tell them he was a despicable man and that it's good riddance. If you don't want to see me again, Mother—and something tells me you don't—bring no more rapists or killers into your bed. If you stay single, or if you remarry a man with honest intentions, I will not return."

As if packing a suit, David placed the bloodless corpse in the body bag then zipped it closed. He hefted the corpse onto his shoulder, then exited his mother's house and returned to Lansdowne Ave and disposed of the corpse in the incinerator. David drew back from the task of disposal when laughter above him caught his attention. He followed the sound to the living room, where he found Gardner and Alex sitting on the couch, with Randal wedged between them.

David studied Alex for a moment. She looked terrified of Randal, and Gardner laughed at her fear. She needed to feel safe, David realized.

When she spotted him staring, she froze. "What is it?"

"You need a weapon."

***

A weapon? Alex felt a shiver of fear wash over her.

Gardner looked at her with furrowed brows. "No. He's not threatening you. Dad's saying you need to be able to defend yourself. You've entered a dangerous world, and you're vulnerable. We need to give you the ability to protect yourself."

Alex leaned away from Gardner, feeling the need to run. She couldn't help but think Gardner had answered a question she hadn't asked.

"What weapon would be effective against immortals?" she asked.

"Machete," Randal said and drew his finger across his throat. "If you want to kill me, chop off my head."

"That's fine for our superior strength and speed," David said. "But she shouldn't have to get that close. That would put her in too much danger. What she needs is a ranged weapon."

"A ranged weapon?" Alex asked. "You make it sound like a video game. If you're talking about guns, count me out. I don't like guns."

"You don't like to protect yourself?" Gardner asked.

"Come with me," David said. The group followed David into the basement.

Alex headed directly to the large steel room at the far end of the basement and placed a hand on it. "What's this."

"That's cold storage." Randal laughed.

"It's an inverted panic room where we store live prey," David said. "But that's not why we are here."

"What happened to the door?"

"A werewolf battered it, but it still holds humans, and maybe werewolves, but we haven't needed to contain any lately."

She turned away from the panic room and looked into the back room, past the stairs. She pointed at the colossal furnace.

"That's where you burn the bodies." Her voice was small. "Are there..." She gulped. "A lot of bodies in there?"

"No, silly," Randal said. "They burn up. And the little pieces of bones fall into the bottom, and we take them out back and bury them."

"Randal." David's look caused the child vampire to stop talking.

"Chill out, Rand. You've freaked her out enough." Gardner touched her shoulder. "Remember. We never kill innocent people."

70

She turned to Gardner. "I know."

"This is the reason we came down here." David pointed to a standing dresser with French doors. As he opened it, Alex's mouth dropped.

Inside the chest, an array of swords in varying lengths and widths that gleamed like trophies. The left side displayed daggers and swords, and to the right, about five different types of bows rested on pegs. Alex stared awestruck into the chest for some time before reaching out and touching one of the weapons.

"Good choice," David said. "That's a bamboo recurve bow from China. It's very lightweight, and you can carry it anywhere. You'll get about a 40-foot range with that one."

"You want me to learn to use a bow?" Alex asked as she slid a hand down its smooth surface. The idea excited her.

"Yes, and maybe…" David glanced over the assortment of daggers until he found one in particular. He pulled a knife from its slot and flipped it, catching it by the blade between two fingers with the hilt jutting toward Alex. She placed her hand on the wooden handle but didn't take it from him just yet. "Use this on anyone who gets too close," he said. She gave him a determined nod and wrapped her slender fingers around the hilt, and pulled it from his grasp. She held it out in front of her in a shaking hand.

"We'll train you to use the weapons, but there is another aspect of their use that will not be so easy to teach. You will have to learn to take the life of whatever might be at the other end of the weapon. It's not an easy thing taking the life of a man who is begging for his life, even if he is a murderer, rapist…"

"Or a werewolf," Gardner said.

Alex looked at him. *Can I do that? Can I kill?*

"You will if you want to stay alive." When both Alex and his father looked at him with questioning stares, Gardner said: "Kill, I mean."

71

"Gar, I'm leaving it up to you to train her. She has to be a dead shot; do you hear me? Her life will depend on her accuracy. It's not easy to kill a werewolf. A shot to the throat will slow him down, but if you can shoot him in the eye, you might be able to hinder the brain long enough to decapitate him. Anything that will stop the heart will kill the werewolf."

"What will kill a vampire?" Alex asked.

David hesitated, then answered. "Nothing short of decapitation will kill a vampire...and the sun, of course."

"You're giving away all our trade secrets," Randal said.

David responded without looking at Randal. "She needs to know everything we know so she can protect herself."

Gardner said, "And so she can feel safer around us." He turned to Randal. "You may be small, but that doesn't mean you're not scary."

"We'll leave you to your work," David said to Gardner. David then motioned Randal to leave with him.

As David and Randal headed back upstairs, Gardner looked around nervously. "How should we start?"

"I don't know target practice?"

"I'll set up targets in the backyard. We have paper targets in the shed. I'll set up bales of hay, which will keep the arrows from getting lost."

Gardner turned to walk away.

"Can I ask you something first?" Alex asked. Gardner turned back to her. After a pause to collect her thoughts, Alex said, "Did you read my thoughts just now?"

"What?" Gardner said stupidly.

"Before, you seemed to know I thought your dad wanted to fight me. It's stupid, I know, but..." She took a breath. "And just now, I thought I might not be able to kill something. I thought about it. And then you answered me. You said, 'You will if you want to stay alive.' You answered a question I only thought to ask. Did you read my mind?"

"Yes," Gardner said softly. "I did."

"Do your parents know you have that ability?"

"No, I haven't told anyone. I never meant to let anyone know."

"Why not? Your entire family is full of extraordinary beings. Your mother has amazing abilities. Why would you hide such a gift from her?"

"Mind reading is an intrusive, abhorrent ability. No one deserves to possess it. I try to control it and prevent it from happening. Sometimes, I slip up. I didn't mean to read your mind. I'm sorry."

"Have you read my mind before?"

"No, this was the only time."

"I don't believe you."

"It's true, I promise." Gardner began to sweat.

"What am I thinking now?"

"I just told you, I don't like to—"

I think you're cute.

He blushed, and she smirked.

"I knew it."

Chapter Seven

He traveled at night, not out of necessity like a vampire but because it was easier to hide. His appearance caused people to run from him. He was Corpse Boy, and it wasn't just his name; it was how he looked. His appearance incited too much alarm around people not used to seeing his mottled and rotting flesh. He moved at night and stayed out of sight during the day. He had nowhere to go after killing the Dark Father and leaving the mansion, but still, he traveled. The Dark Father attacked Jake Shields's family and then created Corpse Boy. Dark Father then experimented on the boy. Yes, he had been Jake once upon a time, but that boy was gone. The Dark Father thought he was creating a vampire, but Jake's corpse turned into something new instead. The Corpse Boy was an immortal zombie who regenerated its rotting flesh by eating insects. The creator had performed several experiments on Corpse Boy by chopping him into several pieces, decapitating him, and burning him, but nothing worked. The Corpse Boy regenerated every time, so Dark Father deemed Corpse Boy indestructible.

Corpse Boy ate maggots on roadkill during his travels, leaving the rotten flesh for the carrion birds. After picking the juiciest grubs from a mashed possum, Corpse Boy wandered away from the road in search of a place to lie low as the day approached.

Corpse Boy spotted an abandoned house well hidden by overgrown bushes and tall grass and took refuge in a shed on the property. Well hidden behind stacks of old car parts and landscaping equipment, Corpse Boy did not sleep. Instead, he simply meditated to pass the daylight hours.

The house Corpse Boy chose for his refuge was not as uninhabited as he had initially thought. Inside the house, a family of settlers had taken up residence. They kept to the bedroom and did not move around or draw attention to themselves. The father was 51-year-old Jack Terrell. He and his wife Libby and son, seven-year-old Scott, had taken over the abandoned house when Jack lost his job at the potato chip plant where he had been an inspector for ten years. The bills had piled up, collectors began calling, and then the eviction notice came. The family left their belongings behind and hit the streets. When they came across the abandoned house, they thought only of seeking shelter for the night. And in the morning, he would move on.

But one night turned to two days. Two days turned into a week. Presently, they had been in the house for over a month, and when no one had come around to check on the place, they figured they would stay until someone chased them off. The bedroom and adjoining bathroom were kept clean. The rest of the house, however, was in disarray. They ate from cans and disposed of the containers by throwing them in the trash left out on the street by neighboring houses. Jack collected food, disposed of the garbage, forbidding Libby and Scott to leave the house.

Jack walked to town and bought food with money he made selling discarded aluminum to recycling centers. Jack had already gone to town to look for a job and collect food the morning Corpse Boy took refuge in the shed. Libby napped. She took a lot of naps since their flight from their once idyllic life.

"Be a good boy and stay close to Mommy, and keep your voice down, okay Pumpkin? Mommy is going to lay down for a while."

"Okay, Mommy." Scott picked up his space shuttle, the only toy he had been able to take with him when they fled their home, and soundlessly pretended the shuttle blasted off into space. After a few minutes of quietly exploring the galaxy, Scott forgot that his mother was napping and added sound effects to his adventure. When she stirred, he clamped his hand over his mouth and stopped moving. When Mommy grew still once again, Scott carefully crept out of the room and resumed flying his shuttle through the universe. He ran through the house, waving his space shuttle up and down, avoiding stars and planets on his journey. Scott stopped the back door, looked back, and waited for his mother to yell at him for not staying with her. When no reprimand came, Scott reached out and opened the door. He stepped out of the house and felt the warm morning air on his face for the first time in weeks. The tall grass and weeds brushed against his legs as he walked toward the side of the house.

He spotted the shed and headed toward it, hoping he would find more toys. He tried to look inside the window, but it was too dark to see anything. Scott looked back at the house. Mommy was not there. He didn't know where his father was, but Daddy usually didn't return until later. Sometimes Daddy returned with food, but not always. Yesterday Daddy had brought home a container with no label, and they had stared at it for a long time. What would they find inside? As it turned out, the can offered obscurely shaped pasta in tomato sauce. It was good. Scott hoped Daddy brought home more of that stuff tonight.

Scott noticed the door to the shed was already slightly open, and he pushed through to the dark, cool interior. There was a stinky pile of rags in the corner next to the door. A bicycle without a front tire leaned against a push lawn mower, placed there to block passage into the shed. Scott had no trouble climbing over the useless equipment pretending he was climbing a remote mountain of trash on a lost planet. He climbed down and pulled a crate toward him and looked inside, hoping to find something fun, but to his disappointment, there were only clothes. There were some shiny machine parts in another box, but they didn't seem like they would be much fun, so he moved on.

As he moved deeper into the shed, he found another box. This one was full of stuffed animals and puppets and other plush toys. They were not quite to his liking, but with little else to occupy his time, he made due.

The puppets had limited entertainment value, and he soon grew bored. He tossed them away without caring where they landed. He worked his way deeper into the shed, pawing through boxes and not liking what he found.

He had just about given up and had decided to leave the shed when he moved a box from the far corner and found the dead boy.

He was not frightened at the sight of the corpse huddled in the corner. Scott stared at the creature, intrigued, excited, confused. Who would have left the dead boy here? How had he died? Should he tell his parents? All these questions swam through his mind. He was not supposed to be there so he couldn't say to his parents about what he had found. The dead boy was his secret, and he used a broken yardstick to poke the dead boy.

When the dead boy's eyes opened, Scott stumbled backward, landing in a tangle of boxes and old clothes.

Without moving its head, the dead boy's glassy, jaundiced eyes flicked to peer at him. Scott stayed in place.

"You're a zombie," Scott said as the dead boy continued to stare at him, neither boy moving. "Are you going to eat me?"

The corpse boy tilted his head slightly, quizzically, and then shook his head slowly: no.

"You don't want to eat my brains?" Scott asked. "Why not?"

The dead boy shrugged.

"My name is Scott. Will you play with me?"

The dead boy tilted his head and nodded slowly. He stood and helped Scott clear away a space in the center of the shed. Then Scott's new friend pulled a box from the pile and emptied the contents on the floor's cleared area.

Scott stared in amazement at what his new friend had found.

The zombie kid meticulously began to assemble the sections of a toy train set. He placed the train on the track, complete with its engine and several little train cars. The caboose went on last, and the tiny conductor dangled from the railing. With Scott's help, they quickly constructed a small city in the center of the room, complete with miniature wooden people and cars. The set even included the miniature road signs and red and white striped crossing gates. By the time Scott heard his mother calling for him, they had created a vast landscape of railroad tracks and crisscrossing streets, with small stations where the train could stop on its circuit around the rails. Scott heard his mother but ignored her for as long as he could. When her voice became more insistent and frantic, and Scott knew he couldn't forget her any longer.

"I've got to go." He groaned. "Will you be here tomorrow?"

The corpse boy hesitated and then gave a slow nod.

Smiling, Scott climbed over the rusted-out equipment and exited the shed. He ran to the back of the house and entered through the screen door. He found his mother in the bedroom, frightened, and with the bed sheet clutched tightly in her fists. Her eyes were wild and filled with terror.

Her darting eyes stopped on Scott, and she visibly relaxed. "Where were you?"

"I was playing," Scott said.

"You promised Mommy you would stay by her side. Where were you?"

"I was in the shed playing with my new friend."

His mother flew off the bed and grabbed him by the shoulders. She shook him firmly but gently. "You let someone see you?" She was almost in tears. Her eyes shot around the room, desperately looking for an escape route.

"It was just my zombie friend, Mommy. He's the dead boy that lives in the shed."

His mother relaxed, let go of his shoulders. "Oh, it's just an imaginary friend." She smiled and returned to the bed. "You know you're not allowed to go outside."

"It's just to the shed out back, Mommy. No one saw me. My zombie friend has a train set out there. He let me play with it."

"Okay," Libby said. "But maybe to be on the safe side, you and your zombie friend should bring the train set in here to play." She had already fallen back to sleep by the time Scott flew from the room to tell his new friend the good news.

He couldn't wait for his mommy to meet the dead boy.

Chapter Eight

Alex pulled the bowstring to her cheek the way Gardner had demonstrated. She held the string lightly with the tips of her fingers and let the arrow fly. And fly it did—right over the target. Gardner laughed. It was not a mocking laugh, but Alex scowled at him anyway. Without even thinking about what she was doing, Alex yanked a second arrow from the quiver and nocked it to the bow. She pulled back and released, nearly hitting the bulls-eye. Gardner stopped laughing.

"Wow," he said.

Alex nocked another arrow and hit the target dead center.

"You're a ringer. How are you doing that?"

"I don't know. I pretend the target is your face and bam." She glared at him.

"Funny," he said without laughing. "Can you do that when you're not pissed at me?"

"I don't know. Go away, and I'll see if I can still hit it."

Gardner's eyes went wide. "Okay, now I know you don't need an arrow to stab something."

Alex's expression softened. "I'm just joking around. Don't be upset."

"I'm not," he said. "We've just done enough for today. Rest up, and we'll start again tomorrow."

Don't be mad. I was kidding, Alex sent the thought to Gardner, and though he pretended to be oblivious, she knew he had and danced around him, teasing him.

They walked back to the house together.

At dusk, the vampires appeared, and Gardner reported Alex's progress.

"Impressive." David gave Alex a high five.

Maggie set the table for dinner. "Come eat, Alex. I cooked roasted potatoes, steamed broccoli, and Tofu."

Randal sat at the opposite side of the table from Gardner and watched him eat.

Gardner set his fork down. "What are you looking at?"

Randal shrugged. "I guess I'm just amazed that a werewolf can be a vegetarian."

"I'm only a vegetarian in human form. I still eat meat in my wolf form."

"Randal stood and stepped away from the table. "I guess I don't see the difference."

"You don't understand because you're not a werewolf."

Randal growled and walked away.

"I was joking. No need to get uptight," Gardner said. When Randal didn't respond, Gardner looked at his mother for support. "He's so sensitive these days."

"I've told you before that you can't treat him like he's an adult. Randal's mind never progressed beyond that of a preteen. He looks up to you, and when you treat him like he's different, it hurts his feelings."

Gardner took a bite of food, swallowed. "I know, but he should know me by now.

"There's something else going on here that you don't see," Maggie said.

Though Maggie made no effort to explain, Alex understood. "It's me."

"Aren't you full of yourself these days?" He took another bite of food.

Alex slugged him on the arm. "You're so dense sometimes, I swear."

"You were his closest ally," Maggie said. "Now, he feels he's lost you to someone else."

"That's ridiculous. We are still as close as ever. I'll make sure Randal understands that."

"Maybe he would like it if you guys included him on Alex's training," Maggie said.

I'm afraid of him.

Gardner turned to her, and she knew he had heard her thought. She gave him a look of warning and stopped him from outing himself in front of his mother.

"I'm not sure," Gardner said to his mother. "But I think Alex is kind of afraid of him. I know she has no reason to be, but..."

"Are you afraid of Randal?" Maggie asked.

She darted a look at Gardner. *I didn't mean for you to know that, and I didn't intend to share it.*

Gardner smiled and placed a hand on her arm. "It's okay. You can admit it."

Alex kept her scowl on Gardner. "I think he's irritated by my presence. His view of me isn't like yours. I think to him I'm not an ally but a nuisance. That makes me nervous. I don't know how to explain it."

Maggie took a seat at the table across from Alex. "If Randal had been allowed to live his human life, he would be in his forties right now. He would have lived and loved and grown old with someone special in his life. Unfortunately, he got denied that life. Making a vampire so young is like the ultimate rub. Randal will never know the joys and sorrows of love and sex. Randal sees Gardner with a girlfriend—"

Gardner dropped his fork. "She's not my girlfriend."

Maggie ignored him. "He sees how close you and Alex are getting, and he knows he cannot have the same thing. Randal may not want a girlfriend, but he doesn't want you to have one either. See what I'm saying?"

"Then I will have to make sure he knows that Alex isn't my girlfriend."

"That won't do any good," said Alex.

Gardner looked at her with a questioning stare.

Alex continued. "Because I'm here. As long as I'm still in the picture, I will be a constant challenger for your attention. Your mother is saying he wants you all to himself."

Maggie nodded. "It's understandable, Alex, after the terrible violence you witnessed and loss you suffered, to have trouble trusting someone who has the power to kill you. Just know that no one in this house would ever harm you, not even Randal. He loves Gardner with all his heart. You have a promise from me that as long as Gardner cares about you, so will Randal. You have no reason to fear him. But if you don't feel comfortable being alone with him, I, for one, will understand."

"Thank you, Maggie. You helped me to understand him better." Alex pointed at the meal on the table. "Aren't you going to eat?"

Maggie smiled. "Like Gardner, I have no taste for meat outside of my wolf form." She leaned in. "And I detest vegetables."

Alex thought a moment. "Are you saying you don't eat anything in your human form?"

Maggie leaned back. "I get all my nutrients from the animals I kill in the wild."

When Maggie stood and walked away, Alex understood that the conversation was over. She and Gardner finished eating. She turned to Gardner.

Thank you for still eating dinner with me, or I would feel out of place. I might starve myself just to fit in.

"Don't worry about that," Gardner said. "I can always eat."

Alex covered her mouth and giggled.

Chapter Nine

Randal exited the house when he couldn't stand to hear that girl's giggle anymore and headed to a neighborhood known for its violent inhabitants. It didn't take long for a nondescript white van to pull up next to him as he huddled, shoulders slumped, on a bench at the bus stop.

The vehicle's tinted window lowered, and a voice barked from the dark interior. "Hey, Kid. Need a ride somewhere?"

Randal looked toward the open window displaying his most frightened expression. "No, I'm okay." His soft voice barely carried over the short distance.

"I have candy," said the voice from within the van.

Randal shivered and turned away.

The vehicle's passenger door opened. "Come on, kid. I won't hurt you."

Randal slowly slid off the bench and shuffled toward the open door. He climbed into the van, closing the door behind him.

The bearded man behind the wheel smiled at Randal. "How old are you, kid?"

"Twelve." Randal's voice crackled with timidity.

The man nodded. "Nice."

The driver reached over to help Randal with the seatbelt. The man's hand moved along Randal's thigh, lingering. Randal looked up, eyes wide and terrified.

"Shh," the man said. "No one needs to know."

Randal lowered his head.

"I'll know." Randal's voice was still timid and childlike, but there was something else there, too; something sing-song, taunting.

"What?"

Randal went for the throat bore the man had time to register how quickly the tables had turned. Randal satisfied his need and decapitated the corpse but left the van sitting in the middle of the street, not caring who found it.

He returned to the park where he was sure to would find the woman. It was near morning when she finally appeared. He approached her.

"Hello, my small creator." She was about to say more, but Randal stopped her. The hour was much too late for chitchat.

"If I join you," he said. "We have to leave this place. We have to go far from here and never come back."

"We will," she said. "That was my plan all along. Wherever you want to go." She smiled pleasantly at him.

"Meet me here tomorrow night." Randal sprinted away.

Randal avoided Gardner and Alex as they frolicked in the backyard and headed to the third-floor room, retreating to his dark place.

Chapter Ten

Alex shuffled through the backyard to the house as she and Gardner returned from training, dirty and tired. He retired to his bedroom, and Alex showered in the second-floor bathroom, but after entering the room assigned to her, she found she wasn't tired. She searched the house until she found Maggie in the computer room.

Alex peered out the window behind Maggie at the rising sun. "Burning the daylight oils?"

Maggie looked up, smiled. "I'm scouting the headlines, hunting."

Alex nearly asked what she meant, but then the meaning occurred to her, and she shivered at the eerie connotation.

"Who is the creep du jour?"

"I think I found something even more urgent." Maggie pointed at the computer screen

Alex came around to read it. *Police seek killer in decapitation case.*

She summarized the article for Alex. "The police are looking for a killer who they believe is on the synthetic drug called bath salts. This killer decapitates his victims and drains the body of blood. Authorities find the body and the severed head in various parts of the city. They believe the victims are killed elsewhere and then planted because they find no blood at the scene where they find the body. Another connection the victims have in this bizarre crime is that they are all known killers, rapists, and drug dealers. The papers have dubbed this suspect the Bath Salts Vigilante."

Maggie turned away from the computer. She looked up at Alex, eyes filled with concern. "This isn't good." She turned back to the computer and shut it down. "There's another monster out there like the Houseguest."

Alex leaned against the sturdy oak desk. "We'll take him down, too."

Maggie glanced at Alex. "You don't understand. This vampire is doing what we do. He's killing rapists and murderers. We can't hunt him. He's us."

"Then just leave him alone." Alex leaned closer to Maggie. "Let him hunt if he's not breaking the code Antony put into place."

"That would be fine." Maggie placed a hand on Alex's arm. "Except this rogue is putting us all in danger."

Chapter Eleven

Cynthia Robinson wrung her hands as she paced her living room. She had already bitten her nails down to the quick and made them bleed and had been exhibiting such erratic behavior since her daughter Alex and her friends failed to show up at the bus stop three days ago. The parents had expected Alex, Amie, and Tom on Monday afternoon. The three sets of parents had waited and waited, but the bus that had picked up their children never returned. Her husband tried to calm her, but she would not relax. She needed answers. She needed to know where her daughter was, and she wouldn't rest until Alex was home.

The police know nothing. No leads, they said. No record that any such contest existed, they said. What did they mean by that? The competition existed because the children were missing. If not, the kids had been spirited away by ghosts. Her stomach was in knots, and her husband George—bless his soul—didn't know what to do. He felt none of the apprehension that plagued Cynthia.

"What do we know?" George said. "They were due back four days ago. What can we learn from the other parents?"

"They know less than we do if you can believe that." Cynthia shook out her hands in an attempt to release her tension. "Amie's parents hadn't even known about the contest." She laughed without humor. "I asked the girl's mother what kind of contest she won, and do you know what she said?"

George didn't have time to answer.

"'What contest?' she said. 'I thought she was spending the night with Alex,' she said." Cynthia made an exasperated groan and paced again. "The boy's father was completely useless. He didn't care if his son ever came home. I think he was drunk." She stopped and faced her husband. "The police were just as useless. They acted like they didn't even care that our kids were missing."

"They have to deal with a lot. I'm sure they gave our situation the amount of attention it warranted compared to all the other issues they are dealing with." George sat forward in his chair. He reached out for Cynthia's hand, but she pulled it away from him and continued her march back and forth across the room.

"Don't make excuses for them."

When the doorbell chimed, Cynthia stopped moving. She stared at the door but didn't make an effort to answer the door.

The doorbell went off two more times in quick succession.

"Don't answer that." Cynthia's voice was barely audible.

"Nonsense," George said and walked to the door.

He unlatched the deadbolt but left the chain lock in place. He opened the door as far as the chain would allow and peered out. He stared at a handsome older woman with silver hair pinned up in a tight bun on the top of her head. She smiled pleasantly at him from the crack in the door.

"Good morning, Mr. Robinson. May I come in and talk to you?" the old woman said.

"What's this about?" George asked.

"Why, about your daughter, of course," the woman said, still smiling. "And where are my manners? My name is Minerva Gould."

George unhooked the chain and allowed the woman to enter, then led her to the living room and offered her a seat. The woman sat down.

Cynthia, back to biting her nails, stood over the silver-haired woman. "What do you know about my daughter?"

"Please sit so we can talk," the woman said. "I do hate having to strain my neck, looking up."

Cynthia dropped into the chair near the window as if forced to do so at gunpoint. "Where is my daughter?" Cynthia said.

"That's why I'm here. I want to explain what is going on so you won't have to worry any longer. The truth of the matter is Alex is just fine, as are her friends and everyone else who went on this trip."

"Why isn't she home? What is going on?" Cynthia asked.

"You see, this was a special event, and we kept our contest a secret to surprise the contestants. This excursion was one of those 'Who Done It?' type vacations. I'm not sure if you've spoken to Alex recently, but the poor girl ran off before she could learn the truth. Have you spoken to her?"

Cynthia sighed. "No, I haven't. But this is not good news. If you've lost my daughter, I'll see to it that you, and whatever company you work for, pay dearly for this."

The older woman's smile vanished in an instant. "We aren't going to learn anything here." Her eyes narrowed, and her mouth curled into a snarl.

"I won't tell you—"

"I told you." The sudden arrival of the man's voice startled Cynthia into silence. She and George looked over at the blond man with a ponytail standing in the living room entrance.

"Who are you? I didn't let you in here. Get out." George stood.

The man stepped forward and forced George back down onto the sofa.

"We can't find your daughter." The older woman continued talking as though the situation had not changed. "We came here hoping you could shed some light on where she might have gone, but you know nothing."

Cynthia rushed over to sit down next to George, throwing her arms around him to stop him from shaking.

"Where is your daughter?" Minerva turned abruptly to Cynthia.

"I don't know," Cynthia said and couldn't understand from where her sudden courage had come. "And I wouldn't tell you if I did."

The blond man said: "I told you the mom and her pup still have her."

"This doesn't prove a thing," Minerva turned to the blond man. "The female and her son could have helped her escape. We won't know for sure if they are the real thing until they return. If they return."

"They'll come back," Roman said.

Cynthia stared at these two strangers—intruders—with a growing bubble of fear in the pit of her stomach. She understood nothing of what these people were saying. They were carrying on a private conversation as if Cynthia and George weren't even present.

The sound of George's whimper caused the woman—Minerva—to turn her attention back to him.

"We'll have to deal with the two of you now, I suppose." Minerva stood.

"I demand to know what's going on," Cynthia said. "You say Alex is still alive, but what about the other children? What have you don't to the parents of those kids?"

Minerva walked around to stand behind the chair in which he had been sitting. "I wouldn't be concerned with them if I were you." She stared Cynthia down. "Their children died like good little sheep."

Cynthia closed her eyes when the blond man began to disrobe. She heard a guttural laugh turn into a growl and hugged George tightly as he trembled and screamed. She kept her eyes shut, even as the blow knocked her across the room, separating her from her beloved George.

Chapter Twelve

When Gardner entered Randal's room, he didn't expect to find the bed neatly made. He turned on the light and stared at the empty bed. Randal never bothered to make the bed before. Randal had once explained his reasons to Gardner. "I refuse to be enslaved to menial tasks for an eternity." Since then, Gardner made it a point to make Randal's bed. Gardner was about to leave the room when he spotted the neatly folded piece of paper on the pillow and picked it up with a mounting sense of dread in the pit of his stomach, the note addressed to him. He scanned it, then searched the room. It had to be a joke.

Gardner squeezed the note in his fist and ran from the room. He stumbled down the steps in a blur of tears and burst into the kitchen where his mother sat at the table sipping tea. Her teacup rattled on the saucer as it slipped from her fingers. She stood and met her son in the center of the room.

"What is it?"

Gardner shook his head, unable to speak, and jammed the note into her hand.

She smoothed out the paper and read:

Gar,

Hey Dude. I don't want you to freak out about this, but I've decided to move on. It's not because of anything you did. I'm searching for myself, and I can't find who I am unless I go out and look. I'm living in a bubble, and there is no way I can see myself doing that. You have to help Alex. I get that, but I have someone I have to help as well. I can create vampires as it would turn out. I have a woman I bit years ago. She doesn't understand our rules, and I have to teach her. She has killed innocent people, and I don't want to see her destroyed, so I'm going away with her. I'll help her understand the code.

We will see each other again because – hey, we're immortals, aren't we? It'd be stupid to think we would never run into each other again someday.

Do what you have to do with Alex. I'll do what I have to do. Just know that I'll always love you and miss you.

Forever,

Rand

"He has threatened to run away before. Being a child-sized immortal is something none of us could hope to understand. One thing I do know is Randal will be okay. He can take care of himself. When he learns how important he is to us, he will return."

Gardner rubbed the back of his hand across his wet eyes. "I should have seen this coming. I need to find him and tell him he can come back. Who is this woman? Did anyone know about her?" He was talking too fast.

His mother placed her hands on his shoulders. "You have to calm down, Honey. You're hyperventilating. We will get through this."

"What's happening?"

When Gardner heard his father's voice behind him, Gardner turned and fell into David's arms. "Randal's gone, Dad." Gardner's voice cracked from the strain of the emotion running through him. "He ran off with some woman."

David guided Gardner into a chair. Maggie handed him the note. David stared at the letter for a long time, then turned to his son. "I didn't know he was able to sire vampires."

"Apparently, he can. Why wouldn't he tell us about this? What does he mean he can't find himself?"

Gardner turned to his mother, but when she had no answers to give, he turned away.

"He said he was afraid we would destroy the woman if we had known of her. Does he not know us better than that? If he cares about her, we won't hurt her. We could have

93

helped him with this woman." Gardner looked up abruptly as if remembering some critical detail. "What if she corrupts him, and he falls to the corruption? It's my fault. All my fault."

"It's not your fault," Maggie said and rubbed his back.

"Stop beating yourself up," David said. "Randal is capable of making his own decisions. And he will do the right thing and come back."

Antony and Alex entered the kitchen, and David explained the situation to them. Antony read the note.

"He will be okay," Antony said. "He is spreading the word about the code. He is stronger than his sire. He will convince her to follow our ways."

Gardner blinked away the last of his tears. "I hope you're right." He turned to Alex. "You ready to train?"

"Are you up to it? Maybe we should…"

"No, I need to get my mind off Randal. Training is just the way to do it."

Gardner and Alex walked out to the training field in the backyard. When everyone was clearly out of hearing range, Gardner stopped Alex.

"I could have stopped Randal," he said.

She gave him a questioning look.

"I could have listened in on his thoughts and seen what was bothering him. I could have seen what he was planning."

"No." Alex's face showed genuine concern. "Just because you can know what others are thinking doesn't mean you should use it to play God. You were right to leave him to his private thoughts. I'm proud of you for showing that kind of strength."

Gardner let this sink in. "We should continue with your training," he said. "You're good with the bow now, but you have to be excellent. To do that, we will have to do something you might not like, but it's necessary."

"And what is that?"

"You have to hunt live animals."

Alex's face became ashen. She seemed unsteady on her feet. "I can't."

"You have to. You need the experience of shooting at moving targets, and you need to know—I need to know—you can take a life if you have to."

"Taking the life of an innocent animal is not the same as attacking a predator that wants to kill me."

"But your ability to shoot when you know it could end a life is an important aspect of what we are doing here. I'm sorry, but this is unavoidable. If you can't shoot to kill, we are wasting our time here. Do you understand?"

Alex swallowed hard and nodded. She collected her bow and quiver, and they headed out to the forested area around the house. Gardner took her to his favorite hunting grounds. They moved swiftly yet quietly through the trees until they came across a doe. Alex aimed. She pulled back the bowstring. Just before she let loose with the arrow, two fawns stepped out of the brush and meandered up to their mother. Alex allowed the bow to drop. She pressed her eyes shut and shook her head.

I can't.

They moved on until they approached a buck. The two followed the animal for about a mile. Once again, Alex aimed. This time she let the arrow fly. The beast was struck in the heart and staggered on its feet. It tried to run but was dead before it could take more than a step. It tripped over its feet and collapsed headlong into the brush.

Alex then took down two raccoons and three squirrels. Gardner kept track of her kills, piling them up. "I'll turn later and eat them for you." He waited for her to protest, but she said nothing. "Just think of it this way; you're not wasting anything."

She nodded.

When another buck entered the woods nearby, Gardner motioned for Alex to take it down. She turned in the direction of the animal. She aimed.

Perhaps it was the wind changing direction or the sound of another animal approaching, but the buck ran.

Gardner pointed. "Chase it down."

Alex gave chase. She moved through the forest at breakneck speed, always keeping the deer in sight. When the animal slowed, Alex aimed. Movement from the left distracted her, and she turned, now pointing at Gardner.

And the bow accidentally released its arrow.

***

The arrow pierced Gardner in the chest to the right of his breastbone. Gardner gasped and dropped to his knees. Blood sprayed from his mouth as he tried to breathe through a collapsed lung. Alex screamed and dropped her bow. She ran to Gardner and held him as he fell into the bed of broken sticks and dead leaves.

Alex ripped the arrow from his chest. Her body shook as she sobbed. She looked at the bloody chunks of meat hanging from the arrow's tip. Removing the shaft had caused even more damage. She tried to stop the blood oozing from the gaping wound with her hands, but her efforts proved useless. She dropped across his chest and wept uncontrollably. After a moment, Alex stood and looked around. She refused to go into shock. She had to find help but dropped back into the dirt beside Gardner. Having no idea where they were, leaving him was out of the question.

Her eyes wild with fear, she wondered what Gardner's mother would do. Undoubtedly, the werewolf matriarch would rip out Alex's heart and eat it. She reached for an arrow. Her fingers brushed against the fletching, and she wrapped her fingers around the shaft, pulled the arrow into her fist. She had no choice but to end her own life before the others did it for her.

"That's a little drastic, don't you think?"

Alex turned at the sound of the voice.

Gardner sat up on one elbow, staring at her.

"You're okay?" Alex stood, relieved yet angry.

"I heal fast. I thought you knew that?"

Alex collected her weapons, trying not to let Gardner see how badly she was shaking. Little good that did, though, since she couldn't hide her thoughts from a mind reader. Still, outwardly, Alex did not let her anxiety show. She allowed her mind to go blank. As Alex concentrated on blocking him out of her thoughts, something soft landed on her head. When she pulled the clothing away, she turned and saw Gardner standing naked a few feet away. He smiled at her and then bounded off. She followed and found him in wolf form, eating her kills. When he had finished, Gardner turned human once again, and Alex threw his clothes back at him. He dressed, and they returned to the yard. She waited for him to apologize, but Gardner only smiled at her, ignoring her anger. She let her anger surface, but still, he seemed not to care that she was mad. Either he was learning to block out her thoughts, or he was blatantly disregarding them.

As they entered the house, they discovered the others gathered around waiting for them. Alex became alarmed. Did they know what she had done in the forest?

"How is the training coming along?" Maggie asked.

Gardner turned to Alex, smiled, and turned back to his mother. "She's ready."

"Good," Maggie said. "Time's up, and we have to go back to New Mexico right away."

Chapter Thirteen

Libby woke from her nap, feeling even more tired than when she laid down. She had a momentary jolt of alarm when she did not see Scott close at hand. When Libby heard him in another room talking to his imaginary friend, she relaxed. Libby remembered Jack returning from the shed with Scott's toy train set.

"I must say, I was impressed with what he did out there," Jack had said. "He had an amazing display, and he did it all by himself."

Libby drifted back to sleep.

***

Corpse Boy hid when the adult came into the shed. After the adult had removed all the train parts, Corpse Boy slipped into the house. He and the boy rebuilt the train set even though the adult male had attempted to recreate what he had seen in the shed. It wasn't even close. After a few hours of playing trains, Scott grew bored and came up with new games for them to play.

Scott set up the rules for the games they played, and Corpse Boy followed the rules, enjoying the interaction with his new friend. He and Scott played cops and robbers and Mars attacks, and Corpse Boy got to play the Mummy in a fantastic horror movie Scott directed.

"Now pretend you kidnapped a *damn's dell in this dress*, and you have to fight her hero rescuer. I'll play the hero. Okay, drop the girl, and fight me." Scott proceeded to wrestle with the Mummy. It was make-believe, and Corpse Boy understood this, so he did not play hard enough to harm his human friend. But Scott wanted realism. Scott twisted the Mummy's hand, first one way, and then the other. He turned the arm around the zombie's back, and then, and then—

Corpse Boy's arm came off with a crack like a dry twig. The severed arm disintegrated in Scott's grip. The boy stared in horror as the dust sifted through his fingers. Scott looked up, eyes wide with shock, as one arm hung limply at Corpse boy's side, the other a mere stump at the elbow.

Scott brushed the remaining dust on his pants. "Gosh, I'm sorry. I didn't mean it."

Corpse Boy looked down at his stump. He turned back to Scott. "It's okay." The voice was a mere whisper through rotted vocal cords. "It'll grow back."

"How long will it take?" Scott asked. He was anxious for his friend to get his arm back.

Corpse boy thought about it. "Tomorrow."

"I didn't know you could talk," Scott said.

Corpse Boy nodded. "Sometimes."

***

At nightfall, Daddy returned, and Scott's rotted friend retreated farther into the house where the family didn't go. Scott ran to his father to see what he had brought home for dinner. Tonight's dinner was in a white Styrofoam box. There was a piece of fish and French fries. He also had several slices of pizza. The food was cold, but it was still good, and Scott couldn't remember the last time he had pizza. It was so good he had two pieces. He asked if he could take a slice to his zombie friend, but his father said no.

"Scott, if you want to take a piece of pizza to your friend, you go right ahead," his mother said. "But not until you finish your dinner.

"Okay, Mommy, thanks."

Libby turned to Jack. "The zombie kid is an imaginary friend. Who do you think will eat the pizza: the corpse that is not there or him? He's going to eat the pizza himself. Let him have the pizza."

"All right. I'll give you that, but why imagine this friend is a zombie?" Jack asked.

"When I was young, my imaginary friend was a ghost," Libby said with a smile. "Jane. I guess these days zombies are the monsters of choice."

"At least a ghost can be explained why it's invisible. But I'll tell you something even creepier than the imaginary zombie friend. Ever since he started playing with this so-called friend, I could swear I smell rotting meat in this place. You don't think he's playing with dead animals, do you?"

Libby dismissed that thought with a wave of her hand. "If he had, I would have seen it. I'm not such a complete basketcase that I don't know what my son is playing with. All he's got are some old toys left behind by the last tenants. I smelled it for a little while too. Maybe you could search under the house for a dead rat or raccoon or something. Honestly, though, you just get used to the smell when you smell it all day."

"I'm out there all day—and most nights— looking for work so that we don't have to stay here. Do you think I want my son and wife living like this?"

"I know you are, baby. I'm not attacking you. Why are you getting so defensive?"

Jack's aggressive posture sagged into something like sadness. "I'm sorry. But until I can fix this broken home, I can't feel like a man." Jack was near tears, but Libby refused to allow him this weakness.

"Jackson Terrell, you are more of a man than anyone I know. You keep us safe and fed when the odds are so against us that it would be easier to give up. You need to stop talking like that: do you hear me?" She shook him for emphasis then kissed him. "I love you."

"I'm done, Mommy. Can I go play with Corpse Boy now?"

She nodded, and Scott ran off.

***

As they lay side by side, Jack wrapped his arms around his wife as if the embrace alone could shelter her from the indignities of their present situation. They made love, ignoring the deterioration and squalor around them.

The following day Jack woke at five and slipped into his clothes. He looked in on Scott as he headed out of the house, noting the smell of rotten meat was most influential in his room. He made a mental note to tell Libby to clean out whatever terrible food was in there.

Jack walked to town and checked through trash cans along the way for any salvageable loot. He placed whatever he deemed worthwhile into the knapsack on his back. Whenever Jack passed a shop with a help wanted sign, he applied for the job, his ritual for the past three weeks, but as of yet, nothing had panned out. Jack would not give up.

He sat on a bench, contemplating his next plan of action, and overheard two women talking about intruders. Jack's ears perked up, wondering if they were talking about him and his family.

"Oh my goodness, Trudy; can you believe these home invasions? No one is safe these days. I heard one woman was shot to death when she walked in on the intruders. They've broken into five houses so far, or so I've heard. Maybe more. That poor woman, they killed her and took the rings off her fingers. Who does that? It's just terrible."

"Terrible," Trudy agreed. The women walked on.

Jack let out the breath he didn't know he had been holding. They weren't talking about him, but the intruders were on the lips and minds of everyone around him. He had heard at least three different stories involving the home invaders and how the police were at a loss to stop them. Jack was only concerned with providing for his family, and when a group of business types left the park and left behind half a box of donuts, Jack placed them in his backpack.

Jack perked up when he spotted a help wanted sign in the apartment complex window. In the foyer, he searched the information board for the location of the office. As he entered the apartment designated as the main office, he gaped at the people shouting and brushing past him as if he wasn't there. It was like walking into a bee's nest — everyone had their jobs to do. Jack made his way through the crowd of people until he found someone he believed to be in charge.

"I'm inquiring about your help wanted sign," Jack said.

"What? I'm sorry I can't hear you," the man in the heavy wool suit said.

"I'm looking for a job. I saw your help wanted ad. I want to apply."

"Oh, the job," The man said. "I see. It includes an apartment and free utility. Have you worked as a superintendent before?"

"I managed an office building in my younger years. I learned all I would need to know then, and I'm good with my hands. I can take a machine apart and put it back together again, even if I've never seen it before."

"Sounds like you could handle this. Write your name and phone number on a paper, and I'll have my secretary set up an interview."

"I'm sorry, but I don't have a phone. I am available any time, any day. I can come back tomorrow or even later today. Just say the word, and I'll be here." Jack did not want to sound desperate, but he felt like this opportunity was slipping away. "Please, I need this job."

"Okay. Be here tomorrow at 9 am and I'll give you an interview. Bring your work experience and credentials."

Jack smiled, showing his straight white teeth, and pumped the man's hand vigorously. "You won't be sorry." Jack danced his way out of the room, looking forward to the return home so he could tell Libby.

Scott gladly took the donuts and vowed to share them with the zombie boy. Libby and Jack barely heard him or cared if his friend was a zombie, or a ghost—or an alien for that matter. They had an interview to plan. In the closet of the room they shared, Libby found a suit that wasn't too moth-ridden. She cleaned it with a damp cloth. He risked using hot water to take a shower. If all went well, they would be long gone before the homeowners learned of the usage. He vowed to pay for whatever electricity and water they used once he had a steady paycheck, anyway.

Jack and Libby checked in on Scott, saw him sleeping with chocolate frosting still smeared on his face, and then retired to their room. Jack was too anxious to sleep, so he lay with an arm wrapped protectively over Libby's slender waist. He almost dropped off to sleep when he heard the noise.

He sat up. He waited, and then he heard it again, a distinct scraping sound. After a moment, he heard a crack, like the breaking of a branch. Jack climbed out of bed and moved to the bedroom door. He peered around the doorframe and waited for his eyes to adjust. He heard the shuffling of feet over the hardwood floor. Standing in his boxers and stocking feet, Jack crept carefully around the corner, heading toward Scott's room.

When Jack first saw the zombie boy, he rubbed his eyes, unsure if he believed what he saw. "You're a real zombie boy?" Jack whispered.

Corpse Boy nodded slowly.

Jack was still staring at the walking corpse when the baseball bat flew at his head. He ducked just before the wood made contact with the side of his head. Jack dropped to the floor and scampered to the wall.

"Look what we have here, Frankie?" the bearded man said and pointed the fat end of the bat at Jack. We got us a darkie squatter in the middle of our latest job."

Another man wearing a bandana on his head stepped around the bearded man. He was holding a gun. "You were right, Paul. Hitting the abandoned houses was a good idea. It looks like we are doing this homeowner a solid and exterminating some vermin."

Jack turned his head and looked into the room where his son still slept. The zombie boy was standing just inside the door frame. With pleading eyes, Jack asked the zombie stranger to get his son out of the house.

***

Corpse Boy understood this request and pulled Scott out of bed, led the sleepy boy to the window, and crashed out the glass with his hand. He then whispered into Scott's ear to run and pushed the boy out the window.

"What the hell was that?" the bearded man asked. "Go find out." But Libby had heard the noise as well, and she stumbled out of the bedroom, distracting the two thieves away from Scott's room.

"Go back, Libby," Jack said. "Now."

"Jack, what's happening?" Panic thickened her voice.

Jack shouted at her. "Just go."

"No," said the man with the gun. "Stay out here where we can see you, or I'll blow your nappy, squatter head right off."

Libby flinched and dropped down beside Jack. Tears smeared the dirt on her cheeks. She peered into the bedroom where Scott was supposed to be sleeping and saw that the bed was empty. As she dragged her gaze toward the window, she spotted the zombie boy.

***

Corpse Boy picked up a shard of glass.

"What's in that room?" the bearded man asked. "You got a squatter kid in there? Come out here, kid."

The bearded man stepped into the doorway and then stepped back again when the zombie exited the room in front of him. Corpse Boy held the glass shard at his side and stalked closer to the intruders.

The bandana man turned the gun toward the thing as it stumbled toward them. The bearded man looked down at Corpse Boy and laughed.

The gunman raised his weapon and fired. The bullet ripped through Corpse Boy's shoulder, but that didn't stop him. The intruder shot again.

"It's a zombie," the bearded man said. "Shoot it in the head, man."

Bandana man blew a chunk of Corpse Boy's head away. As maggots wiggled out of the hole and dropped to the floor, the gunman emptied the clip, but still, Corpse Boy did not fall.

The bearded man looked at the bat still in his hand and swung with all his strength, but Corpse Boy easily dodged the weapon. Corpse Boy slashed the glass shard across the back of the man's hand with a speed only an immortal could achieve. The man screamed and dropped the bat. He clutched at his bleeding hand.

Corpse boy did not hesitate. He drove the shard of glass into the bearded man's belly and then twisted it. He pulled the bloodied piece of glass out along with an extended length of intestine. The wounded man tried to push the bloody purple rope back inside his body. Corpse Boy stabbed him again. And again.

The gunman reached into his boot for the second gun but did not have the opportunity to use it. Corpse Boy turned to the gunman next and stuck the piece of glass into his throat. The man dropped the gun reached for the shard of glass jutting from his neck.

He yanked it out and dropped it. The shard shattered.

Desperately, the wounded man clapped his hands over the bleeding wound. Blood bubbled through his fingers and over his hands. The man looked down at the blood pooling around his feet. Dark ribbons of fluid poured from his fingers and added to the sticky mess on the floor. He vaguely heard the mewling cry from his partner. "My guts are coming out. Oh, Frankie. It's my guts coming out of me."

Corpse Boy turned to the couple cringing against the wall. He raised his hands to show them he was not a danger to them. They nodded their understanding. When Corpse Boy heard the police sirens blaring in the background, he left the house through the broken window.

***

Jack and Libby exited the house to meet the police. Their statement described how Jack and his family had been staying in the house when the intruders came. Jack and Libby both confirmed the series of events that led to the demise of the home invaders. In the official story, Jack, having heard the intruders entering the house, rushed to Scott and broke the window. He sent Scott for help. After Scott was away, Jack picked up a shard of glass and fended off the armed intruders, mortally wounding them.

A forensic team determined that the intruders' gun was the same gun that had killed the woman in a previous break-in. Jack received a reward from the mayor, along with a key to the city. Scott loved the attention the reporters showed him. He knew he could not mention his zombie friend to the reporters, though.

When the apartment manager learned Jack was the man looking for work the day before, he quickly offered Jack the job. Jack accepted, and he and his family moved in immediately.

After the media circus died down, Jack took Scott back to the house. Scott ran into the shed and found the zombie boy in there waiting for him. His missing body parts had regenerated, and Scott was glad about that.

"I have a new home," Scott told him.

Corpse Boy nodded.

"Will you stay here?" Scott asked.

Corpse Boy shook his head slowly.

"Where will you go?"

"Home," Corpse Boy said.

"Where do you live?"

Corpse Boy didn't answer right away. He thought about it then said, "Where my Dark Father created me."

"Will I see you again?" Scott asked. Sadly, he already knew the answer.

Corpse boy shook his head.

Scott threw his arms around his zombie friend and hugged him tightly but was careful not to break off any other body parts.

***

When Scott was gone, Corpse Boy started on his long journey back to the house where his immortal voyage began, where he belonged. That was if he belonged anywhere at all.

Part Two: The Pack

Chapter Fourteen

Maggie approached the hacienda's gate, trying to tame the squirrels tumbling around in her stomach. Outnumbered and inside and behind enemy lines, she needed to be on her guard at all times. If Maggie had any acting ability, this would be the time to shine. Gardner's and her lives relied upon this pack believing she and Gardner wished to join them. She took a deep breath, turned to Gardner, and smiled. His smile strengthened her and filled Maggie with a confidence that hadn't been there a moment ago. She pressed a button that made no noise in her ears but assumed it alerted the people inside of their presence. The blond man with the ponytail answered the call, and his face filled the monitor next to the button she had just pressed. "Just a second," he said, and his image disappeared. They watched him stroll up to the gate, taking his time. He introduced himself as Roman. He smiled a devious smear of pink lips that made Maggie's skin crawl, and then he hit a switch that opened the gate. They walked through, and he led them up to the main house. Their guide didn't speak but stole glances at Maggie randomly. She didn't like the way he was looking at her, as if she had a steak bone tied around her neck. She shivered when his eyes touched her skin.

Minerva met them in the foyer smiling, but she frowned when she did not see the girl. "You did not bring the prize?"

Maggie stepped forward. "She is safe," she said to the silver-haired woman.

"I don't want her safe. I want her dead body here, in front of me."

Maggie forced herself not to flinch at the woman's growling voice.

Maggie studied Minerva and now understood why their first meeting had unnerved her. The older woman's brown aura was pulsating. Maggie pondered the significance of this strange alteration to her ability but could not guess why she saw this. "She is safely tucked away until I know we can trust you. Once you show us good faith that you are willing to let us join, we will deliver her to you."

"Very well." The older woman sighed. "Follow me."

Minerva's mild demeanor returned. Maggie followed the older woman, still wondered what caused her aura to pulsate. Was insanity the reason? Maggie didn't think so. No one was more insane than the Houseguest, and his black aura didn't throb like this. Her ability said Minerva was different in some way that Maggie did not yet understand. For now, she understood the simple fact that Minerva was dangerous.

***

Maggie and Gardner each brought with them two bags. Those bags were taken to their room by Hispanic servants. Gardner, a master at the art of inconspicuous inspection and with incredible peripheral vision, surveyed their surroundings. He used it to scope out their possible exits in the event of a hasty escape. Gardner could also see the red-haired girl staying off to the left but keeping pace with him. He sensed more than saw the blond man, Roman, staying close as well. Gardner considered listening to their thoughts but was concerned they would *feel* the intrusion, alerting the group to his ability. Then everything he and his mother planned would unravel. He would not play that hand until he had no other choice.

As he walked through the hacienda, Gardner was continually being distracted from his task by the place's beauty. The walls seemed to be carved rather than built. He reached out with one hand and touched the wall, shocked by the smooth, cold stone surface. He followed his mother and Minerva to the building that housed the bedrooms. His Mom's room was down the hall on the right side, his door to the left. He had hoped their bedrooms would be attached, giving them better access to each other, but their quarters were too far apart, and there was no possibility of going unseen from room to room. As Maggie continued to her room, Gardner connected to his mother's mind. He wanted to hear her if she was in danger. He ignored her casual thoughts ("want to pluck out those eyes..." and "gives me the shivers..."), but if she cried out—even if only in her mind—he would know.

He entered his room and looked around, wondering what poor soul had occupied this room before him. He did not have his mother's ability to sense past tragedies, and he was grateful for that.

Gardner's bags were on the bed when he arrived at the room. He unpacked quickly, then went investigating. He walked through the halls and into the courtyard that connected all the buildings. He took note of the gated alley Alex had described, knowing it led to the secret garden. Gardner didn't give the gate much notice because someone observed his every move. He didn't want his viewer to suspect he knew more about the hacienda than he should.

He didn't have to look to know the red-haired girl was following him. He walked through the main building and into the area where the pool lay shimmering in the sun. The water falling from the fountain gave the impression that it was a flowing brook and not an artificial thing. He walked past the pool to the double doors leading to the banquet hall. He expected the doors to be locked, but they were not. He entered the room, trying not to expect dead bodies, though it was hard to hide such emotions. But the room was clean and empty. He made a note of the vents without actually looking at them. Those vents had saved Alex's life, he realized. Had the vent she chose led back inside the hacienda somewhere and not to the outside, her fate might have been tragically different. He shuttered at the thought.

Rose entered the room as Gardner examined the intricate carvings on the large table's surface in the room's center. He had been looking for signs of blood but saw none. He looked up and nodded at Rose. She walked over to him and sat on the table in front of him. She looked around the room and sighed as if saying, *what could be more exciting than me?* She turned her attention back to him and waited for him to speak. When he didn't, she spoke up instead. Her voice sounded childlike and innocent, and he had trouble believing her to be a violent killer.

"This is my favorite place in the hacienda." She flicked a wrist to indicate her surroundings without taking her eyes off Gardner. "We've had so many grand parties in here. When the room is full of people, and everyone is laughing and shouting, the sound reverberates off the walls, and the room just comes alive."

Gardner cringed at the thought of what — or who — made up the main course at these parties. "Perhaps Mother and I will get to join in on those parties one day." He kept his face emotionless, playing it off as if he could think of nothing more exceptional.

"Perhaps," Rose said. She peered into Gardner's eyes for a moment and leaned forward when she spoke again. "I want to see your wolf." She smiled. "I'll bet you make a beautiful wolf, don't you?"

Gardner laughed. "I've never seen my wolf."

She flashed him that devilish smile again. "Do you want to see mine?"

Gardner's smile faltered. "Now?" He gulped. "You can change without aid from your alpha?"

"I can change whenever I want. As long as we are under the influence of Mother's care, we can change whenever we wish. The freedom we feel is exquisite. The best part is remembering the wolf. Before I joined this pack, I couldn't remember what I did as the wolf. Mother allows us to recall our wolf's memories."

"The old woman," Gardner said. "She's not your real mother, is she?"

114

"No. When Minerva took me in, I was an orphan. I grew up in one foster home after another. I got bitten at the age of sixteen when a foster family took me camping. The wolf killed the entire family. I hid in a tree."

"Was it...?"

"Minerva? No. A different pack attacked me. At first, I didn't know what had happened. I kept waking up in different places from where I fell asleep, and I would be naked. Then I started finding half-eaten corpses nearby. It didn't take me long to know I had eaten them. By the time I met Minerva, I knew what I was and what was happening, but I still didn't know how to control the wolf. Minerva helped me control and helps me to remember everything when the wolf comes out."

Maggie was Gardner's link to his wolf, but he wasn't about to tell this murderous girl anything personal. Gardner believed opening up to the minds of this pack would be a tremendous advantage, but he just couldn't take the chance that they might somehow sense his presence in their heads. His mother never suspected, but that meant nothing. He knew nothing of these strangers. What if one of them had a similar gift and found out he was poking around in there? He and his mother would be dead before she could even blink out for help.

"Did you name your wolf?" Rose asked, and Gardner tilted his head inquisitively. She laughed at his comical gesture. "We've all named our wolves. The wolves have their separate personalities, so they shouldn't just be considered random nameless animals. I named my wolf Fox. Roman, the creative type that he is, named his wolf." She rolled her eyes. "Bethany named her wolf Dingo. Herman's wolf is named Husky. Vince named his wolf Pup. He's the newest to the group, so I guess it's appropriate. If you and your mother join the pack, we will expect you and your mother to name your wolves."

Gardner tried to keep his expression blank and unassuming, but he found this practice of naming their werewolves a bit egotistical. It seemed downright disrespectful. Werewolves were not pets to be labeled. They were wild beasts—an extension of the murderous and violent part of human nature. Werewolves were a side of them that required constant attention and control, not names.

"What is the name of Minerva's wolf'?" Gardner asked.

Rose looked up from the table where she had been tracing the wood's grain with her finger. "Mother," she said as if he should have already known. "When we address Minerva, it's as if she and the wolf are the same."

"I see," Gardner said, but really, he didn't.

Rose studied him intensely for a moment and then relaxed and smiled. Gardner believed that when a person smiled—genuinely smiled—it showed in their eyes. Gardner noticed Rose's smile never touched her eyes. He had trouble believing Rose had any real emotion behind her smile. He imagined she wore a friendly mask merely to put the other person at ease. Or perhaps it was meant to distract and disarm, lowering her opponent's guard. Either way, Gardner had no intention of trusting this girl.

Rose went back to work, outlining the intricate patterns in the table's design. "Many years ago, Minerva had a husband named Arthur. We were at Yellowstone Park on vacation, and we came across some campers, so we decided to hunt. They seemed an easy lot, but Arthur died. Minerva had been distraught over the loss. She expected to have Arthur with her forever. Things were tough for us for a while. We lost control of our wolves because Minerva refused to lead us. It was Bethany that came up with the campaign to bring our prey to us. The idea intrigued Minerva enough to bring her back from the abyss. It's been a flawless run until now. That little bitch you and your mother captured was our only mistake in the past fifteen years. We

116

need her back. Minerva wants proof of life, so I hope you haven't accidentally eaten her or something like that."

"She's alive for the moment," Gardner said.

"Not for long. I think Minerva will agree to your terms if it means getting her back. Why do you want to join our pack, anyway?"

"It's mostly my mother's idea. She believes we will be safer in a pack rather than on our own."

Rose nodded and seemed to accept the lie. "I'm not privy to their committees, so I can't tell you what they will decide," she said. "I hope they let you in. I'd like to run with you sometime." She smiled her devious smile again, and Gardner had no trouble understanding what she meant: I want to see you naked.

He blushed.

Something in Rose's smile changed when she saw him squirm. He saw a flash of warmth in her smile. She reached out and touched his hand. Her soft, warm flesh lingered on his for a moment, and then she pulled him toward her. She leaned into him, closed her eyes, and pursed her lips. Gardner considered pulling away from her, but something told him spurning her now was the worst thing he could do. The other alternative—accept the kiss—would also lead to trouble. Luckily, Gardner didn't have to make that decision.

"Rosie, what's going on?" Herman said.

Rose broke away from Gardner and leaned back. "Nothing."

Herman stared at Gardner with obvious contempt.

"Nothing was going on, sir," Gardner said. "She was just telling me—"

"Telling him about the rules around here," she said quickly. She shot him a look of desperation, and he understood the information she had relayed had been privileged and not for his ears.

"The rules," he said.

"Make sure you adhere to them, little man," Herman said and fixed Gardner with an icy glare. "You guys shouldn't be in here. Rose, take him back to his room."

"With pleasure." She took Gardner by the hand. After Herman had gone, she added: "What should we do when we get there?"

"You can tell me these rules," he said.

Rose pouted.

Chapter Fifteen

When Maggie heard Gardner's door open and shut, she stepped into the hall and watched him walk away, considering going after him, but decided to give him privacy as he performed his surveillance. She returned to her room and closed the door. She opened the suitcase with her clothes in it and unpacked. Maggie was putting her toiletries away when a knock on her bedroom door stopped her. She opened the door to find a servant girl standing in the hall. The small Spanish girl nervously handed Maggie a piece of paper and then ran off. Maggie wondered if the girl knew what these people were or what they did. She closed the door and studied the folded piece of paper. It was a formal invitation. She opened it and read the heading: From the desk of Roman Strong. The rest of the note was handwritten.

Café Jean Pierre.

3 pm

I'll pick you up at your room. Be ready.

She looked at the clock next to the bed, which read 1:34 pm. She sighed, tossed the note on the dresser, and headed to the bathroom. She took a shower and dressed for a night on the town. She was applying the finishing touches to her makeup when at precisely 3 pm, a loud rap echoed through the room. She checked her dress one last time in the large mirror attached to the dresser and opened the door. Roman stood there, smiling.

"You're ready." He sounded shocked. "I thought all women liked to keep the man waiting."

"I'm not all women," she said.

"I like your hair. You're beautiful with your hair up like that. And that dress is exquisite. I'm very pleased."

"I'm glad you approve."

If he picked up on her sarcasm, he didn't show it. "You're a beautiful woman. How could I not?"

"You're not so bad yourself," she said.

She was surprisingly impressed with his look. He was tall and muscular and filled out his black tuxedo well. His hair was not tied back in a ponytail but hanging loose to his shoulders. He looked like an international spy. She let him take her by the arm and lead her out to the driveway's turnaround and the Yellow Porsche Cayman waiting for them.

"Nice car," she said, and it was, but that wasn't why she said it. She knew he wanted her to say it.

The ride to the restaurant was quiet, but Roman kept stealing glances at Maggie as he drove, always smiling. He sped, obviously not afraid of getting pulled over. Maggie stared out the windshield, uncomfortable with the silence and his attention. She tried to avoid him, but clearly, he refused to be ignored. He caressed the shifter as he accelerated. She figured he imagined the lever was her leg or perhaps a part of his anatomy. She sighed when they finally pulled up in front of the restaurant. Roman passed his keys to the valet, then opened her door. She nearly fell onto the sidewalk getting out. Roman held the restaurant door for her, but she took the handle from him and allowed him to take the lead. He confirmed his reservation, and the maître d turned to the nearest hostess. "Please direct Mr. Strong and company to table seventeen." The maître d then passed a menu to Roman and a smaller card to Maggie. She followed Roman to the reserved table.

The restaurant smelled of freshly baked bread, garlic and herbs, and other French savory cuisines. Maggie had to admit she liked this place. Roman made a great choice, but she would never admit that to him.

Why is he trying so hard to impress me?

He pulled out her chair, and she sat reluctantly, allowing him to push her up to the table. As she glanced over the menu, she realized there were no prices. Although she bristled at the thought of giving up her independence, she allowed him to place her order. They started with wine.

Roman requested a bottle of Romanée Conti. Maggie whispered to the waiter as he was about to slip away that he ordered wine with his name in the title. The waiter huffed out a laugh and hurried off to fetch the expensive red. He returned with a cart carrying the wine and two glasses. After the waiter poured a sample into a glass, Roman swirled it, sniffed it, and then tasted it. He nodded his approval and allowed the waiter to refill the glass and then pour Maggie's. Roman then ordered ratatouille as the soup, Boeuf Bordelaise for himself, and the seafood special for Maggie. She rolled her eyes and cringed at the thought of having to smell fish all night.

As the waiter served Roman's food, he made grand gestures meant to mock Roman, though Maggie's date did not seem to understand the mocking tone. She struggled not to laugh, especially during one hilarious performance when the waiter stood behind Roman, pretending to throw up all over his head. On another trip by them, the waiter mimicked Roman throwing money to his adoring fans. She couldn't help it; she laughed out loud. When Roman turned to see what was so funny, the waiter stood statue-still with a white towel across his arm.

"And will the lady require a doggie bag this evening so that the mister can take her food home and eat it?"

Roman turned to face back at Maggie. She struggled to stop laughing.

"What?" Roman said, unsure if he had heard the young waiter correctly.

The waiter exaggerated every word. "Do you want to take her leftovers home and eat them?"

Maggie stifled a giggle. Roman growled at her, and she straightened up. The waiter walked away.

As Maggie picked at her expensive meal, she could feel Roman's eyes watching her. He made several disgruntled noises and tried to engage her in conversation, but her gaze and her attention were elsewhere in the room. She decided that if she talked to him, she would choose the topic.

"I didn't get a chance to talk to Gardner today," she said. "Did you happen to know what his plans were for the day?"

"Rosie was keeping him entertained, or so I believe." He didn't want to talk about the young ones.

"I would like to see him when we get back," she said.

"I'm sure you will. The kid's probably back in his room already, albeit not alone." His smile turned greasy again, and she turned away.

She hoped Gardner had more sense than to be alone with that girl.

"So why did you bring me here?" she asked.

He seemed not to understand the question. "I like the restaurant," he said.

But not our waiter. "No, I mean, why did you invite me out on this...?" She couldn't bring herself to say the word date.

"I wanted to get to know you. If you want to join my pack, I want to know if you are worthy."

"So, this is — what, an interview?"

"No," Roman said quickly. "Let's just say it's more of a business meeting."

"So, you invite me out to this expensive restaurant, you order the most expensive bottle of wine on the rack, and then you seem to be trying to woo me with kindness. Can you blame me for being suspicious?"

Roman smiled. "This is just what I do."

"Thank you for dinner," she said, not sure what else to say.

"You're welcome. I just wish you ate some of it."

Maggie didn't reply.

There was a moment of silence while Roman dug into his food with ravenous hunger. When he finished, his fork fell to his plate with a tremendous clatter. "I can't help but wonder where you are keeping our mutual friend. Is she tied to a post somewhere? What did you do with her?"

And there it is. The real reason we're here. Maggie lowered her head to hide a smile. "The most I can tell you is that we are keeping her safe. More than that might give away our upper hand. Tell your *Mother* she will be delivered when we are part of the fold."

Roman stared at Maggie for a long time, then shrugged and took a sip of wine.

After dinner, the waiter brought a dessert menu. Maggie and the waiter shared a knowing glance. "Surely madam would like something sweet?" the waiter said in a charming French accent.

"I couldn't eat another bite," she admitted.

"You didn't eat anything," Roman grumbled.

"Monsieur would have a dessert?" The waiter didn't look at Roman as he spoke.

Roman glanced over the list but felt no need to order dessert if Maggie wasn't eating. He closed the menu and handed it back to the waiter.

Now the waiter looked at him. "Perhaps the Mister could benefit from a French-to-English dictionary. Surely Monsieur hasn't spent enough money yet."

Maggie openly laughed.

Roman reddened. He leaned toward the waiter and growled: "I could buy and sell this place just for the sole purpose of firing your ungrateful ass, so stuff it. How is that for spending money, you little jerk?"

"You'll be doing me a mighty great service. I'm an actor, by trade, and the extra time would allow me to work on my craft." The French inflection morphed into a persuasive English accent. "That you for your business, sir. And your money. Come back again any time."

Maggie stifled a laugh. "Your acting is excellent."

Roman pointed a thick finger at the waiter. "You think I owe you something, don't you?"

"Not at all, sir." The waiter bowed. "You're the king of all that you survey, sir." The waiter backed up and scurried off.

Maggie stifled a bout of giggles.

When Roman pounded his fist against the table, she realized the waiter had no idea of the danger Roman posed. Maggie's posture changed from pleasant to protective.

"He's having a little fun, Roman," she said. "You don't have to get angry."

The waiter walked away.

Roman plucked the napkin off his lap and threw it on the table. He paid the bill and turned to Maggie. "Are you coming?" He left no tip.

Roman turned and was out the door. Maggie withdrew a one-hundred-dollar bill from her purse and left it on the table. She winked at the waiter as she passed. He bowed to her.

Maggie rushed to catch up to Roman, convinced he really would have left her behind. She stood behind him as they waited for the valet to deliver the car. The tires squealed and gave off acrid black smoke as Roman drove away. Maggie turned and watched as the people around them coughed and waved their hands in front of their faces.

For most of the ride, Roman was silent. Maggie felt the tension inside the car but said nothing. She didn't want to further infuriate Roman by saying something to invoke his rage again.

"I have bent over backward for you tonight," he said as they pulled into the compound. "You were rude and ungrateful. That's not how someone who wants to join our pack should act."

"You're correct," she said. "And I'm sorry you are upset, but if tonight was about getting to know me—who I am—you're not going to do that by opening doors for me and ordering for me. If you expect me to swoon and hang on to your every word, you are looking at the wrong girl. That's not me. I'm cheeky and abrasive. You were flaunting your money and your fancy car, and even the waiter could see through you. I will say and do whatever I wish. I have to keep my individuality intact. I'm sorry if this means I'm not meant for this pack, but something tells me Minerva will not be concerned with how I treat you."

"You said you were sorry twice, so you're forgiven."

"Thank you."

He had utterly missed the vague apologies for the sarcasm they were, and that made her smile.

"Of course, you can keep your individuality," he said. "I think I was more upset with that infuriating waiter than with you."

"Forget him," she said, hoping the kid would fall off Roman's radar. "You are a successful, rich, and handsome man. He is probably a struggling student who was jealous of what you have. He means nothing."

Roman turned to Maggie and smiled. "He *will* be nothing when I see him again."

Chapter Sixteen

Minerva paced in her room like a caged panther. She glanced at the bedside clock and noted the time: five minutes since the last time she checked. She paced and tapped a slender finger against the back of the opposite hand. The woman huffed, perturbed by the slowness of time. When the knock finally came, she stopped pacing, fixed the bun on the top of her head, and bid her company enter. Bethany stepped through the door, followed closely by Vince. He closed the door once he was inside.

Minerva put the finishing touches on her appearance and turned away from the mirror to face her children. "What news do you have?"

"Not good." Bethany lowered her head. "We returned to the campsite where Roman had first seen their RV, but it wasn't there. We then systematically checked all campsites within a one-hundred-mile radius with no luck. They did not park the RV anywhere near us...that we could find."

"So then, where is she? How many more are helping them? Have they tied her up and put her in some deep dark hole somewhere? So help me, if they killed her before I have a chance to torture that little bitch, I'll..."

"Tear out your bun?" Vince said.

Minerva glared at him. She wasn't in the mood for jokes.

"Do you suppose they have another werewolf watching her?" Bethany asked. "If so, why would she ask to join our pack? That would mean she practically has a pack of her own, wouldn't it?"

"We cannot harm Momma bitch and her mongrel pup until we know the answer to that question," Minerva said. "But the minute we have the girl, anyone who helped her escape will pay with their lives."

"We won't give up the search," Vince promised. "I'll head out with Herman as soon as we can get away."

Minerva straightened her back militarily. "We will double our efforts. I want two teams out there looking for the RV. It should be the easiest thing to find. Roman called it a castle on wheels. How many RV's out there could be as big and extravagant as all that?"

Minerva left her room and started down the hall to the main chambers. Bethany fell into step beside her, and Vince raced to keep up with the two women. When they reached the main sitting room, decorated with antique Spanish art and sculptures, she took a seat in one of the Spanish wicker chairs. Bethany sat on the ottoman. Vince stood to the right of Minerva.

"Where is the Momma wolf now?" Minerva asked.

"Roman took Maggie out to dinner, hoping to get information from her regarding the whereabouts of the RV and the girl," Bethany said.

"He's sniffing out the wrong foxhole," Minerva said.

"He'll get intel, I'm sure," Vince said.

"He is about as sharp as a plastic spoon," Minerva said. "She'll never fall for anything he might try. More likely, he is out to woo her with his masculinity and his wealth. Both of which will not impress her if she is the woman I believe her to be. Where is her whelp?"

"The boy is with Rose," Bethany said.

"Another useless endeavor," Minerva said. "Rose doesn't know anything about the intricacies of seduction or reconnaissance. How can we expect her to get intel? And she better keep her pretty little mouth shut."

"She won't be a problem." Bethany leaned in closer to Mother.

Minerva wasn't so confident. Rose had always been loose-lipped when it came to secrets within the pack. The girl played by her own rules, a weak link.

Minerva secretly blamed Rose for Arthur's death. It had been Rose who insisted on hitting the campers that fateful night. If they had gone on their way, Arthur would still be alive. The notion that the entire group was a little excited by the idea of attacking the humans meant nothing to Minerva. Rose had insisted on the attack, and once it had begun, there was nothing they could do but continue until all the humans were dead. It was Arthur's own rule never to leave survivors. Ironically, one did survive. After being bitten by Arthur, the man had escaped. The strongest human in the group had delivered the fatal blow that brought Arthur low. That man, at least, had been taken down. But the one that got away still haunted Minerva. Who was he? Where was he?

Mother picked up a small brass bell on the stand next to her chair. She rang it then placed it back on the podium. Within minutes, a young Hispanic woman arrived, bowing at Mother's feet. "I wish to have a glass of tea," she told the young woman. "Specifically, African red tea with an orange slice, chilled with ice, and please do not let the tea bag sit so long this time. The last batch was so strong it tasted like cough syrup."

The woman nodded and scurried off.

Returning to the topic at hand, Mother leaned forward, shaking her finger at Bethany. "That girl is the key to wrapping this up. We get our hands on that girl, and we can end this. We must find that girl."

Bethany took Mother by the hands. "We'll do all we can to find her."

Mother pulled her hands away. "See that you do. I detest the idea of allowing that bitch, and that son of a bitch, to join our ranks. Once we have the girl, kill them all."

The young woman returned with the iced tea and set up a portable tray. Ice cubes clinked in the glass carafe as she poured the amber-colored liquid into three frosted mugs. She handed one to Mother, one to Bethany, and the last to Vince. Bethany took a tentative sip from her glass then placed the drink back on the tray. Vince downed the tea in one long swallow, then proceeded to crunch on the ice that had fallen into his cup until a stern look from Mother stopped him. He set his glass on the tray and returned to his post at Mother's side.

Mother took a sip from her glass, tested the flavor, and then nodded her approval. She dismissed the young servant.

"I want to speak with Roman as soon as he returns," Mother said. "He will head up this hunting expedition. He has a nose for this sort of thing. Vince, please see to it he comes to me when he is back from his excursion."

"I will, Mother," Vince said.

"Bethany, dear," Mother said as Vince walked away. "I fear my drink needs something a little stronger. Would you please fetch a bottle of brandy?"

Chapter Seventeen

As Roman pulled up to the walkway, Maggie climbed out of the Cayman and raced inside the hacienda. She didn't want him holding any more doors for her or telling her how pretty she looked or—heaven forbid—inviting her to his room.

She went looking for Gardner and found him still talking to Rose in his room. She asked the girl to leave. She hugged Gardner as if she had expected never to see him again.

"What's going on?" he asked. "You're shaking."

"It's probably more out of anger than anything else. I should never have agreed to that dinner."

"You went on a date?" Gardner said with a laugh. "With who?"

"Not a date," she said quickly. "Roman took me to a restaurant to discuss the terms of our joining the pack, I think. But the night was a total wash."

"Sounds like a date to me…and you're sure dressed like you were on a date."

She scowled at him. "You don't like how I look?"

"You're beautiful," he said. "That's the point I was making."

She dismissed the date talk and told him about the trip to the restaurant. She explained the confrontation between Roman and the waiter and her fears that he would retaliate against the kid. "It was a nightmare. But the real problem is the suspicion I had during the ride home. In it, Roman confronted you, accusing you of something. He was, and I feared for you in this vision. I want you to watch out for him. They may suspect we are not all that we say we are."

"We're not," Gardner reminded her. "We are here intruders, and these people are a suspicious bunch. But we have to see this through to the end. We can't back out now if for no other reason than to keep Alex safe. But I think the answer to taking this pack down is in here."

Maggie shook her head. "They will never invite us into their pack."

"We don't need them to," Gardner said. "If we just hold them off for a couple of days, I think we'll have the answers we're looking for."

"I can't help but think they are maneuvering us into position for something else. The only thing we have going for us right now is the pack doesn't know where Alex is. We have to keep her away from them and hope they don't decide to kill us and try to find her on their own."

"You are just working yourself up, Mom," Gardner said. "Besides, I think we may have an ally inside the pack."

Maggie stopped short. "You do? Who is it?"

"Rose," he said. "She seems genuinely oblivious to everything that's going on here. She truly thinks we are pledging membership to the pack. I'm not sure why but I think they are keeping her out of the loop. She has a lot of information to pass on to us, and she's very eager to do it. I'm going to work on her."

"Keep in mind that she is as dangerous as the rest of them. I will continue to keep up the pretext that we want to join the pack."

"Tell me more about Roman and this waiter," Gardner said.

"It was quite funny. The waiter had this way of pushing Roman's buttons that was downright hilarious. I think he might be an actor or something because he moved in and out of different accents, as though changing hats. He was very clever. I started to worry we were taking it too far, though. Roman was angry that the waiter was picking on him, and he was mad at me for laughing. I worry that Roman might want to do something drastic against the waiter, seek revenge, you know?"

"Mother, stop tormenting the vicious monsters," Gardner said.

Maggie laughed and hugged him. "I've missed you. I hate that we are apart all day."

"We have to mingle. It looks conspiratorial if we are spending too much time together," Gardner said.

"I know. I just don't like it, that's all." Maggie tried to smile, but inside, she still felt nothing but sadness. "I hate when you are out of my sight. And being surrounded by these savage beasts? Forget it." She shook her head. "I can't think straight."

"I can take care of myself," Gardner said.

A memory struck Maggie. "I know, honey. When you said that just now, I remember when you were four years old, tying your shoes. I offered to do it for you, but you brushed me aside and said, 'No, Mommy. I can take care of myself.'" Tears threatened to spill from her eyes.

Gardner hugged her and then held her out at arm's length. "I really can, you know."

She smirked. "I know." She dabbed at her eyes with the knuckle of her index finger. She strode to Gardner's bathroom and stood in front of the mirror. She used a tissue to wipe away aberrant makeup. Gardner stood behind her and watched her.

"I can't stop thinking of Randal, Mom. What if he returned and found we are gone? He should be here helping us." Gardner closed his eyes and sighed heavily.

Maggie considered her words carefully. She said her words softly, gently. "Randal never really understood why we hunt only terrible people. We have to remember he was turned at a very young age and never achieved an adult's mind. Now, he never will. He is perpetually trapped in the state of pre-adolescence and will, therefore, struggle with the concept of right and wrong.

"On top of that, he watched his human family get slaughtered. He has to deal with these demons. He might even have committed violence against innocents. If so, we will have to come to grips with his actions."

Gardner's voice cracked with disbelief. "He wouldn't do that."

"I'm not saying he did. I'm just afraid he might have." Maggie pulled Gardner around and encouraged him to lean against the sink. "I read an article before we left about bodies that were being drained of blood and decapitated and then left to be found by the authorities. I think that is Randal's work."

"Why would you think that? Randal would never put us in danger that way, exposing us like that."

"I'm not saying he's doing it intentionally, but the victims are all criminal types. I think he has inadvertently started an investigation. The tabloids are calling him the Bath Salts Vigilante. Does that remind you of anyone?"

"The Houseguest? Are they calling him a serial killer?" Gardner let the words hang in the air like smoke. "That's all the more reason he shouldn't have gone away. The guilt will consume him."

"It's the reason I rushed you out here. When I pieced it together that Randal was the Vigilante in those articles, I knew that your concerns would override your judgment when you learned about this. We have to deal with this situation first. Randal will be okay until we return. I promise you that when we return, I will devote every waking minute to finding Randal and bringing him back to the group. Nothing he has done—or will ever do—will take him from our hearts. We will find him and make him understand that we are behind him, now and always."

Maggie could see the fear and confusion in Gardner's eyes. She brushed a hand through his dark and shiny hair. She stared into his handsome face. "I'm sure he will return," Maggie said. "And when he does, you cannot ask him what he has done while he was away. If he tells you, you mustn't judge or condemn him for anything he may have done while he was away. We will forgive him for anything. Do you understand that?"

Gardner nodded. He studied her for a moment. "I would never judge Randal. But do you think he did this?"

"Yes," she said. "The police see it as the work of a deranged killer on a psychotropic drug, but what I see is a cry for help."

"Poor Randal." Gardner's shoulders sagged.

"Yeah, I know," Maggie said. "But right now, you need to put this out of your head. Randal will be okay. I miss him too, but we have to make it out of this place alive to help him. Let's resolve the issue at hand, make sure Alex is safe, and then we can spend all the time we need to bring our lost little sheep back into the flock."

Gardner nodded. "It's time to stop playing games. Roman is a dangerous predator, and we have to make sure he doesn't hurt anyone on our watch."

"Be careful, Baby."

"I will."

She kissed his cheek and left his room. She trusted that he would do everything in his power to stay out of danger, but she worried about him just the same. Sometimes, she even wondered if it had been her biggest mistake turning him. But then she thought of his beautiful, caring heart and was glad he would be around for longer than just one lifetime.

Chapter Eighteen

Roman stared at his naked form in the mirror. He ran his hands over the stiff muscles in his arms, his chest, and down to his stomach. Feeling aroused, Roman pulled the rubber band from his ponytail and shook his head, letting long blond hair fall into place around his shoulders. Roman stepped out onto the veranda and allowed the cold night air to blow over his naked flesh. He stepped off the deck and squished sand between his toes. Roman smiled, lifted his face to the night sky, and laughed. He enjoyed his nakedness, and the freedom nudity provided him. He allowed the change to take over. The muscles under his skin quivered and reshaped; bones transformed into lupine dimensions. The skin sagged and reformed over his new animal shape. He dropped down to all fours, and blond fur coursed in waves over his newly formed body. He scratched at the dirt, enjoying the sand under his paws. Sniffing at the earth, Wolf bolted across the sand and away from the hacienda.

Chapter Nineteen

Martin Humphreys was only working at Café Jean Pierre until his acting career took off. For a while, he had worked the dinner theater circuit, but that was a waste of his talent. No one watched the show. In the best scene, guests complained to the waitresses or looked down at their plates, totally oblivious to his work. More recently, he had landed a part in a New Mexican theater production of The Miracle Worker. It should have been his big break, and it would have been if he had landed Captain Keller, Helen's father, but at the last minute, the role went to the theatre manager's son, and Martin got the part of James, her brother. He had two big scenes totaling a whopping seven words. What a breakthrough role that turned out to be.

That was sarcasm, folks. Do you know what that is? No? Let me teach you something —

He'd been better off working the dinner theatre scene. At least then, he'd had lines, even if no one was watching. He had the classic good looks, the charismatic personality, and the drive, so why wasn't he getting auditions?

Waiting tables would not get him discovered, but at least it paid the rent. Martin left the restaurant, waved goodbye to Claude, the cook, and headed through the dark streets toward his apartment. He had contemplated moving out to California or — if he wanted theater work — New York City. But Martin wanted to be in movies. He wanted a sitcom. California was more to his liking.

Martin strolled down the street, looking into the darkened windows of closed shops as he passed them. His body felt tired, but his brain was spinning. He hoped by the time he made it home, usually around midnight, he would be able to fall into bed and snooze. The past couple of nights, however, sleep would not come. Maybe it was his job, but the more likely culprit was the caffeine tablets he downed every four hours just to perform his job. To entertain himself, he had taken up toying with the customers. He was a master at doing voices and accents. He sometimes would start with a French accent, return and use a Texas accent, and confound them with a Canadian accent. The looks he got when he did this were priceless. He laughed now, thinking about how they would turn to their partners or wives and ask: "Was he just speaking with a French accent a minute ago?"

Priceless.

Looking at the path ahead, Martin saw a crowd of disruptive-looking youths coming his way. The kids, who seemed to range in age from 14 to 17, were shouting, hitting street signs, and knocking over trash cans. He could walk past them and risk having this group of ten or so kids harass him and possibly cause him bodily harm, or he could skirt past them by ducking into an alley and move over to the other side of the block until they passed, returning to his side of the street after they were gone. He chose the latter because he liked what his face looked like in its present condition.

He had read somewhere that humans are the only animal on the planet known to ignore their inner sense of self-preservation and go headlong into danger. And when Martin's inner voice told him the alley was not safe, he proved this theory by ignoring his inner voice and stepping into the gloom of the lane.

Vague shapes lurking in the darkness could be trash cans or trolls crouched to attack. The black form with jutting, irregular angles could be the bow of a sinking pirate ship or a dumpster. His imagination was working harder tonight than he recalled on previous trips through town.

Martin moved halfway down the alley, then stopped and looked back the way he had come. No light entered the black hole of an alleyway. He could hear the group of kids moving closer. He tried to blend into the darkness, afraid that if one of the kids looked, they would see him. He considered walking to the other end of the alley, back into the lighted street, but the aisle seemed monstrously long suddenly. Also, he feared the kids would see him moving and give chase. He crouched behind a dumpster until the group had passed. He sat and listened. The little hoodlums were suddenly moving too slowly. They seemed to have picked the end of this alley to stall their progress, and if they decided to turn and come down the lane, they would discover him.

Look, guys, a coward hiding in the shadows. Let's rearrange his face.

Martin's imagination was too vivid for his good.

Fearing a confrontation, Martin crept along the wall, concealed by the dumpster, toward the other end of the alley. Damn, but this seemed like the longest alley in the city. Leave it to him to find the one lane that didn't end.

When Martin heard the growl, it sounded as though it had come from everywhere at once. Suddenly the kids weren't his only concern. He stopped moving and looked around for the dog but could see nothing. At the other end of the alley, the group of shadows started moving again. He came within a few feet from the opposite entrance when a light-colored wolf appeared. It growled, and its blue eyes — its strangely human blue eyes — narrowed, and its lips pulled back in a snarl showing its jagged row of dagger-like fangs. It took a step toward Martin.

"Nice doggie," Martin said and took a reflexive step back.

The wolf moved closer, sidestepping and then following Martin with its eyes. It stepped to the left then glanced back over its right shoulder. Martin wasn't sure, but he thought the wolf was inviting him to run. No, not asking him, daring him.

"I don't think so." Martin turned and ran back toward the other end of the alley. The kids, he saw, had moved on, leaving that entrance open. But the kids were the least of his problems, had never been a problem. He could handle a few kids but hadn't wanted to. Now a more significant and dangerous threat had arisen to teach him a lesson in humility.

Martin was halfway through the alley when the tawny wolf leaped over his head and landed, skittering on its paws in front of him. The wolf turned. Martin skittered to a stop, face to face with the animal, and lost his balance falling back on his ass.

The wolf charged him, snapping and growling. Spittle flew from its jaws, and it nipped at Martin's flailing limbs. Martin shuffled backward and managed to get to his feet. He turned, and in a blind panic, ran from the wolf. Martin had forgotten another rule of survival—never turn your back on a charging animal. But Martin wasn't worried about rules. He just wanted to be away from the wolf at his heels. He sprinted back toward the entranceway where the wolf had first appeared.

The sound of wolf paws on the blacktop, and heavy breathing in his ears was a constant presence behind him. Martin stopped running when teeth gripped his shoe, tripping him. He spun around to face the slathering terror above him. The wolf stopped charging and stared at Martin. The animal's gaze dropped to the ground, and when it looked back, Martin was almost sure he had seen those evil eyes somewhere else.

What did I do to you? The animal was going for his throat.

Just as the wolf sprung, its momentum stopped as a second wolf leaped over Martin's head, driving back the tawny wolf. The second wolf's fur was so black it appeared almost blue. And the black was a male, Martin knew, because as it bounded over his head, Martin could see its testicles dangling from its underbelly. The two wolves came together in a snarling mass of razor teeth and fur. Martin felt the weight of the animals pressing against him as they rolled over him in their struggle. Martin pushed his back against the brick wall in an attempt to escape the fury of the two opposing animals. He felt their hot breath, and saliva dripped on his face. The musky, wild scent of animals was a constant presence in his nostrils, choking him. A paw caught him in the groin, and he doubled over in an explosion of brilliant, white-hot pain.

Then the fight moved away from him, and he could see the animals in action. The tawny wolf was more prominent, but the black wolf was faster and more powerful. The black wolf moved and dodged every attack made by the tawny wolf. The black snapped and bit into the tawny, tearing away chunks of fur and bloody flesh. The black wolf snarled and nipped, driving the tawny wolf back and back. Finally, the tawny wolf had had enough and ran through the alley, disappearing around the corner.

Martin froze in place when the black wolf, panting from the exertion of the fight, turned and stared at him. The wolf padded up to him, sniffed his shoeless foot, and then sniffed his crotch where Martin had peed himself.

"Oh, that. Well, you see —" When Martin looked up, the black wolf was gone.

Martin stood and shook one leg and then the other to get the sodden fabric off his skin. He shivered from the cold wetness at his groin but also from fear.

Seeing nothing around in either direction, Martin bolted from the alley, running down the street, and didn't stop until he locked himself inside his apartment.

Chapter Twenty

Alex stood beside David, looking out at the expanse of desert in front of her. Her exercises had been exhausting, and she needed a rest. David had admitted that he was impressed with the level of mastery Alex had shown over the bamboo bow. David had agreed to be her target. Shooting arrows into someone she considered a friend was a daunting prospect, but her accident with Gardner had conditioned her to handle it. And besides, David had insisted.

At first, it seemed that David was not in any danger of being hit. The arrows flew harmlessly to the place where David had last been standing. His vampire speed took him to a new spot by the time she had loosed the arrow. But Alex watched David and anticipated his movements. She adjusted her aim to let the arrow fly to the spot where she believed David would appear next.

The first arrow hit David in the leg. Alex screamed and dropped the bow. David quickly assured her that he wasn't hurt. After that, he was fair game. By the end, David looked like Saint Sebastian, with arrows sticking out of him in every direction. Alex watched David's wounds healed as soon as he removed the shafts.

"Now I want you to start aiming for strategic body parts," he had said. "You can't hurt a werewolf by shooting him in the leg, but shoot him in the heart, and you just might. The wound won't heal until I remove the object. A shot to the heart, or in the eye deep enough to penetrate the brain, and you might just kill him."

Alex listened as he talked. There was no doubt David was Gardner's father, she concluded. Except for the hair and eyes, which Gardner had undoubtedly inherited from his mother, the son was the father's spitting image. Both were extremely handsome. Staring into David's beautiful green eyes made it difficult for her to concentrate on his words.

David said Vampires didn't have hypnotic abilities. He continued to lecture her, but she still wasn't listening. *That's not entirely true, is it?*

From what Maggie had told her about David's human existence, Alex understood he had harbored this charismatic talent even then. "He could charm an oyster from its shell," Maggie had once told her. She understood that now.

"...pulling an arrow from its eye will put the brakes on its forward motion." David stopped talking. "Are you listening to me?"

Alex snapped back to attention. "Yes." She started. "It's just...are you telling me to aim for your eyes?"

"Like I've told you before, it can't kill me."

"Yes, you've told me it wouldn't kill you, but does it *hurt* you? Do you feel pain?"

David smiled. "No, there is no pain. I feel the pressure when it hits, and I can feel the weight of it in my skin, and I can even feel the tug when removed, but I feel no pain. The eye will regenerate. I do not bleed, and I have no brain function. These facts aren't true for the werewolf. A shot to the brain or the heart will kill it."

"Do stakes to the heart kill you, like in the movies?" Alex felt a little weird asking, but her curiosity was too high.

"No. Antony might be able to explain where that myth came from, but I don't know."

"He still scares me," Alex said before she could stop herself.

David's eyes widened. "He does? Why?"

Alex considered her reasons. "For starters, he's so old...or aged. He's lived a long time. Looking at him is like peering into an abyss. The knowledge he must have acquired over the centuries is mind-boggling,"

"Antony?" David said with a disbelieving expression. "He's dumb as a box of rocks."

"A box of rocks?" Antony emerged from the darkness and joined them. "Really?"

142

David froze. Alex gasped. David turned to her and whispered, "Don't you hate it when he does that?"

Alex looked nervously at Antony. His gaze back at her, head slightly tilted, studying her, made him seem harmless enough, but still, she shuddered in his presence.

"You do not have to fear me. I have dedicated over a thousand years of my existence to preserving human life. I do not expect to assuage your fears with my words, but I do want you to hear it directly from me that you are in no danger from me."

"I didn't mean to offend you." Alex felt the heat of tears stinging her eyes.

Antony smiled. "I am not offended." His smile faded. "But I am sad that I cause you to fear me. I will never harm you. I hope you can see it in your heart to accept my apologies."

"No," Alex said quickly. "I should be apologizing. My fear isn't from any belief you would do me harm. I'm in awe of your experience. My mere eighteen years pales in comparison. Your centuries of existence are very intimidating."

"My centuries are not that impressive. I have lived a long and sheltered existence. Do not waste any more time fretting over such trivial matters. We are a team. We must now work toward the same goal of protecting the population from the pain and violence inflicted by such vile creatures as these werewolves."

"I don't know about you, but my sole purpose for going after these bastards is revenge for my friends." Alex's fears lifted, and the previous fire and passion returned in her eyes.

"That too," Antony agreed. Then changed the subject. "How is the training going?"

Alex turned to David for an assessment of her progress.

"This girl has the reflexes of a cobra. I don't know any human who can shoot a target moving at the speed of sound like she can. And she doesn't just have the reflexes. She has the accuracy too. I counted four kill shots."

"This is good news," Antony announced. "But we should get back to the RV and head out. We do not want to spend too much time in one place. The Werewolves might be able to track us down. We do not want to get caught off guard."

They headed back to the Zephyr.

"I have something for you," Antony said to Alex.

"A gift?" she asked.

"You can call it that."

Inside the Zephyr, Antony retrieved a wooden box from inside his steel sleeping chamber. He placed the crate in front of Alex, and she stared at it for a moment before making a move to open it.

"It's not even my birthday," she said.

"This gift could not wait," Antony explained.

The box was about the same size as a dozen roses, but something told her there were no flowers inside. She reached out and unlatched the clasp. She flipped the top back and peered inside, unsure what she was looking for. She removed the object from the box. It was a curved blade with an intricately carved handle. Gingerly she began to toy with it, careful not to cut herself on the extremely sharp edge. When she gripped the weapon by its hilt, she realized the blade flipped out and away from the handle. She flicked her wrist, and the curved blade snapped into position.

Now she knew what it was. "It's a scythe."

"It's got an edge as sharp as my katana," David said. "We have to train you at handling the blade, so if they trap you in close quarters, you have something to protect yourself with. It's my design, too. I made it to fold away so you can easily carry it with your bow and extend it with a flick of the wrist."

"Thank you," Alex said. She began swinging the scythe in a figure-eight pattern. Then she turned the blade at David's head.

David caught the blade in his hand just as it was about to connect with his neck. Alex flushed as David stood with the business end of the blade inches from his neck. "This isn't a toy," he said. If you take my head off with this, I'm done. That is one way to kill a vampire."

"I'm so sorry," she said. "After shooting you in the heart with an arrow, I started believing I couldn't hurt you no matter what I did."

"Next rule," David said. "Do not swing sharp objects at my neck."

Chapter Twenty-One

Gardner found his mother in the ballroom sitting at the piano. He walked up behind her and watched her fingers pass over the keys without depressing them. After a moment, she dropped her hands at her sides without causing even a tingle from the chords. She sighed heavily.

"What were you playing?"

Her piercing scream echoed off the walls and reverberated through the empty room.

Gardner pulled his hands away from his ears. "I'm sorry. I didn't mean to startle you."

"How long were you standing there? I guess I'm a little tightly wound these days." She placed the palm of her hand at her heart.

Gardner seemed to be the only one with the ability to sneak up on her like that. "Only a few minutes."

Maggie looked around the ballroom with a dreamy expression. "If this place wasn't so full of evil people, I could get used to it here."

Gardner had snuck up on her before, but she had never reacted as she had just now. He supposed that being literally in the wolf's den could do that to someone. "Being here has your nerves frayed to the breaking point. We should call this off and sneak out."

"No, we're going to see this through."

He sat down beside her and mimicked her finger motion. When he thought he had it correct, he started to play. The music he played was haunting and familiar. When he finished, he turned to her. "I know this song."

Maggie gaped. After the shock wore off, she found her words. "Did you learn to play that just now while watching me?"

"Yes," he said as if it were the most natural thing.

"It's Chopin Etude Op. 25 no 7. I used to play it for you when you were a baby. I haven't touched a piano since you were four years old. How could you know how to play that?"

"I don't know. I've always had a knack for learning by watching. My friends in school used to get a kick out of it. They would show me dance moves just once, and I could perform it perfectly."

"How did I not know this about you?" she asked, astonished.

"There's a lot you don't know about me. That's kind of why I'm here to see you."

"What do you mean?" she asked.

Gardner turned as if expecting to see someone to be standing in the doorway. "I'd rather not talk about it here. We have to go somewhere no one can hear us."

Maggie was intrigued. "Okay."

They left the ballroom and walked along a path that led them away from any buildings. Maggie stared at Gardner for several minutes as they walked. "Okay, I can't take it any longer. What's going on?"

Gardner started to speak several times and only managed a syllable or two before he stopped and tried again. At last, he found the words he had been unable to form, and once Gardner started talking, he didn't stop.

"I hear voices. It started when I turned 14 but didn't come to full strength until I was—you know—turned. I started noticing that I was hearing people talking when their mouths weren't moving. At first, I thought I was going crazy—schizophrenia, or something; hearing voices and all that—but I didn't hear imaginary voices: I heard thoughts. I wasn't hearing what people were saying; I was hearing what people were thinking. When I started hearing thoughts that I wasn't meant to hear, I learned to shut the thoughts out. So instead of strengthening the ability, I was strengthening my resistance to it. Now I can turn it on and off at will. When we first arrived here, I was afraid of turning this ability on and alerting our hosts to my ability. But the longer we stayed, and the farther behind enemy lines we seem to have fallen, I think we should take the risk. I started gradually at first. I listened in on Rose's thoughts. She has no direct knowledge of this pack's workings, and she showed no recognition of my presence inside her head, so I moved on. The next person I peeked in on was Roman. I learned he planned to kill the waiter at the restaurant he took you to. I followed him and stopped him from finishing the poor guy off. I don't think he knows it was me, but I'm sure he suspects. I haven't seen him yet, but I can guess he's mad. What do you think?"

Maggie just stared at him. Tears glistened in her eyes.

"What do you think?" he asked again.

"I'm lost for words. You read minds? Mindreading surpasses even my abilities. How have you hidden this from us for so long? And you exposed yourself? You should have said something to me sooner. And you said you fought with Roman? Gardner, he could have killed you."

"He's not that tough," Gardner said.

"He's dangerous."

"Yea, I know, but what about my proposal? Should we use my ability on the pack? Find out what the pack is hiding from us?"

"I have to calm down and collect my thoughts. I have to consider all the possibilities surrounding this idea. This ability could change everything. Why hadn't you told me about this sooner, and who else knows about it?"

"Alex is the only other person who knows," he said. "I accidentally used it on her. She figured it out."

Good for her, Maggie thought. *I'm your mother, and this went unnoticed by me. She figured it out within days of meeting you.*

"Well, it's because I had trouble hiding it from her. I couldn't tune her out, so when I reacted to what she was thinking, she started to suspect."

Are you reading my thoughts right now? Maggie thought.

"Yes. Mom, don't turn this into a parlor trick."

Maggie slapped a hand over her mouth and giggled uncontrollably.

"Did you sense me in there?" he asked.

"I'm not sure. Do it again."

I love you, Baby, his mother thought.

"Mom." He groaned. "I know you love me. You have to make it harder than that."

Maggie giggled again. She thought: *I'm very proud of you taking on Roman like that, but it was perilous. I should have been with you.*

"I had control of the situation the whole time. Roman didn't even know it was me, not for sure. And I caught him by surprise. I had him running with his tail between his legs, literally."

She laughed and hugged him. When she pulled back, he waited for her analysis.

"I had no sense of you in my head. Even my premonitions didn't warn me. You have an amazing gift. You should have told me sooner."

"Okay, you know now. Are we going to test it? Let's confront Roman. I'm going to listen in and see if he suspects me as the werewolf that interrupted his attack last night. We'll also find out if he can sense me in his head."

"Sounds dangerous," Maggie said. "But I think we need to do it."

They walked around the compound, trying to pinpoint where Roman might be without having to come out and ask someone. They found him quite by accident when Gardner gave up the search and headed for the kitchen.

"What's good?" Gardner said.

Roman chomped into a sandwich. "Roast beef," he said through a mouthful of raw meat. "Rare, just the way I like it."

Gardner's stomach roiled. He could only eat meat in his wolf form. The thought of eating meat sickened him otherwise.

149

"Is there any left?" Gardner asked.

Gardner stopped caring what Roman was saying. He started listening inside Roman's head.

Little pup, was it you last night who interfered with my kill? No, you couldn't possibly be anywhere large enough to stand against me. If you had been there, I would have torn your throat out and ate you for a light snack.

I'd like to see you try. Gardner tried to send this thought into Roman's head, but if Roman heard, he gave no indication.

"Sorry, kid. I ate it all." Roman dismissed the boy and his mother and walked past them.

When he was gone from the room, Gardner turned to his mother. "Looks like my ability is a one-way receiver."

"Yes, but we have to make sure. Try it on the girl, Rose, again. I want to be there when you try it on, Bethany and Minerva. If something goes wrong, it will take both of us to stop them. And if I have to, I'll astrally project and bring Antony and your dad, so we should do it at night."

"Okay," Gardner said.

They returned to Maggie's room. She wanted to know more about his unusual gift, and Gardner told her everything he knew, all he understood to be true about how to control it. She didn't interrupt.

"I was worried that if people knew I could invade their thoughts, they would be mad at me," he said. "I guess I was ashamed."

"Never be ashamed, Honey. Your gift is a blessing, something given to you for a purpose. I guess I should have told you from the start just how important your gift would be, but I didn't want you to get discouraged if you never developed one. I could have helped you through your discomfort and helped you to use it only when necessary. I'm sorry you had to carry this burden alone."

"There's more," Gardner said.

"What is it?" Maggie asked.

"It's Randal. I feel I could have protected him better if I had used the ability to see what was troubling him. I should have helped him."

"Sometimes people have to help themselves. Even if you had used your ability to see what was troubling him, it doesn't mean you would have had the answers to solve his dilemma. Only he can do that. Chances are good he would have seen your interference as prying. He may even have resented you for it. You did the right thing."

"Alex said the same thing," he said.

"She's right."

"I miss him."

"I do, too," Maggie said. "I helped that boy more than you can know in the beginning. I saved him from being destroyed."

"By who?" Gardner asked. He was expecting her to say some horrific monster or some terrible event. The answer had him floored.

"Antony," she said. "He felt he was going to be a danger to himself and others, so he had concluded to destroy Randal. I talked him out of it."

"Thank you," Gardner said. "I'm sure Randal appreciated that, too."

"I can't take all the credit. Randal proved to be respectful and upstanding. Even though Randal didn't have the maturity to understand what he was and what he could do, our little friend learned fast. And thanks to you, Randal learned compassion. He was your protector and your best friend growing up. He worshiped you, cherished you. Having you gave him a part of his humanity back. Something he had lost when the killer murdered his human family. I have no doubt Randal will return to us—to you."

"I love you, Mom," Gardner said.

I love you, too, Maggie thought. *I can say it without opening my mouth, and you can hear it, but I must still voice it.*

She whispered into his ear. "I love you, too."

Chapter Twenty-Two

Gardner walked along the stone pathway that meandered around the buildings of the compound. He was not actively seeking Rose but found her sitting on a stone bench with the steel tag: IN LOVING MEMORY OF ARTHUR GOULD.

"What's up?" he said.

She looked up at him but didn't answer.

"Mind if I sit with you?"

She didn't respond but nor did object, so he sat. Gardner pretended to take in the surroundings as he secretly connected to her mind. He listened for anything she might know about the pack's intentions toward his mother and him, but she wasn't thinking of anything. Gardner looked for any sign she could sense his presence inside her head. If she knew he was inside her head, she gave no notice. He received no thoughts from her, so he came right out and asked her.

"What are you thinking about?" he said.

"I'm thinking about how much I hate this place," she said. Gardner had to reach down into what felt like a dark tunnel to find this thought, but finally, it was there.

"How can you hate such a beautiful place? It's amazing here."

"Okay, I don't mean the place. I mean the people." She stopped and looked around, searching for spies. "I get this sense that something is going on, and no one tells me what it is. As if I'm not worthy enough to be in the loop, I guess."

"Why don't you leave?" Gardner said.

"I can't." Her voice was stern, almost angry at Gardner for suggesting it. But then she spoke softer. "I'll lose my protection. I can't go back to living the life of a lone wolf. I just have to put up with being treated like an outsider to keep the pack's benefits. I'm sure it's the same for you and your mom, right. I mean, isn't that why you two want to join. You're not joining because you like the people."

"You're right." Gardner didn't want to lie but could tell her nothing of his real reasons for being there.

"How is it you and your mother became werewolves? Was it at the same time?"

"No, she changed first, getting turned when I was young, somehow managing to keep me safe. She bit me when I was nineteen." He couldn't say it was intentional because that would imply she had control over the wolf inside her. He didn't want Rose to know his mother had that ability.

"What about the wolf that bit her? Wasn't he in a pack?"

"No, he was a loner, too. The wolf is dead now." *So far, so good. No real lies there.*

"What happened to your father?" Rose asked.

"Mom killed him." It was out before Gardner realized what he'd said and looked at Rose to see if she believed him. He wasn't sure but thought he'd just told his very first lie. He may have lied as a child, but he didn't remember.

Rose laughed.

"Good for her," she said.

Gardner searched Rose's thoughts. She did believe it.

I can do this. I can say anything. I have to remember to tell mom she killed dad. I hope she gets as big a kick out of that as Rose did. And will the others buy this if Rose mentions it to someone?

Rose seemed to be a dead end. She either didn't know anything about the pack, or she just didn't care enough to give it any thought. Everything inside her head had to do with how the world affected her.

"I'm curious to know more about that feast here the night my mom and I first approached your pack," Gardner said and gaged her reaction to this question. "Do you guys host that kind of thing often?"

153

"About once a year," she said. "I ate three people that night: one of Herman's nerds and two pretty girls. I was a real pig."

Gardner shuttered at the loss of life and the cruel way she talked about it. He cringed as she reminisced about eating the pretty girls. "We hunt hikers and vacationers for the rest of the year."

She loved killing, he realized. She loved it and would never stop. She would have no place in his group. He swallowed hard as he realized that he would have to destroy her with the rest.

Gardner remembered Randal once asking him, "Why do we have the right to decide who is bad or good?"

Gardner had thought about this question before answering. "We use the rules of society to make that determination," he had said.

Randal had not seemed convinced. "It's a society we are no longer a part of."

Gardner didn't remember how he had responded; he only remembered the topic had been far outside his realm of expertise. He thought maybe he had directed Randal to Antony for an answer. Gardner had been mature enough to understand that the principles his mother and father passed on to him were just the way they had to be. Still, he could see where Randal did not have that level of maturity. Rose had also been turned immortal without that guidance and sophistication, but where Randal had been willing to accept and obey others' governance, Rose cared about Rose.

Rose's voice broke Gardner's concentration, and he looked at her. "What?"

"When are you going to give us that girl?" she said again.

Here it is. Gardner groaned inside. *Time to get real.*

"When my mother deems it's safe to trust your pack, and after Minerva agrees to let us join," he said.

"What if she doesn't let you join?"

"Then I guess we go on our way, and we take the girl with us."

"Mother will never let that happen," Rose said.

Gardner felt a rock settle in the pit of his stomach.

"I don't think you realize it yet, but there are only two choices for you."

"And what are those?"

"Simple. Either you give us the girl, and Minerva lets you join, or you give us the girl, and we kill you and your mother."

I'd like to see you try. "Well then, for our sake, I hope Minerva accepts us."

"This would be the first time." The doubt in Rose's voice was unmistakable.

"First time for what?" Gardner asked, though he already knew the answer.

"The first time that someone came to Minerva asking to join. The last member to join the pack was Vince. Minerva found him traveling the roads and wreaking havoc across the countryside. The officials started an investigation when people thought his victims were the work of some maniac. He was too close to home, so she took him in to control him and stop the investigations. None of us asked to join. Minerva and Author came to us. All of us."

"But has anyone asked to join and were turned down?"

"Not that I know of."

"So, there is still a chance for us."

"I guess." She didn't sound convinced.

"Have you ever seen other werewolves besides your pack?" Gardner asked.

"Yes, we've come across other competing packs. We've always executed them."

"Have you ever lost prey that you have bitten and created a new werewolf?"

155

"Not since Arthur. He bit someone who got away. It was the same night he died. We never knew what happened to that one."

It struck Gardner then that he and his mother were already a part of this pack. He and his mother were, in fact, from Arthur's line. But it seemed of little importance since they weren't trying to get into the pack. He would remind his mother of this fact since there was a potential to exploit this angle.

Gardner and Rose sat in silence for a while. When Rose started showing boredom in his company, he reached into her thoughts one last time. What he heard gave him a chill, and he had to walk away.

Rose thought: *I wonder who will kill him when Minerva orders his death? I think I'll pass. I like him.*

Chapter Twenty-Three

Maggie flinched as a sharp knock reverberated through her room. She slowly opened the door and peered out at Minerva standing in the hall. The woman's thin-lipped smile was as tight as the bun on her head. Maggie couldn't imagine it was a comfortable hairstyle, with the hair pulled, so snug there seemed to be stress marks on her scalp. The older woman stood outside the room with her hands clasped behind her back, a straight posture, wearing a heavy black polyester dress and sensible shoes.

"Good afternoon," Maggie said before her shock was too evident. "And what is it I can I do for you, Ms. Minerva?"

"It's time to discuss your integration into the pack," Minerva said. "We want the girl, and if allowing you to join us is the fastest way to get her, I see no reason to put you off any longer. You're in. Welcome to the pack. I'm here to take you to your permanent home."

Maggie just stared at Minerva for a minute. The inauguration was happening too fast. Then panic set in. She found Alex, and now the game is over. Maggie wished Gardner was there to hear Minerva's thoughts. She struggled to hide her nervousness.

"We all have our own apartments on the compound. You and your son will also have an apartment. You don't mind sharing with Gardner, do you?"

"Not at all," Maggie said. She stepped out of the room and closed the door. She followed Minerva down the hall. "Although, I can't rightfully speak for him." Maggie laughed, not letting on that she thought this woman was leading her into a trap. She wished she had time to astral project to the Zephyr and see if Alex was still safe, but leaving her body now would only put Maggie in more danger. She would just have to wait and see how this played out.

Minerva turned to Maggie. "Once integrated into the pack, I will need to know what you and your son taste like."

Maggie stopped. "What?" She worked to swallow the lump in her throat.

"Yes, we need to know what your tastes are. What type of prey do you prefer? Rose likes pretty girls, and Bethany enjoys men who sexualize women. Vince likes buxom blonds. Herman prefers homosexuals. I wouldn't be able to tell you what that is all about, but..."

"I get the point," Maggie said, and they continued walking. She had to think fast. A hesitation might alert Minerva to the lie. "I'm partial to bodybuilders, and Gardner prefers ethnic women." Maggie's words came out seamlessly. She was sure she sounded natural and honest.

Minerva nodded. "We will have to include them in our next roundup."

Bile rose in Maggie's throat at the appalling way this woman spoke of humans like cattle. She tried not to let the horror show on her face and swallowed her purge with an audible gulp. Minerva took the lead, and several times the older woman turned back to look at Maggie as if checking to see if she still followed. Maggie's skin crawled every time the older woman's eyes fell upon her. Maggie smiled, however. She was determined to show no outward signs of distress.

The woman stopped at the building looking like the rest of the hacienda, though apart from the other facilities. Maggie imagined the horrors she would find on the other side of the door, and her façade broke.

With a trembling voice, she said: "I was wondering if this is a good time to tell you something that I've meant to share with you."

"What is it, dear?" Minerva asked. Her voice was cold.

"It's the real reason why we have approached to join your pack," Maggie said. Minerva's expression changed from that of boredom to one of curiosity.

158

"Please continue," Minerva said.

"Gardner and I are already practically part of the family," she said. "The werewolf who bit me was the man who your Arthur bit in the Yellowstone National Park."

Minerva's unyielding face showed no sign of shock or surprise. "Please continue."

"I was bitten by a werewolf who later told me of the attack on him in the Yellowstone Park. When Gardner turned eighteen, I bit him on purpose to protect him. We traveled together ever since, looking for the pack that created him, and by default us, and after many years, we finally tracked you down."

"What became of this man?" Minerva asked.

"He's dead," Maggie said. "I killed him."

"He's dead then," Minerva said with a deep sigh of relief.

"Yes."

Minerva smiled, and happiness converted her cold demeanor into something friendlier. "I have something to confess also." Minerva opened the door to the building. "I could smell Arthur's blood in you the minute you showed up at my door. I've always known what you just confirmed."

Maggie peered wide-eyed into the doorway at an adobe-style home, decorated with what looked to be ancient Mayan artifacts and expensive and rare paintings on the walls. The carpeting looked so thick and luxurious that Maggie couldn't wait to feel the fibers under her bare feet.

I could live here.

The building had a cathedral ceiling, with a winding staircase that led to the two bedrooms. The kitchen had an island with a sink in it. The faucet with an adjustable neck came down from the ceiling. Two chains controlled hot and cold water. The stove blended into the counter so well to be invisible until the burners came on and the hotplate glowed red. The entire apartment was fully furnished right down to the pots and pans and vases filled with flowers right out of Minerva's private garden.

"When can we move in?" Maggie asked.

"Today," Minerva said. "Right now."

Maggie lost herself in the beauty of the place and had to remind herself. I'm not really going to live here. It's all make-believe. Yes, it was only temporary, but she was going to enjoy every minute spent in this new apartment. Maggie walked through the house with Minerva, and there was nothing pretend about the awe the place instilled in her. From the smile on the older woman's face, Maggie understood this was the reaction Minerva had been expecting.

Though this new home seemed more private, Maggie thought that the pack could still monitor every word she and Gardner said or hidden cameras could see everything they did. Even the bathrooms and bedrooms afforded them no privacy. The group could overhear every word spoken, and every action watched. They weren't safe, no matter how luxurious their new home appeared to be.

"Now I want you to sit and tell me about this man who bit you." Minerva led Maggie to a leather sofa. "What happened that brought you into contact with him?"

Maggie settled into her seat as she worked out the story she was going to tell. She decided it had to be half-truthful if she to sell her story. As Maggie made a show of enjoying the comfort, the story began to form in her head. She felt comfortable adding to the account once the general plot began to form.

"He was a tenant," Maggie said. "My husband, David, and I owned a house, and we took him in as a border. Gardner was a baby at the time, and we needed money. He was a quiet sort and paid his rent on time. We had no reason to dislike him. He had been living in our guesthouse for six months when he failed to control his change. David heard a noise near the guest house and went out to check on it. The wolf killed David and then came after me. I managed to get Gardner into the panic room, but it bit me before I could get to safety. We waited out the night in the panic room. When the wolf turned back into the man—his name was Dylan, by the way—I locked him in the panic room. Using the intercom, I forced him to tell me everything he knew about what he was and how it had happened. That was when I learned about your pack and the events—as he told them, anyway—at Yellowstone. I traveled with this man for many years, always sure to cage ourselves up and put Gardner somewhere safe."

"Amazing," Minerva said. "What happened to this man, this…Dylan?"

"I killed him." Maggie spoke in a hushed tone. Her story had begun to fall apart as she talked of the way she killed Dylan (ripping out his heart), but she couldn't change it now. Maggie couldn't tell by Minerva's stony face if she had bought the fabrication, but she supposed it didn't matter. The story served the purpose of buying Maggie and Gardner more time.

"I like that you ripped out his heart," Minerva said. "Quite apropos. It's what his friend did to me when he killed Arthur."

When Minerva seemed sufficiently informed, she stood and walked out. Maggie quickly swept through the apartment, looking for anything that could be hiding a small microphone or hidden camera. She removed mirrors and framed pictures, vases, and knick-knacks. There seemed to be nothing unusual about any of them. If the group bugged the house, she couldn't prove it.

Later, Maggie sought out Gardner to inform him of the move. They walked in a section of the compound where they knew no one could hear them. She told him that the new place was not to be trusted, and they quickly worked out code words that would not alert any unwanted ears to their plans.

161

Maggie stopped and turned to face Gardner. She lowered her head. "What did you learn from our little red-haired girl?"

"I didn't learn much about the pack from Rose," he said. "But she learned a lot about us. I told her that you killed Dad."

"Interesting," Maggie said. "And unfortunate, because in the version I told Minerva, Dylan killed your Dad."

"What do we do?" Gardner asked.

"Nothing," Maggie said. "And pray they never compare stories."

Chapter Twenty-Four

Night arrived, and heavy clouds blotted out the moon. The dark form crept across the sand, crouching low. Although human in shape and color, glowing blue eyes saw clearly in monochromatic night vision due to the wolf's high ratio of rods to cones. Another aspect of this wolf that differed from a full-blooded member of the lupine species was the oddly shaped head. This creature's skull was slightly larger than an ordinary wolf's head, although it would take a well-trained eye to see the mutation. This head held the humanoid brain of a man-wolf hybrid. As the yellow-furred creature stalked through the darkness, it lowered its snout and sniffed. It had picked up the scent of the girl about an hour ago and pursued her now. The werewolf also located tire tracks from a big vehicle, possibly the RV Wolf sought. Tonight, Wolf would leave little doubt why he was best suited to do all the tracking."

Wolf bounded through the night, kicking up clumps of sand, having picked up a strong scent leading to the girl. She was close, very close. He had reached a full run by the time he had reached the source of the smell.

Wolf stopped. He glanced around but saw nothing. He padded over to a well-worn area where tire tracks and human footprints crisscrossed in an endless pattern. Wolf lowered his snout to the sand and sniffed. He turned left and then skittered to the right, sniffed. Here the odor was more pungent, so he moved across the sand to the thing that had led him to this place. Crouching down, Wolf sniffed the broken arrow. The girl's scent was all over it. He growled, angered that the girl had slipped away from him. The overpowering odor left no doubt she had been there recently. But she was not there now.

He sniffed the arrow again. It was all he could smell. He tried to find a new trail, tried to discern which direction the vehicle had gone. He could begin the search anew, but the damn arrow clouded its senses.

Wolf stood over the projectile, lifted his leg, and a bright yellow stream of hot urine streaked out of his prepuce and struck the arrow with uncanny accuracy. When the urine stream ended, he kicked at the sand with his hind legs.

With the scent on the arrow destroyed, Wolf would have a better scent trail to follow. He paced the spot where the RV had cut several tracks leading in all directions, and the path was weaker, but he dismissed all irrelevant smells and focused on only one. The wolf located the girl's scent again, though faint as it was, and managed to determine which tracks were freshest. He moved through the desert once again, although at a slower pace this time. It wasn't long before he realized he was heading into town. Town's Folk didn't take kindly to wolves, and Wolf had crossed that line before, even to the point of getting shot at, so he ran back to the place where the human form had carefully laid out his clothes. Wolf transformed into Roman and dressed. He climbed into his Cayman and drove into town. He parked his ride in a garage where he knew no one would see it.

He walked through town with his hands in his pockets, whistling. It was 11:30 at night, and most shops were closed, but he did pass several tattoo shops and liquor stores still open. Two restaurants served late diners, but alas, his pal from Café Jean Pierre seemed absent from the establishment. I'm not finished with you, my friend. But you will have to keep for now. Little Miss was who he needed to deal with right now.

After fending off a few prostitutes and a bum selling socks, Roman found the RV in the parking lot of a closed department store. Windows glowed with dull yellow light, and shadows moved across the illuminated rectangles. He found a secluded place and crouched low to watch. He waited for someone to emerge from the vehicle, but no one did. When he felt it was safe to approach, Roman moved in a lazy zigzag pattern toward the RV's back, where there were no windows.

Inside, two male voices were talking, but he could not tell what they were saying. Roman moved along the RV's right side, looking back to see if anyone observed his actions. There was no one around. He concentrated on the people inside the RV.

He stopped at a window and dared to peek inside.

The girl was lying on the bed. In another room, a boy with blonde hair and a brown-haired man talked casually. Roman could only hear the conversation pieces, but he didn't care about what they were saying. What most concerned him was that neither of these men had the scent of a wolf on them, and even if they were wolves, neither of them could have been the black wolf who had interrupted his attack the other night.

Roman's mind kept turning back to the pup. Could it have been the skinny kid that night? It didn't make sense. The raven-coated wolf was significant, as big as Wolf, but this kid was nothing. How could a mere boy turn into such a formidable opponent?

Roman realized he had broken the cardinal rule of stalking and lost focus. His obsession over the mystery wolf caused him to fail to notice the girl had climbed off the bed and had approached the very window under which he crouched. She squinted at the darkness beyond the window, trying to make sense of the shadows. Roman pressed his back against the RV and stayed low. Had she seen him?

"What is it?" Roman heard one of the men say.

"I thought I saw something out there." The girl's reply was much closer and her words louder.

"Get back from the window," said a mysterious male voice. "I'll go check it out."

Roman transformed into Wolf and ran off, leaving no trail any mortal could follow.

Chapter Twenty-Five

David drove into town so he and Antony could feed. David went first and selected three men who had been victimizing the tenants of a housing project. Three in one location: perfect. Antony found a youth who was killing bums, a would-be rapist who stalked a young girl, and a john who had beaten the hooker until she was nearly dead. He fed quickly and still managed to get the girl to the hospital before she died. The hospital administrators would not help the girl until she resolved the issue of insurance. Antony placed a call, and when the hospital received one hundred thousand dollars, the girl suddenly found herself in good hands. She would live. Their feedings had been quick. The prey barely even knew what hit them. They were both back in the RV with Alex by midnight.

As Alex lay on the bed, not really able to sleep but too tired to do anything else, she scanned through Maggie's small collection of books. In the other end of the RV, she could hear David and Antony discussing their kills that night and how they had chosen to dispose of the bodies. They glanced at Alex several times, and she at them. She was restless, antsy, and they thought they knew why. "She wants this to be over," Antony said. "Just like us, she wants to charge into the fray and destroy the enemy." David agreed; he wanted that, too. And she was okay, maybe even good enough to stand her ground in a fight. Her instincts were remarkable. She was getting so good with the bow she could hit David even as he moved at vampire speed from one destination to another. David didn't want to be the werewolf that went up against her in battle.

She stood and walked to the window, looking out nervously. David saw her. "What is it?" he asked.

"I thought I saw something out there," she said.

David stood. "Get back away from the window. I'll go check it out," he said and quickly moved to the door. He stepped into the Zephyr's doorway and looked outside along that side of the RV but saw nothing. When he felt Antony's presence behind him, guarding the door, David stepped off the Zephyr's platform and walked along the side of the RV. He glanced around the back and then moved to the other side, circling to the front until he was back at the door again. To be safe, David checked under and on top of the vehicle. He walked around to the side where Alex had said she saw something and looked more closely. It was then that he saw wolf tracks leading away from the Zephyr.

"Time to go," David said as he climbed into the driver's seat. The RV sped out of town in a matter of minutes.

Chapter Twenty-Six

"They weren't wolves," Roman said. He had debated going to Minerva with his find, knowing she would be overly critical of his handling of the event. In the end, he decided to tell her and get help.

"What were they then?" she said. "Ordinary men? Why didn't you tear their throats out and bring me the girl?" Her chest heaved with the exertion of her words. "You had her in your sight, and you let her go." Minerva seethed. "I can't stomach failure, Roman. You know this."

"I didn't fail you, Mother."

Mother's anger did not belong with Roman. She had fallen for that raven-haired bitch's lies. Mother started to believe Maggie wished to join the pack. Now that she knew Maggie was secretly harboring the little darling, Minerva wanted to rip something apart. Unfortunately, Roman would prove to be just as good a target as anything.

"They weren't ordinary men," Roman said. "I would have been a fool to walk in there not knowing what I was dealing with. But I know who they are now and how they are eluding us. Do you doubt I'll find them again? How low has your opinion of me fallen, Mother?" Roman's eyes burned with unshed tears.

Minerva pulled her blonde warrior into her breast and held him there, indulging him. "I know you did what you could," she said. "I appreciate everything you do for the pack and me. You keep us safe." Abruptly, the nurturing posture became a threatening one, and Minerva squeezed Roman's neck in a massive headlock. "But if you fail me again, I will snap your neck like a stick."

She released him.

Roman stepped away from her. She didn't acknowledge him as she walked away. Roman watched her go, with rage building inside him. His muscles tensed, and his body vibrated. His teeth clenched, and spittle flew from his lips as he howled in rage.

Roman decided he would no longer concern himself with the black mystery wolf. His sole concern would be the girl, as it should have been all along. He would only rest when he brought the girl's head to his beloved leader. The male protectors—whatever they might be—would be torn apart where they stood.

The following night Roman recruited Herman to help him. "Mother is upset that I found the girl and didn't bring her back with me, but without backup, I was unable to secure her capture. I ask you to come with me, and together we will get the girl."

Herman blinked. Roman never requested help before. He didn't know how to respond. "Okay," he said dumbly. "What do you need me to do?"

"Follow orders; kill when I tell you to. I located the girl, but she has two protectors. I will take one, and you will need to dispatch the other. They are riding around in a large RV. They never stay in one place for long, but I'm confident I can find them again with little effort. Stay with me, but stay out of my way. I'll do all the work. You are only there for backup. Are you ready for this?"

"I'm ready," Herman said eagerly. He was excited that Roman needed his help.

Roman and Herman climbed into the Cayman and headed out into the dark desert night. For the first time, Herman sat in the sports car, caressing the leather seats and asking questions that Roman did not answer.

The car stopped abruptly, and Roman exited the vehicle. Immediately, Herman followed. They stripped out of their clothes and transformed. The blond wolf and the brown wolf ran together through the desert, searching for the girl's scent. Wolf stopped abruptly, and Herman's wolf, Husky, struggled to keep from crashing into him. Wolf turned back and growled a warning: *be quiet.*

Husky whimpered and lowered his head submissively. Wolf sniffed the ground. He walked one way but lost the scent and returned to where the smell was more potent. He located the scent, turned back to Husky, and chuffed: *this way.*

The wolves sprinted through the desert side by side, panting and kicking up sand. After several long minutes, the tawny wolf skidded to a stop. The brown wolf backtracked and stood with his brother behind a boulder, the RV about one hundred yards in front of them. Using his eyes, Wolf told Husky to move to the left. The tawny wolf stepped from behind the boulder and moved right. As the two wolves slowly approached the RV from the north and south, the tawny wolf took the side with the door.

Wolf began his assault at a trot, unsure of a plan even as he approached, but the closer the vehicle loomed, the faster he ran. He slammed into the side of the RV at a dead run hard enough to make it lurch to the side. The RV rocked and came crashing back down, swaying. The girl screamed inside the vehicle. There was movement. Wolf then attacked the windows, tearing at the screens and pounding his paws at the glass hard enough to crack it. The two protectors exited the vehicle leaving the girl alone inside.

They were not mortal men, just as he had suspected. Now that they were out where he could see them clearly, he knew they were vampires when he saw their gleaming teeth sparkling in his preternatural sight. He had not recognized their scent. He had never gone up against a vampire before, and now he had to contend with two? Vampires could move quickly, much faster than he could ever dream of moving. That was just fine; moving faster only meant he could kill them sooner. When they attacked, he would bite off their heads in a snap of his powerful jaws.

But the vampires would not act on his provocation. They would not leave the door unattended. He needed them both to move away from the door so his brother could enter the vehicle and take the girl. He stopped backing away and charged them instead. They dodged him quickly, but they did not seem to be aware of what he was doing. As they dodged his attacks, keeping him in sight at all times, they slowly moved away from the door and toward the back of the vehicle. They were not aware of the second wolf.

Wolf leaped onto the roof of the RV. His paws skittered noisily on the slick surface until he recovered his balance. The blonde turned and watched as the vampires climbed onto the roof with him. The taller one came first, and before the vampire had regained his footing, the tawny wolf flew into him. The vampire and wolf flew from the roof in a tangle of limbs and fur. They hit the sand and rolled, only breaking apart after having gone twenty yards from the RV. Wolf went for the vampire's throat, but the immortal was able to fall back and avoid a fatal bite that could have removed his head. The vampire gripped the wolf in a bear hug and attempted to crush the life from the animal, but Wolf used his powerful hind legs to jump out of the vampire's grip.

The vampire and werewolf circled each other. The second vampire appeared, flanking the tawny wolf. The wolf swiveled his body, refusing to allow the vampires to corner him. He growled a warning. With agility and reflexes to match the vampires, Wolf was able to avoid their coordinated attacks. Wolf saw Husky at the door of the RV. The time had come for Wolf to turn the tides of this battle.

Wolf latched his teeth onto the flailing foot when the younger vampire fell back to avoid Wolf's snapping jaws. Now the second vampire understood this was not a game. Wolf needed only to clamp down at full force to remove the foot. He did not want to lose his hold just yet, however. Wolf dragged the vampire several more yards from the RV. As expected, the other vampire followed. The second vampire attacked, protecting his pinned comrade. Wolf released his hold on the vampire in his jaws and dropped back. He snarled a warning as the two vampires converged on him again.

But now, the true intentions of the werewolf's attack became apparent.

Inside the RV, the girl released a terrifying and gut-wrenching scream. When this caused the closer vampire to turn to the RV, Wolf leaped. His sharp fangs bit down deep into the vampire's shoulder.

The second vampire ripped the tawny wolf off his companion. The wolf came away with flesh in his jaws that turned to acrid dust in his mouth. The animal flew for several feet, kicking and flailing to gain balance. The wolf landed with a thud and a yelp, but he quickly worked his feet underneath him. He staggered momentarily and then advanced.

The shorter vampire said: "Go, I'll take care of this one."

The vampire with the torn shoulder disappeared in a wisp of ozone and a crackling breeze.

The wolf wished for the power of speech to tell his remaining opponent it was already too late.

Chapter Twenty-Seven

A closet and a bathroom made up the very back of the Zephyr. This area was separated from the bedroom by a door. A short hallway separated the bedroom from the kitchen. The living room area adjacent to the kitchen consisted of a sofa and loveseat on the right side and a faux fireplace and widescreen TV to the left. The driver seat and passenger seat made up the very front of the vehicle. The only door (besides the emergency hatch in the ceiling above the kitchen) was located just behind the passenger seat. The girl had been sitting on the loveseat and the vampires on the sofa when the wolf attacked.

"Do you miss the sun?" Alex asked.

"Sometimes," David admitted.

"I honestly do not remember the sun," Antony said.

The vehicle rocked as grating metal and crackling glass caused Alex to scream. The entire RV tilted to the side as if struck broadside by a bulldozer. David and Antony were on their feet at once. When they heard the wolf growl, they understood. Alex moved to the driver seat when the vampires exited the vehicle. She tried to keep track of the action but could not see past the other chair.

She watched the tawny werewolf confront the vampires. It growled. When the vampires moved forward, the wolf backed up. David placed a hand on Antony's chest, discouraging him from following. David stayed close to the door. When its first plan wasn't working, the wolf flew at them. It wasn't fast enough to surprise them, but that wasn't what it was trying to do. The wolf charged them but dodged in time to avoid being trapped by the vampire's powerful grip. The wolf charged again and again, but David managed to push it back. The next time Antony got a piece of it but was unable to hold it. The wolf scrambled free once again. It ran toward the back of the RV, and Alex followed along inside the RV, not wanting to lose sight of it. She heard its nails clicking on the roof of the RV. Alex's chest burned red hot as she turned and waited for the animal to enter the emergency hatch up there.

David leaped onto the roof. The werewolf took David off the top, throwing him several yards from the RV. The werewolf and the vampire grappled. The vampire struggled to gain a firm grip but was unable to pin the werewolf down. David tried to get the wiry wolf around the neck but only managed to lose his balance and fall backward. The wolf clamped down on his ankle, but the wolf did not bite through. David struggled free and stood.

Antony joined the fight, flanking the wolf, but the animal would not be taken from behind, either.

This wolf is one brutal monster. He's quick and intelligent and seems to have the vampires always in his sights.

The stalemate lasted for several minutes. It seemed the vampires were finally closing in when the werewolf attempted to break away from the fight.

David and the beast grappled again.

Alex was a smart girl. She knew to stay inside the vehicle as the monsters fought outside. Alex spotted the second wolf approaching from the far side of the RV. She struggled to find a way to lock the door before the second wolf reached the door. The door buckled inward, and she knew the door would not hold for long.

The wolf tore at the door until it had pulled a corner of the door away. She raced toward the back of the Zephyr. She dared to look back. The brown wolf was on its belly, worming through the hole it had caused in the door. She gasped in mute horror as the thing completed its entry into the vehicle and then stood on all fours. It shook out its fur and stalked toward her. She could swear she saw the beast grinning.

Herman, she thought. *This one is Herman*. She knew this because Herman's eyes were green. The other brown-haired pack member, Vince, had brown eyes. She called his name. It stopped momentarily but continued its advance quickly. She had managed to distract the wolf long enough to stretch out her hand and touch the familiar handle of something to her right. Just as her groping fingers latched onto it, the wolf leaped. Her hand came around in a reflexive motion.

She screamed.

Chapter Twenty-Eight

David reached the damaged door in a panic. He tore the door from its hinges and entered the Zephyr. He stared at the back of the RV in disbelief, unsure of what he was seeing. Alex was there in the hallway leading the bedroom, covered in blood. He approached slowly. As he reached her, he pulled her protectively to him and searched her body for injuries. She was unharmed. He hugged her. As he glanced over her shoulder, he finally understood what had happened.

The scythe lay in a puddle of blood. Next to the blade, a naked headless corpse of a man lay sprawled in the bedroom. The head had landed in the corner, near the dresser. She and the vampire stared at the mess. Her chest heaved from the adrenaline coursing through her. She was crying and laughing at the same time.

David stepped out of the Zephyr and strode to where Antony and the werewolf grappled. Neither seemed able to give the other a fatal wound. At his approach, the vampire and werewolf stopped fighting and looked at him. David lifted the head of the slain man and held it out.

The werewolf instantly turned into a naked man with silky blond hair falling over his shoulders. He ran at David. David threw the head, and it plopped wetly against the naked man's chest, leaving a red splotch there. The man stopped as if he had run into a brick wall. The blonde man glared down at his friend's dead eyes and torn flesh. He touched the blood on his chest. The man looked up at David and glared with deadly intent at him. The man lifted his hand and pointed at David, marking him for death.

Then the man turned into the tawny wolf again and ran into the darkness. David thought of giving chase to stop the wolf from warning the others of what had happened but knew he had to stay and protect Alex from any other attacks. David and Antony disposed of the head and its corpse.

"I'm sorry," Alex said after she had cleaned herself up. "Because of what I have done, Gardner and Maggie are in terrible danger."

"This isn't your fault," David said. "They can take care of themselves. They will agree you are the priority here. You had no choice but to do what you did."

"There is a good chance Maggie had already seen this in a vision," Antony said.

Alex had another idea. "If we get closer to the hacienda, I might be able to get a message to Gardner," she said.

"How?" Antony and David both asked.

"I can't tell you yet, but I can do it. You have to trust me."

"Even if you can," Antony said. "We can't risk it. We have to get you farther away from the hacienda, not closer."

"No," David said. "I think she knows what she's doing. I'm taking us closer."

Antony shrugged, and David started the Zephyr.

Chapter Twenty-Nine

Wolf ran, snarling and snapping at nothing. He was senseless with rage, wild and chaotic. He couldn't tell Mother how wrong this attack had gone. She would blame him. She would blame him for Herman's death, and she would punish him.

Wolf howled.

Chapter Thirty

Rose stared at the note the little Hispanic girl had handed her: *See me. Mother.* Rose swallowed her nerves and obeyed the summons. She stepped into the large and fragrant bedroom and moved timidly to the high-backed wicker chair where Mother sat. Rose kneeled. The older woman held out a gnarled hand and invited Rose to take it. Mother's long and bony fingers encircled Rose's tender pink hand and continued to apply pressure until the girl was cringing in pain. Mother was old, but she was a powerful wolf.

"You've been spending a lot of time with the boy, and I want to know what you have been talking about," Mother said without expression.

"Nothing, Mother," Rose said between gasps. "I have said nothing."

"That's not what I asked you." Mother's crushing grip slackened, but she did not let go of the girl's hand. Rose was in tears. "I want to know what he's been telling you."

"He told me about how his father died," Rose said. "How he became a werewolf, and why they want to join the pack."

"Did he now. Why do they want to join us?"

"He said he and his mother are afraid of hunters. They want protection."

"I think I'll have you killed," Mother said.

Rose felt the world loosen around her. She felt her grip on the pack fall away as Mother released her. Tears fell onto Rose's cheeks as she looked up into Mother's stony gray eyes. "Why?"

"When I brought you into the pack, I was sure I could shed you of that insolent behavior of yours. But here you sit today, and still, you defy me. I am tired of the trouble you continue to cause this pack."

"Mother, please don't do this. I love you, and I love the pack. I have never done anything or said anything that hurts the pack. My rebellious spirit is merely an act. I have always been on my own, and it is hard for me to play nice when others resent my presence." Tears welled in Rose's eyes, but this display meant nothing to Mother.

"If you wish to continue being a part of this pack, you must do something for me," Mother said.

"Anything." Rose rubbed the tears from her eyes. "I'll do anything."

"Work on the boy. Report to me everything he does and everything he says. Get him to confide in you. Get him to tell you everything he knows about us. Do you wish to know what we know? I'll tell you now: that boy and his *mother--*" the word came out as if it should have been a crime to use that word to describe Maggie. "Have no intention of joining the pack. They never planned to give us the girl. They have help protecting her as we speak. If Roman and Herman are successful, she will be in my grasp soon. And the boy and his mother will be dead. But in case something does go wrong, I'll need what you learn to crush them. Find out where they are hiding that girl."

"Yes, Mother," Rose said, and any trace of playfulness was gone. "You will have your answers as soon as I have them."

Mother smiled, and with the smile, Rose felt her connection to the pack return. She sighed.

"Good. That's what I like to hear. Now please have tea and cookies with me." Mother tinkled a little brass bell near her chair, and a Hispanic serving girl appeared almost instantly. Mother placed her order, and the girl scampered off. Rose sipped her tea cautiously when the girl returned with the treats, wondering if Mother had poisoned Rose's food. When she felt safe, she relaxed, but Rose ate the cookies the same way. Rose was happy Mother wanted to have tea and cake with her, but manners were not Rose's strong point, and the red-haired girl feared everything she did or said would offend Mother.

Rose endured tea with Mother.

Chapter Thirty-One

Gardner, there is danger, do you hear me?

It was Alex's voice.

Gardner, if you can hear me, send your mother to the Zephyr. We have information you'll need to hear. Please, Gardner. Send her to us so we can explain what has happened.

"Mom." Gardner staggered, nearly blind, into the hallway, wearing only a pair of loose cotton pajama bottoms tied at the waist.

"What is it?" she said. She met Gardner in the hall.

"The Zephyr. Go to the Zephyr. They've had trouble. Alex contacted me and said you need to go to them so they can explain. That's all I know," Gardner said.

Maggie didn't hesitate. Gardner had to catch his mother when she went limp. He carried her to a chair.

Chapter Thirty-Two

Maggie blinked to the Zephyr and glanced around, alert to danger. She spotted the three sitting around the table. Alex gasped when she popped into existence, and David and Antony turned to face Maggie

"You're not in danger?" Maggie asked.

"They attacked us, but we managed to defeat the wolves."

"What happened?" Maggie asked. "And why are you so close to the hacienda? It's dangerous to be this close."

"We had to get closer," Alex said. "We needed to be in range for Gardner to hear me. It worked."

"How are things inside the compound?" David asked. "Has Roman returned?"

"Nothing was happening at the hacienda," Maggie said. "Explain to me what is going on."

"Roman and Herman attacked us," Alex said. "Roman fought the guys while I had to fend off Herman. I killed him."

Maggie stared at her. "You killed Herman?" she said when she found her voice again. "Good for you."

"Roman got away," David said. "We figured he returned to the compound for reinforcements."

"We haven't heard anything yet. Get away from the hacienda. It's almost dawn, and Alex will be a sitting duck once you're both incapacitated. Get her to safety, and I'll find out what's going on at the hacienda. If Roman is still out there, he won't stop. Go." Maggie turned to Alex. "Be safe," she said.

"I will," Alex assured her. With a firm nod of agreement, Maggie returned to her body.

She snapped awake and looked around, disoriented.

"Mom," Gardner said, and she focused on him. "What do you know?"

"Alex is safe for the moment," she said. "They were attacked. Roman got away, but she killed Herman."

"Good for her," Gardner said and smiled.

"We have to find out what is happening around here. Find Rose see what she knows. It seems to me this place isn't aware of Herman's death yet, or they would have stormed our apartment and killed us in retaliation by now."

Gardner went in search of Rose. Maggie searched through the compound's main building for the angry mob, but she found no one. She searched the kitchen and discovered the refrigerator door was open.

"Can't get enough of the roast beef?" Maggie asked the person behind the door. Bethany stepped back and closed the door. The surprise must have been evident on Maggie's face because Bethany smirked.

"I don't touch the stuff," Bethany said. She was holding a diet soda and a slice of cold pizza.

"Sorry, I thought you were Roman," Maggie said.

"Roman is on an errand. He hasn't returned yet."

"Oh? What kind of errand?"

"The kind that you don't need to concern yourself with," Bethany said. She tossed the pizza slice in the microwave and started it up for 30 seconds.

Roman hasn't returned. He is probably afraid of telling Mother that Herman is dead, Maggie thought.

Maggie left the kitchen and located Vince in the living room, watching football on the large screen TV. He had his stocking feet propped up on the coffee table. He was eating popcorn. Maggie sat down in the recliner adjacent to him and stared up at the screen. Vince ignored her for a few minutes but began stealing glances when she did not get up and leave.

Maggie looked over at him and smiled.

"I was bored," she said. "You don't mind, do you?"

"No," Vince said, suddenly disinterested in her again.

"You wouldn't happen to know where Roman is, would you?" she asked.

"Wasn't my turn to keep track of him," Vince said through a mouthful of popcorn.

"And Herman? I suppose it wasn't your turn to keep track of him either?"

"No," Vince said.

No one knows where they are, and no one cares.

They must do this all the time: disappear for hours on end with no communication. They weren't even concerned.

Maggie left Vince alone to watch the game and went off in search of Mother. She was the last Maggie wished to interrogate.

If Mother didn't know what had happened to Herman, they were in the clear, at least until nightfall.

Maggie found Mother in the secret garden. As the Gate squeaked upon Maggie's entrance, Mother looked up.

"Good morning," Mother said.

"Good morning," Maggie replied. "Do you need help with anything?"

"No," Mother said. "But I could do with a little company. What's on your mind, Child." Mother shifted her basket from one arm to the other. Maggie took her free arm and walked mother to her next destination. Mother released Maggie's arm and pulled out her trimming shears. As mother clipped roses, Maggie took them and placed them in the basket. "Careful of the thorns, Dear," Mother said.

"I'm aware," Maggie said.

"You seem anxious. What's on your mind?"

"I've been looking for Roman," she said. "I thought I would invite him on an outing. I enjoy his company."

"A date?" Mother said, not hiding her incredulity. "I'm sure he'll be home soon." Mother turned away, but Maggie could see the older woman's smile.

Chapter Thirty-Three

Gardner found Rose wandering the grounds, deep in thought, and Gardner saw something different about her. When he said hi to her, she looked up and noticed him for the first time. At the sight of him, her demeanor changed drastically. She smiled brightly and threw her arms around him. When she pulled away, there were tears in her eyes. She wiped them and tried to hide them as best she could. When she found her voice, she said: "I was hoping I would see you again."

"Why the warm greeting?" Gardner asked.

"I wanted to ask you a favor," she said.

He was cautious. He said nothing.

"I want you to give me the girl."

"Alex?"

"I guess that's her name. I don't know. I don't care. I need to give the girl to Mother. If I don't do something soon, she's going to abandon me. I can't be alone again, I'll die; Mother is desperate and wants the girl. We have Roman out looking for her, and he's a good hunter. He will find her."

"Not that good," Gardner said softly. Either Rose didn't hear him, or she didn't care what he said. She ignored the comment.

"Here's the thing. Mother threatened to kick me out of the pack. She doesn't think I pull my weight around here, I guess. I don't know why she turned on me. It doesn't matter, but if I convince you to turn her over, Mother will love me again."

"It's not my call. You'd have to ask my mother. It's up to her what we do with the girl."

Rose nodded. "That makes sense."

"What's with all the urgency all of a sudden? Has Roman found her yet?"

"I don't think so. Mother is very upset. I don't know why, but she has this crazy notion that you and your mom never wanted to join the pack. She thinks you're protecting the girl. That's crazy, right?"

Gardner didn't laugh.

"Mother is wrong, right? Now that you're in the pack, you'll give us the girl. Let's end this sordid affair so things can go back to the way they were. I want it to go back to normal around here."

Gardner couldn't hold back anymore. His face turned red with anger. "Normal?" He spat out the word like a piece of rotten fruit. "You call this hellish place normal? You are far from normal. What you've all been doing here is evil, not normal." He had already gone too far, so he decided to go all the way. "What you're doing isn't normal, and it isn't right...it's sick. We're not here to join you; we're here to stop you. We're here to *end* you."

Rose gaped. Gardner's chest heaved. As his words sank in, her expression turned from one of confusion to one of utter loathing. Her face crumpled inward, and she bared her teeth. She seethed, panting like an animal about to charge. Her fists balled into small white cudgels that she used to beat him in the face and chest. He warded off her blows, but he did not fight her.

"You've ruined everything." Her blows became weaker as the tears came. He pushed her away, and she staggered backward. He stared at her, disgusted, yet still, he pitied her. She sobbed and looked around as if lost. She turned back to him. "You're dead," she said. Then the sobs came back, and she mumbled, almost inaudibly: "We're all dead."

Then she ran away.

Dawn came, and Maggie and Gardner came together. They didn't go back to the apartment, and they didn't want to end up cornered. The front gate was not an acceptable option for escape, and they didn't dare confront anyone from the pack just yet. Maggie found a relatively safe section of the compound, and they holed up to wait out the day. Maggie blinked back to the Zephyr after the sunset. Alex, David, and Antony sat anxiously huddled on the sofa. They stood in unison when she appeared.

"It's no longer safe there. We need you to come as soon as possible."

Chapter Thirty-Four

Maggie returned to her body and came out of her confused state to see Gardner's wolf locked in deadly combat with the ginger wolf and the brown wolf. She turned, black fur spread rapidly across her lupine form. The female raven wolf joined the fight. The male black wolf drove the ginger wolf back, snapping and drooling, then turned its vicious attack on the brown wolf. The raven she-wolf clamped powerful jaws onto the ginger wolf and flung her across the courtyard. The ginger howled and then landed with a grunt and a yelp.

Maggie's wolf immediately turned on Vince's wolf and bit down on the back of his neck. The female raven wolf twisted and struggled to subdue the brown wolf, forcing it to release its grip on Gardner's wolf. The black-haired male broke free of the brown wolf's crushing jaws and rounded to press the attack.

The ginger jumped over the black wolves and joined the brown wolf.

Maggie's black female charged forward, focusing her attack on the ginger wolf. Gardner attacked the brown wolf in a snarling flash of teeth and claws. The two wolves tore into each other, ripping and snapping. The black wolf gained the upper hand when it managed to knock the brown wolf off its feet. But the brown wolf quickly regained its footing, narrowly escaping a deadly lunge from the black-haired male. The black female couldn't break away from the ginger wolf without turning her back on the bitch. She had strength and speed over the ginger, and when Rose's wolf tried to double-team Gardner, Maggie snapped powerful jaws on the ginger wolf, pulling it away from her son.

The black female and the ginger wolf circled, staring each other down as the black male and the brown wolf fought fiercely. Gardner leaped onto the back of the brown wolf, pinning him down. With great effort, the black wolf pushed the brown wolf in place with his body's weight. The brown wolf's front feet splayed out in front of him as his back feet kicked frantically for purchase but finding nothing. The brown wolf could not get into a suitable position to get his feet back underneath his body.

Then the black wolf went in for the kill.

The brown wolf waited helplessly as the black wolf maneuvered his black muzzle into position and, with razor-sharp teeth, tore out a gaping chunk of the brown wolf's throat. The brown wolf whimpered weakly as the gurgling blood spurted from the wound. The blood loss was too substantial and the damage too significant for the brown wolf to recover. Somewhere behind him, the red wolf wailed, a tearful sound that caused the black wolf to step away from Vince's now human corpse. The black female allowed the ginger wolf to pass. The ginger coat slipped away, and the human form, naked and vulnerable, stood there in stunned silence.

Maggie changed back next. Gardner turned last. Maggie and Gardner dressed back into their shed clothes and watched as Rose walked over and examined the remains of Vince's body.

"This pack is not going to survive the night," Gardner told the pale and naked girl. "Go collect whatever belongings you hold sacred and leave this place; because if you stay, you will die."

Rose stepped away from the corpse. Without the slightest sense of indecency over her naked body, Rose turned to Gardner. She had tears in her eyes, and Vince's blood smeared across her face.

"Take me with you," she said. "I can't be alone. I'll die on my own. If you take this pack from me, I will not survive. You might as well kill me now, with Vince's blood on your face and his flesh in your teeth."

Gardner shook his head slowly and with great sorrow. "We can't trust you," he said. "You are not capable of feeling compassion and love for others. You would not fit in with our way of life. You have tasted too much human flesh ever to stop."

Rose's shoulders sagged as if the weight of his words had landed there. She made no move to cover her naked breasts. Tears streamed down her face, causing clear streaks through the blood.

"This is my fault," Rose said as if someone had asked. "I went to Vince after my confrontation with you, Gardner, and told him you were not here to join the pack at all. I told him of Mother's belief that you were protecting the girl. I got Vince worked up in a lathering rage. I wanted Vince to attack you and punish you for the horrible things you said to me. I sent Vince after you to make

186

you suffer, but now Vince is dead. And Mother is going to blame me for this."

"It's what you deserve," Gardner said. "You sent him here to kill me."

"No, not to kill to scare, to hurt, but not to kill."

Maggie stepped forward. "He's a violent killer, Rose. He would never settle for injured. He came here to kill my son."

She snatched up the tee-shirt Vince had shed when he had transformed and put it on. The shirt hung halfway down her thighs.

"You'll regret this," she said. "You'll wish you had killed me here when next we meet because – "

"Pray that we never meet again," Maggie said, cutting her off. "Because if he doesn't kill you, I surely will."

Rose turned away from them and ran into the darkness. Maggie stood next to her son, and together they watched her disappear.

"Do you think it was wise to let her go?" Maggie asked. "We should go after her."

"And do what?" Gardner asked. "Kill her? Take her prisoner? If we had killed her, it would have been a slaughter."

Maggie knew he was right. Still, as wrong as it would have been to execute her, she couldn't help but think they had made a mistake letting her go. She hugged her son, loving him more for his mercy than any other trait he possessed at that moment.

"But if she does anything to jeopardize your safety or the safety of anyone we love, she's dead meat," Maggie said.

Gardner smiled. He looked around, suddenly aware that the pack could ambush then at any moment. "We should get someplace safe and wait for Dad and the others to arrive."

"You're right, but our apartment is no longer safe. Where can we go to be hidden until we have sufficient backup?"

Gardner glanced around.

"High ground," he said. When Maggie looked at him puzzled, he elaborated. "The roofs."

Chapter Thirty-Five

Rose left the compound as instructed, first by Mother and then by Gardner. She ran shoeless through the sand. Rose ran and ran and ran. Then she stopped running. Where was she going? Rose didn't believe the pack would lose the coming battle, and she didn't want to abandon her family, but she also couldn't depend on her group for protection anymore. Even if Mother and the others won the battle, and by some twist of fate, Rose survived, Mother would order Rose's death for sure.

Still, if the pack survived the coming clash, it would not be without casualties. Vince was proof of that. If Mother survived, she would be stupid to turn Rose away as she licked her wounds and rebuilt the pack.

Rose turned and looked back at the hacienda. She cursed Gardner and his mother. If Rose returned, she would need to avoid Mother and the other pack members. Rose had failed to subdue the young wolf, and Mother would not forgive her for that. Nor did she want Gardner or his mother to see her. Rose knew of a place to hide until the fight was over.

If Mother won this fight, the older woman would beg Rose to come back into the fold. If Gardner's side proved to be the winner by some chance, she would attack and kill the fool when he was at his most vulnerable.

Rose would not kill Gardner or the girl. Instead, she would scurry away once the coast was clear, but she could dream.

Rose was still under the benefits of Mother's protection and could always change at will if she needed to.

Rose returned to the compound, moving through the shadows like a wraith. Rose stayed close to the walls and avoided lighted areas. When she heard voices, Rose stopped and listened, only venturing further after the talkers were gone. Rose inched through the compound, circumventing a collision course with the forces about to be released therein. She was a ghost. No, she was...

"The monster," she said aloud. She hadn't meant to speak, but it was what she was thinking. "I'm a monster. I am a killer."

She repeated this as if it were a mantra, something she said to inspire herself.

Rose moved swiftly past the swimming pool to the Banquet Hall. Glancing around to be sure she was still alone, she opened one side of the large oak doors and slipped into the crack she had made. She closed the door silently behind her.

In the stillness of the room, Rose waited and allowed her eyes to focus on the surrounding darkness. Fox would have no trouble seeing in this darkness, but she had no desire to transform just yet. Besides, she needed to be the slender young girl to fit in the space where she planned to go. Fox was too bulky and awkward to squeeze into the vent.

Rose located the vent the girl had used to escape the night of the feast and climbed in. She'd gone in there before; when Mother learned, this was how the girl ran, and she, Rose, was the only pack member small enough to fit inside. Rose had gone in, but of course, it had been too late. By the time Rose entered the vent, the girl had met up with Gardner and his mother. They had spirited her away to safety, leaving Rose to climb around inside the ducts looking for the one that got away.

But Rose learned that she enjoyed the space. She had climbed through the vents and explored the compound from a new vantage point. After being forced into the small space by Mother, Rose readily entered the area to be alone. Now, she would hide until the moment when she could emerge as

as the monster.

Chapter Thirty-Six

David drove the RV at top speed toward the hacienda, causing it to hope and bounce over the rocky ground. Alex sat in the passenger seat, strapped in, but still holding on for dear life. Antony stood between the seats.

"You cannot help Maggie and Gardner if we tip over, David." Antony placed one hand on David's shoulder while using his other hand to brace himself with the RV ceiling.

When Maggie departed abruptly and then didn't return to tell them everything was okay, David flew into a panic. Antony managed to calm him down and convince David to drive, but now the Zephyr's speed as it soared across the desert concerned Antony. The vampires could survive an accident, but Alex was still in danger. The only aspect of David's driving that gave Antony comfort was David's agility and reflexes. David reached the outskirts of the compound in forty-five minutes. He stopped the RV a quarter of a mile from the hacienda, intending to walk the rest of the way.

Alex collected her bow and quiver, as well as the scythe, which she secured to the belt sheath. The three headed out of the RV.

"David, wait," Antony said as David was about use vampire speed. "We should approach together."

Even before David could respond, the naked blond man jumped off the Zephyr's roof and transformed into the wolf. The wolf charged at Alex, but David intervened. Using his hands to deflect the teeth and claws, David deflected the wolf's advance. The wolf bounced off his hands and tumbled backward, quickly regaining its footing and charging again.

When Antony tried to assist, David waved him off. "I can handle this," David said. "Go help my son."

The wolf was on him again before he finished his plea. Trusting David to handle the blonde wolf, Antony lifted Alex off the ground and ran with her. He had run holding humans before; he and Grace had run together, and he knew there would be no ill effects to Alex from moving so fast. She might have a bit of disorientation for a second or two when they stopped, but no physical harm would come to her.

When The wolf tried to chase the fleeing vampire and the girl, David refused to allow him to go. No matter how many times the wolf attempted to run off, David forced it to stay and fight. Eventually, the animal realized it would have to defeat David before it could continue after the girl. The wolf charged, tearing at David with blind rage. Slavering teeth and raking claws tore at David, ripping him open and leaving massive gashes that healed quickly but returned just as quickly. The wolf relentlessly attacked David. The Vampire, knowing one blow from those massive paws could take his head off, David dodged and weaved, but still pressing his attack on the wolf.

David had dropped his sword in that first savage attack but spotted it now several feet from him. He tried to work his way to it, but his attempts seemed futile as the wolf drove him farther from the lifesaving weapon. David abandoned the sword for the moment to keep his enemy in front of him.

David attempted to use vampire speed to gain an advantage, but the werewolf's reflexes were too prodigious. David had another advantage he could use against the wolf: his inability to tire. He didn't have the strength to overpower the wolf completely, but the wolf breathed air and blood pumped through its heart. And although werewolves had pronounced stamina, they still could weaken and grow tired. This monster showed no sign of exhaustion, however.

David fought on. He sustained injuries—and healed—and inflicted wounds, but still, there seemed to be no end to the battle. He deflected an attack and dodged the wolf's lunging jaws. If those teeth had made contact with David's neck, the beast would end his immortal life. The wolf seemed to know that severing the head and little else would kill David. The creature's powerful jaws snapped and stretched to get at David's throat. David's attempts to trap the wolf in a deadly headlock seemed to fail at every try. If David didn't end the battle and soon, the werewolf could very possibly endure till the first light of day, forcing David to die by sunlight or try to hide from the sun leaving the werewolf free to go after the girl. He struggled not to allow his concern for Gardner and the others to distract him, which could turn this battle against him. They would have to do without him for now. He had the priority of keeping this beast at his throat from taking off his head. David dodged another attack and sprung forward, never giving the creature a moment to rest while never giving it a chance to inflict a fatal blow.

Chapter Thirty-Seven

Gardner saw Rose creep back into the compound from his perch on the roof. She had stayed in the shadows and had hidden against the buildings to avoid being caught by Bethany and Minerva as the two cased the grounds, but Gardner knew she was there. Rose did not see him, nor had the others shown any acknowledgment of his presence as he listened in on bits and pieces of their conversation. He had understood that Roman had not returned with any news of the girl.

After they moved on, and Gardner felt safe to move, he tried to locate Rose again. He wanted to keep her in sight at all times, but he could not find her after going from roof to roof. Gardner gave up the search for her and returned to his mother. Gardner nudged his mother when he saw Antony appear at the north wall. Antony had been carrying Alex but placed her on the ground and steady herself. Gardner flung himself off the roof, rolled, and landed in a crouch in front of them. Reflexively, Alex reached for her bow until she saw it was Gardner. She released the bow and hugged him instead.

"Showoff," Maggie said as she dropped from a hanging position at the roof's edge. She hugged Alex and then Antony.

"Where's my Dad?"

"Where's David?"

Both questions came out at precisely the same time.

"He is fighting the blond wolf as we speak," Antony said.

"Roman," Gardner uttered. "He'll kill my dad. We have to go back and help."

"Your father can take care of himself," Maggie said. "We have our own set of problems to deal with."

"No," Gardner said more forcefully. Speaking in hushed tones to that point, Gardner spoke at full volume now to get his point across. He wasn't about to leave his father at the mercy of that maniac with teeth. "We have to help him."

"Bickering already?"

Gardner spun around to face Minerva as the older woman stepped from the shadows of a building. The statuesque woman, Bethany, folded her arms across her chest, smiling.

"Family reunions are so touching," Minerva and turned to Bethany. "Don't you agree?"

Bethany made no reply. Minerva shrugged and turned back to the group of intruders in front of her. She raised her hand and then lowered it again.

On cue, two wolves with black fur stepped out of the shadows and surrounded the two women. Maggie stared at the new arrivals, dumbfounded. Gardner looked at his mother questioningly.

As if hearing her son's unspoken question, Maggie said: "Servants. She has bitten servants and made them werewolves to bolster her forces." These new wolves would be weaker and less experienced, and therefore easier to dispatch, but they would be enough of a distraction to give Minerva and her surviving pack members the upper hand. How many other servants had the woman transformed into killer pets? There were dozens of servants running around the hacienda. Were they all werewolf assassins now?

When Minerva's eye landed on Alex, Gardner stepped reflexively in front of her. Minerva smiled at him.

"I finally get to see the girl who caused all this trouble," Said Minerva. "I should tell you now that I paid a little visit to your family. Your mother and father back in Ohio; they are no more, I'm afraid."

Alex stepped out from behind Gardner. "What did you say?"

"You heard me just fine. I killed your parents. I ate your father. His flesh tasted exquisite, so full of fear and despair."

Alex screamed in rage. Gardner placed a hand on her shoulder, but she shrugged him off. In an instant, she knocked an arrow to her bow and released it. The arrow flew straight and true, but one of the black-haired wolves jumped in the way, and the arrow sank deep into the shoulder of the protective wolf. Gardner stayed her hand when she threatened to send another bolt at the old hag. She relaxed her grip on the bow.

"Wasting arrows is not part of the plan," Gardner said.

With her rage in check, Alex's shoulders slackened, and she groaned, pushing her face into Gardner's shoulder. She cried, and deep, hitching sobs shook her body. Gardner held her until she had recovered. Alex turned back to the fight, pushing her sorrow deep inside herself. Now was not the time to grieve. If what the woman said was true, Alex would have to work through not only the grief and sorrow but possibly the guilt of knowing she had left them to be unwitting and vulnerable victims. But none of that mattered right now. Right now, living was a top priority; surviving and revenge.

"If you hand her over, you can walk away, and I won't have to kick your asses," Bethany said, still standing beside Minerva.

"You know she's not going anywhere," Gardner said.

"She's not the only reason we are here," Maggie said. "I wasn't lying to you about being infected by your husband, Arthur. What was a lie was that the man who Arthur bit, Dylan, was a close friend. We are here to clean out the werewolves who wiped out his friends that night in Yellowstone Park. During our hunt for your pack, we learned about all the atrocities committed by you. We are here to end your reign of terror."

At the mention of Arthur's name, Minerva's smile faltered, but she quickly recovered. The Injured wolf limped over, and Minerva plucked the arrow from its shoulder. She tossed the shaft into the sand in front of her. She did not take her eyes off Maggie as she performed this task.

"So be it," the silver-haired woman said with cold finality. There was no longer that fake hint of cheerfulness in her voice. She was a businesswoman now, and her business was death. Her body language said she would conduct her interaction with the detached efficiency of a predator.

The attack seemed to come at once and from several different directions. Maggie spotted two wolves charging from the left and started her transformation. At the same time, Gardner transformed. The two wolves hit the group at a dead run. Antony flew off his feet. Maggie's wolf turned on the nearest of the attacking wolves and tore a hole in the beast's neck. A swipe of her paw took the beast's head clean off.

Two more wolves appeared from behind the building and joined the fight.

Gardner bit down on the throat of a male wolf that had appeared after the initial attack. With a twist of his head, Gardner tore out the wolf's throat. Gardner swallowed the meat and bone in a single gulp. The animal writhed and spasmed until it

195

reformed into a human corpse. He barely finished with that attack when the next wolf hit him. In a flurry of snarls and growls, Gardner's wolf fended off this new assailant.

Antony regained his feet and grappled with the wolf that had confronted him. He reached into the sheath at his hip and removed the knife hidden there. The werewolf fighting him took note of the blade and backed off.

Two more werewolves appeared to join the surviving three already pressing the attack. The wolves moved on Antony, but Alex nocked an arrow took one out with a well-placed projectile through the temple. The animal spun in the dirt and landed in the form of a naked human woman. Antony swung his knife and tore through the neck of a second attacking wolf with such force the animal's head came off cleanly.

The third wolf ripped a large chunk of flesh from Antony's arm before he could pull back, but the injury quickly healed. The werewolf turned its attention to Alex and charged her before she could get another arrow in her bow.

The wolf leaped, and she reached for her scythe but was moving too slow. She would not have her weapon out before the beast hit her.

From the side, Gardner's wolf flew at Alex's attacking wolf. The two wolves collided in midair. The wolves landed, and Gardner's wolf got back his feet in an instant, while the attacking wolf landed on its side, struggling, mortally wounded with a broken back. Gardner's wolf landed on it and snapped its neck before the back injury had a chance to heal. The Hispanic man died staring at the night sky.

Almost as quickly as it had begun, the fight was over. Littering the ground were the bodies of two males and four females. Maggie knew that these poor souls had had no control over their actions. They probably didn't even know what had happened to them. Minerva had been in total control of everything they had done. Maggie looked back at the building where Minerva and Bethany had been standing.

The two women had vanished.

Chapter Thirty-Eight

David believed the wolf had finally begun to tire. Its attacks were slower and less frequent. The wolf's attacks became easier to deflect. He took this opportunity to glance around for his katana. He saw the steel glinting in the moonlight far to his right. When the next attack came, David dodged in that direction, bringing himself another few feet closer to the weapon. He moved backward as the wolf stalked toward him. The wolf glanced briefly at the ground behind David with his cunning human eyes, possibly seeing David's plan. The wolf attacked again, but this time did not go after David. The wolf leaped past him, putting itself between David and the weapon, thwarting David's plan to retrieve the sword.

David was determined to get his sword back. He dashed toward the weapon. When the wolf countered his move, David held out his arm to deflect the beast. The wolf clamped its teeth on David's forearm. David dragged the wolf with him as he rolled toward the sword. The wolf bit down, crushing through the flesh and bone, and nearly severed the arm. If the wolf pulled back or had shaken the arm, David would lose the arm forever. He abandoned his attempts to retrieve the weapon and focused on getting the wolf's deadly teeth off his arm. He punched at the wolf's head and pried at the muzzle with his free hand. The wolf only seemed to bite down harder with those powerful jaws. David stopped trying to force the jaws open and tried a new approach. He gripped the wolf by the throat and dug his fingers into the animal's windpipe.

This action worked, and the wolf released its grip. David pulled his arm free and shoved the wolf backward. At the same time, he fell back and reached for the sword, which was now almost within reach.

The wolf came again with renewed energy and power. It snarled and growled and barked its fury as it tried to rip David's stomach open. Once again, David had to abandon the weapon to keep from having his insides torn out. Would that kill him? He didn't think so, but he liked his guts where they were and didn't want to lose them. He fought the wolf off yet again, but the fight had pulled him further away from the sword.

The wolf and the vampire rolled and lunged, locked a battle where neither combatant could gain the upper hand. The wolf tried for David's throat again, but David ducked his head and shoved the wolf off balance with his shoulder. The wolf tore a chunk from his ear, but the collision's momentum put the wolf awkwardly on his back. As he struggled to gain his feet, David flew backward and rolled. He had no choice now; he had to turn his back on the wolf and make a play for his sword. The wolf was on him at once. The pressure of the animal's weight on his back prevented him from making the last few inches to his sword, and he, once again, turned his attention to the animal. David struggled to turn under the wolf's weight and face the wolf. He gripped the wolf around the throat and squeezed. The wolf shook and raged in his grip until it was able to break David's hold. The wolf backed off. David took this chance to crab-walk backward until his hand finally found the sword, following its blade to the hilt.

The wolf pounced at him, but he was able to grip the katana tightly and bring it around in an arc. The wolf probably knew the fight was over even as it leaped. It flew at David, ignoring the weapon. David aimed for the animal's neck. The momentum of his swing pulled him forward, lifting him off the ground and putting him on his knees. The sword finished its arc, cutting the leaping wolf in half at the middle. The bloody entrails oozed from the bottom half of the human form. David watched in stunned silence as the top half of the man, his blond hair streaked with sweat and blood, and plastered to his face, continued to crawl toward David.

David stood and walked over to the destroyed creature. He drove the sword through the man's skull and ended the fight.

David wasted no time climbing into the Zephyr and starting the engine. He pointed the large vehicle toward the hacienda and drove at speeds of which Antony would not have approved.

Chapter Thirty-Nine

Gardner felt more than heard the Zephyr as it struck the hacienda's front gate doing 85 miles an hour. The vehicle plowed through the steel gate, twisting it into scrap metal. The RV didn't stop, busting through walls as if made of cards and uprooting small trees along the edge of the winding driveway. Clay pots exploded. The Zephyr finally came to a stop halfway through the front door. Gardner, Alex, Maggie, and Antony had begun a systematic search for Minerva and Bethany after surviving the werewolf underlings' initial attack.

David caught found them passing through the courtyard to the gate to the secret garden. David pulled his son to him and hugged him tightly. He didn't want to let him go, but Gardner pulled away.

I love you so much.

"I love you too, Dad, but we have work to do."

Gardner smiled at the confused look on his father's face.

"I'll explain everything to you when we are through with this place," Gardner said.

"Okay." David placed an arm around his son's shoulder as they walked. "So, fill me in, son. What's happening?"

"Vince is dead, and we're hunting Minerva and Bethany. They are sending servant werewolves after us, but they've only proven to slow us down up till now. I take it Roman is no longer an issue?"

"He—how shall I say—fell apart."

"As well as the servants, we also have to watch out for Rose. She's here somewhere, too, but I doubt she'll pose much of a threat on her own."

The five moved as one entity, searching each building, and each room in each building, in a systematic sweep. Gardner opened his mind to capture the surviving pack members' thoughts. Still, he wasn't getting anything save the occasional word in Spanish, wishing he had taken that language instead of French in school.

The buildings in the northernmost section of the compound had been thoroughly checked and eliminated. The group moved on to the south end. If they had no luck flushing them out there, they would have to split up and recheck every place simultaneously. If that turned up nothing, there was a good chance they had escaped somehow, through an underground passageway maybe, or some other escape route.

Maggie astral projected throughout the compound to root out their quarry, but this caused her to slow down the group lest they leave her behind, but David didn't like the idea. He did admit it could save them some time.

"I'll stay with her while the rest of you keep searching," Alex said.

"No, that's too risky," Gardner said.

"He's so cute when he tried to be forceful, isn't he?" Maggie said. "The women have spoken. Move out. We'll be okay."

Cursing under his breath, Gardner was pulled away by his father. "No sense arguing about it," David said with his hand gently gripping his son by the back of the neck. "We're wasting time."

After a minute, Maggie and Alex were alone.

***

The courtyard was quiet. Maggie took a seat on the nearby bench.

"How does this work?" Alex asked. She had seen Maggie astral project before, but she didn't know the mechanics of it.

"My body stays here, but I project my mind somewhere else. I can't explain how that works or why people can see my apparition, but I'm not there. It's like a ghost of me or something. I can't move, which is annoying, but through practice, I can pop in and out in an instant. If I want to move around, that's how I do it. Your job is to protect me. I can hear you if you shout to me. Any trouble shout out to me, and I'll come back to my body."

"Okay, that sounds easy."

"It's not," Maggie said ominously. "Ready?"

"Yes," Alex said, but she wasn't sure that she was.

Maggie's head dropped back, and she sat with her hands in her lap, seeming to be looking up at the stars. Her body was a statue. Alex thought it was eerie seeing her this way, not blinking or moving at all. Alex readied her bow and scanned the

200

surroundings for any movement. The courtyard was as still and quiet as a tomb.

Maggie blinked into the banquet hall, but the room sat dark and empty. She popped out and appeared inside Minerva's apartment but still saw nothing. Maggie blinked out and in again, entering each room. She next appeared in Bethany's apartment, also with no luck. She appeared in the main hall, checking every angle without success.

She crossed paths with David and the others briefly and told them where she had been. Gardner asked about Alex, and she assured him the girl was safe. As they moved on, Maggie continued her sweep of the grounds. She appeared and reappeared in one room after another, finding nothing. Maggie considered the idea that the werewolves had fled when she heard Alex scream Maggie's name.

Chapter Forty

The night had gone quiet around her. Alex felt guilty that she would be missing out if any action arose. She tried not to look at Maggie's lifeless body. It was just too creepy seeing her sitting there with her blank eyes staring at the cloudless night sky. The stillness gave her mind time to think back on what she had learned earlier that night. Specifically, Alex recalled Minerva's admission that she had killed her parents. Alex took a deep breath and put thoughts of her parents out of her head. The top priority was surviving the night. She focused her attention on the surrounding buildings and rooftops. There were only two open routes into this particular courtyard, and both were directly in front of her. Someone could easily approach from atop the roofs, but Alex would see their silhouettes against the night sky. There were several windows into the courtyard, but it was so quiet, the sound of a window creaking open would instantly draw her attention.

The night must have been playing tricks on her. She thought she had heard sounds coming from one of the buildings to her left several times, but after looking, she saw nothing. There were no open windows or doors, and the rooftop was clear. She kept her mind alert, checking on Maggie and looking left and right. She scanned the rooftops and then started all over again after she had checked everything.

When the attack came, Alex hardly believed what she was seeing. The ginger wolf seemed to materialize from nowhere in the buildings' vicinity to her left, from the place the sounds had issued. The ginger wolf approached slowly at first, staying low to the ground. But it picked up speed as it grew closer.

The wolf that killed Amie, Alex thought. Alex stared in dumb fascination as the beast charged.

Alex snapped back to her senses in an instant and released an arrow. The bolt flew wide and so harmlessly past the wolf it hardly moved to dodge the attack. Alex knocked another bolt, pulled back until she anchored her thumb to her chin, and let loose. This time the wolf had to roll and dodge the missile, slowing her forward progress. Alex reached back and brought out another arrow, slapped it into place, and let fly. The arrow nicked the hide but didn't stick and deflected away harmlessly.

The wolf was ever closer now, almost too close for her bow to serve her appropriately. She abandoned the arrow for the scythe, but it wasn't on her back. She looked down at the weapon lying at her feet. She glanced back to the wolf.

"You killed Amie." Alex screamed and pulled an arrow from her quiver. Alex had no time to prep the bow, so she dropped it. As the wolf leaped on her, Alex drove the bolt into the ginger wolf's right eye.

The wolf squealed and went down, falling back and writhing in pain. The wolf pawed at the shaft sticking out of its eye socket without success. When it heard Alex readying another arrow, the wolf darted to its right and raced quickly down one of the alleyways. Alex sent another bolt after it, but the weapon thumped harmlessly off the terracotta wall.

She hadn't killed the wolf, but she doubted it would be back any time soon.

Alex held her bow at her side and turned back toward Maggie. During the fight with the ginger wolf, Alex failed to notice Bethany had come in from the courtyard's opposite side. Bethany had been standing quietly in Alex's blind spot and grabbed the girl's bow from her hand before Alex had any time to register what had happened.

Alex screamed: "Maggie."

Bethany gripped Alex in a tight embraced and covered her mouth so she couldn't scream for help.

***

But Maggie had already heard the call, and she returned to her body. After a second of reorientation, Maggie spotted Bethany dragging Alex toward an open window to the right and raced toward them.

"No closer," Bethany said. "I'll kill her. I would have slit your throat while you were incapacitated, but any movement would have given away my position before I was ready to act."

Maggie stopped. Bethany held Alex in a grip that could easily snap the girl's neck in one quick movement. Maggie studied

203

her opponent for a second. If they wanted the girl dead, she would already have killed her. In the time that it had taken Maggie to return to her body and reorient herself, Alex could have already been dead, and Bethany could have fled. Her orders weren't to kill the girl herself because Minerva wanted the pleasure of that act.

Bethany then did something Maggie hadn't thought she would do.

Bethany threw the girl to the ground and snapped her bow in half. Alex crawled through the dirt, away from the statuesque woman.

"Mother wants the girl, but she gave me the privilege of killing you. She said no matter what else happens, she wanted you dead in retribution for Arthur's murder." Bethany began her change. Maggie, too, transformed into the wolf. Within minutes the two black wolves were circling each other, each seeming to wait for the other to make the first move.

Maggie's wolf attacked, snapping and snarling. It moved in and bit down on the other wolf's foreleg, nearly snapping the bone. The second wolf howled and bit into the flesh on the back of Maggie's wolf.

The wolves broke apart.

***

Alex stayed low to the ground and well clear of the battling wolves. She realized she could hardly tell the wolves apart once they came together in a ferocious bundle of muscle and fur.

Maggie's wolf continued to press the attack. It leaped at its opponent with a ferocity that even made Alex flinch. Bethany's wolf evaded the deadlier attacks, always backing up. What was she waiting for? She didn't seem to be trying to fight back at all. The wolf simply dodged and pulled back.

Then it became evident that Bethany's wolf was leading Maggie to an open alleyway. In the alley, Alex saw the second wolf crouched and waiting. Alex wanted to scream a warning but was afraid the distraction might cause Maggie's wolf to lose focus. Alex reached for her bow but remembered too late that it was gone. She then crept along the ground to where her scythe lay.

Once in hand, Alex bolted for the alley and the hidden trap waiting there.

Alex unsheathed her scythe and swung it with all her strength at the wolf in the alley. This wolf caught Alex's movement turned on Alex instead. As Alex brought the scythe down in a deadly arc, the wolf snapped its teeth together mere inches from Alex's wrist. But it was too late for the wolf. The scythe continued its sweep, and the wolf's head flew from the body, rolling and landing near the battling wolves.

Bethany named her wolf Dingo in honor of her Australian ancestry. Now she looked down at the severed head of a distinctly Hispanic human male. Dingo then looked up and saw Alex standing over the servant's decapitated corpse, which Bethany had instructed to assist in this kill.

Dingo's human-shaped eyes narrowed, and a vicious growl escaped her black lips. Razor-sharp teeth snapped together, and the wolf darted at Alex, those eyes insane with hatred.

Maggie's wolf was there to prevent the deadly confrontation. The wolf protected Alex by biting into Dingo's neck with tremendous force. With an audible snap that even Alex could hear, Dingo's spinal cord severed. The advancing wolf dropped instantly to the earth, whimpered once, and then died. Bethany contorted into her human shape for the last time.

Maggie transformed as well, donned her discarded clothing, and walked from the courtyard. Alex followed close behind. Alex explained to Maggie how the ginger wolf had attacked and how Alex had jammed an arrow into the wolf's eye.

"She didn't die," Alex said. "She ran off, and it's now cowering somewhere with one less eye."

"That wouldn't kill a werewolf," Maggie said. "But she can't regenerate a new eye. With only one eye, I doubt Rose will be willing to attack again so soon. She'll be too afraid of losing the other eye. I doubt she'll be back, but we can't count her out just yet. Right now, our priority is Minerva. She is the oldest, smartest, and most powerful of them all. She is the real danger, and from what I gathered from Bethany's words, Minerva is still here somewhere. We have to find her before she finds us."

"We should find the others as well. A united front will give us better odds," Alex said.

Maggie nodded in agreement.

"I know where they headed. Follow me," Maggie said.

Chapter Forty-One

It was in the ballroom where Antony, Gardner, and David finally located Minerva. She was sitting at the grand piano playing some soft notes when they entered. They stood watching her in silence for several minutes. They weren't even sure if she knew they were there until she stopped playing and dropped the cover down over the keys with a resounding twang of vibrating strings deep inside the instrument.

She turned and faced them. She did not seem upset to see them. As outnumbered as she was, they had expected her to be more afraid. But she was not. She seemed pleased to see them.

"Welcome to the party. The last party these walls will ever see, I suppose. You have come into my home and have systematically executed my family. Not very friendly of you, I'm afraid. As we speak, either my Bethany has killed your sweet Maggie or has been killed by her. Since I had expected Bethany to arrive by now with Alex in tow, I'm guessing the latter is true. That would mean I am alone now."

"If you are hoping we'll feel sorry for you, it's not going to happen," Gardner said.

Minerva turned a vicious glare at the boy. After a second, her face softened, and she smiled.

"I've never expected anything of the sort," she said. "I'm just stating the truth as I see it. We have lived in peace for many years, picking only those that the world would not miss. We fed on nobodies and derelicts; we fed on those that even the media would not care to report."

"You fed on innocent people living as best they could under the circumstances, and you had no right to end their lives," David said.

"I have every right," Minerva said, showing anger for the first time. "I have the right of a species to survive. We did what every animal does; we fed on the weak and infirm. By plucking out the weaker of the species, humanity gets stronger as a whole. It's the natural order of things. We were only doing what comes naturally to us. Then you come in here with your superior attitudes and say what is right and wrong with our ways. Who gave you the right to decide our way of life is wrong? You've killed us not for food or your survival. You've hunted us for sport."

"Hunting serves its purpose, too," Gardner said. "It prevents a species from growing out of control. And you and your evil pack were out of control."

Minerva stood up from the piano bench and walked across the floor to a table set up with a floral centerpiece and a candle on each end. A tablecloth covered the mahogany wood, and Minerva played her finger across the table to the first candle. She waved her hand over the flame. Then Minerva picked up the candle and poured the melting wax onto the back of her hand. She winced at the pain but then smiled.

"I've ensured that no one will leave this place," she said as she replaced the candle and wiped the wax from her hand with a napkin. "Not me and not you." She turned away from the table and addressed the company at the other end of the room once again. "But that doesn't mean I'll go down without a fight."

The older woman unbuttoned the dress she was wearing and stepped out of it. Standing naked in front of the men, the woman changed into the silver-haired wolf. Her change was lightning fast, and she was charging at them even as Gardner was starting his transformation. The silver wolf charged at Gardner full speed. Antony tried to stop the attacking wolf, but she knocked him away without stopping her forward momentum.

The silver wolf kicked with powerful hind legs and sent David flying. Even moving at the speed of sound, the vampires could not get a grip on Minerva's wolf. Gardner finished his transformation and joined the effort to bring down the silver beast. She seemed to be playing with them, leaping at them only to push off their chest and dodge away. Mother quickly changed direction and swept through, taking first David and then Antony right off their feet. She snapped at them, but they moved out of the way of her jaws with a crackle of vampiric speed.

David pulled his katana from the sheath at his hip, but no matter how fast he swung the blade, he could not connect with the wolf. She allowed him access to her neck, only to swoop out of the path of the sword before it could touch her. David slashed and jabbed and chopped, but to no avail. The silver wolf clamped down on David's wrist. Gardner's wolf pounced. The silver wolf released David's hand or risked opening its belly up by the black wolf's snapping teeth.

The silver wolf backed off to reformulate a new plan.

Then something began to happen that the silver wolf did not anticipate. Gardner's wolf moved ahead of the silver wolf's attacks. If she flashed to the left, the black wolf was already there. If she leaped, the black wolf leaped first. She and the black wolf danced in a parody of mirror movements.

The silver wolf dodged right, then quickly back to the left, but the black-haired wolf anticipated even this and was there to block her attempt to break free of his trap. The silver wolf backed up a few more steps. She backed up until she ran out of space. She crouched down and snarled at her opponent. She snapped at him in an attempt to push him back, but he only stepped back and forward again to keep her against the wall.

The silver wolf rolled to the left and then back to the right. In a desperate attempt to be free of her position, she leaped high over the black-haired wolf's head. Gardner's wolf knew she was planning this and jumped also. He latched onto the silver wolf's throat and did not let go, even as the two wolves hit the floor and rolled. Gardner's wolf bit down deeper. The silver wolf thrashed and bucked, rolled and tugged, but still, the black wolf held firm. Blood began to flow, turning the silver wolf's throat crimson.

Sometime during the silver's wolf's failed attempts to throw off the black-haired wolf's deadly hold, Maggie and Alex arrived at the ballroom. Maggie clamped her hand to her mouth at the sight of the two wolves whipping and rolling across the floor. She wanted to help, but she was as useless as the vampires. With the animals so intertwined, there was no hope of stabbing one without the risk of piercing the other.

This fight to the death between the silver wolf and the black wolf could not be interrupted without causing a switch in advantage, which the black wolf had at the moment. The black wolf growled as he ground his teeth together and continued to rip into the flesh of the silver wolf's neck. The skin under his teeth knitted together and repaired itself as fast as he cut into it. He reopened the wounds with a vicious shake of the head, and the blood flowed again. This approach wasn't working as the silver wolf was not only repairing the torn flesh but regenerating the lost blood. He had to inflict damage that the silver wolf could not fix.

He had to rip out her throat.

His teeth clamped down tighter, readjusting to include more and more flesh, muscle, and bone. He felt the delicate bones of the windpipe under his teeth. He leaped with his hind legs and whipped his head around, lifting the silver wolf off the floor. He shook violently at the silver wolf's throat, refusing to release his teeth. A satisfying crunch and a whimper from the silver wolf signaled to the black wolf the fight was over. He flung the silver wolf across the room, and it landed in a heap under the grand piano.

The silver wolf transformed back into the older woman. She reached up and placed a hand at her torn throat. The blood poured in rivulets between her fingers. The damage was too extensive and could not repair itself.

Across the room, the black wolf dropped the meat and bone that had been Minerva's throat. Everyone looked at the woman sitting up against the grand piano leg. Blood flowed steadily from the torn flesh and ran down between her breasts to puddle on the floor around her. She brought her legs up to a sitting position with legs bent at the knees. She dropped her hand away from her torn throat and tried to speak but only managed to cough up blood. Her eyes cleared, and she smiled. With one bloody hand, she waved goodbye. Then the hand dropped back into her lap, and she died.

A vision came to Maggie in a flash of fire and death, and she understood why the woman had waved. "Oh, God. There's a bomb."

Without hesitating, the group turned and ran from the ballroom. David led them back to the main gate where the Zephyr had plowed through the wall and came to a rest. Did it still run? If it was out of commission, they were all dead.

"How much time do we have?" David asked as he attempted to start the Zephyr.

"Less than a minute," Maggie said.

Alex moaned.

***

The Zephyr started, and David quickly backed it out of the hole he had made. When he was free of the compound, he turned the wheel sharply and drove away. David pushed the massive vehicle to sixty, seventy, eighty miles an hour when he looked in his rearview mirror and saw the explosion. David watched the growing fireball, and it became chillingly apparent that they were not going to get out of the blast range in time. He thought about his son, about Antony. David thought about the budding romance between Gardner and this vulnerable human girl and wondered if any of them would live through the pending blast. As the shock wave hit them, he did all he could to keep the Zephyr moving, but the sand and the sheer size of the vehicle were conspiring to hinder their escape.

"Hold onto something," David shouted. And then the Zephyr was spinning, tumbling out of control.

Chapter Forty-Two

Deep inside the hacienda, the Hispanic male servant received the order to start the timer. When the woman died, her control over him ended, and he looked at what he had done. He cried out and tried to stop the bomb. "¡Oh, Dios mío, ¿qué he hecho?" He sobbed as he frantically but ineffectively attempted to turn the timer off.

His decision to flee from the bomb came too late. He was halfway out the door when the bomb went off and incinerated him.

***

The heat and pressure built up, and the building blasted into dust within seconds. The fireball continued to expand, destroying everything in its path. The fish in the koi pond vaporized. Still, the explosion pushed outward. The shock wave traveled just a few seconds ahead of the fiery show, blowing up all buildings and plants in its path. The fireball shot skyward, but the heatwave pushed along the ground, picking up speed. It hit the Zephyr at one hundred and fifty miles an hour, twisting its metal and tossing it like a toy through the air. The vehicle broke apart and continued to spin across the ground in three different directions, fanning out and leaving metal and plastic debris trails. When the explosion was over and the Zephyr stopped rolling, the survivors began to move. David was the first to emerge from the wreckage. He stood and staggered toward the compartment where he had last seen Gardner. His son was there, still and unmoving. He rushed to the boy, checking for vitals.

David helped his son from the wreckage when Gardner coughed and sat up.

Antony staggered from the debris farthest from the main wreckage and joined the other two survivors. Maggie was the next to come out of the pile, doubled over and holding her side. She had internal injuries, but she was confident she would heal.

Gardner staggered over to his mother and hugged her tightly. She groaned in pain but was glad to see him in one piece. She tolerated the pain. Gardner abruptly pulled away and looked into his mother's eyes. He had tears streaming down his cheeks. "Alex," he said. "I can't hear any thoughts coming from her."

They called her. Antony checked the rubble he had been in, but she wasn't in there. David and Maggie checked the smaller piles of debris. Gardner tore through the most significant part of the wreckage, pushing distorted and burning furniture out of the way. When he saw the sofa overturned and smoking, he panicked. Gardner hefted the bulky piece of junk and tossed it aside but saw only legs visible under the heap of smoldering cushions. Fearful of what he would find but needing to know if she was all right, Gardner pushed the pillows off her.

A cut over her right eye bled profusely, and her clothes had burned away in places, but her breath came in steady, low wheezes. He shook her gently, and she turned and looked up at him. "Did I survive?" she asked hoarsely, then coughed on the smoke circling her.

Gardner laughed through his tears and pulled her into a firm embrace. When they separated, he helped her to stand. He tore off part of his shirt to staunch the blood flow coming from her head wound.

She had twisted her ankle, and they suspected a concussion, but otherwise, she seemed okay.

The five staggered out of the wreckage. Alex looked back at the hacienda's smoldering ruins and then walked away with her friends and protectors. The sun would rise soon, and the vampires needed to find shelter. The others would have to make it to the nearest town and get medical help and transportation back to Philadelphia. When the vampires rose the following night, they would meet them back at the house.

Antony and David found an abandoned shack, pulled up the floorboards, and took shelter in the earth beneath the floor. Maggie Alex and Gardner found a road and received help from an elderly couple. They drove the injured group to town.

"Looks like y'all were in a car accident. Is that what happened?' the old man asked.

"Luke, mind your business," the woman said with a nervous chuckle.

"Saw a massive light in the sky. That wasn't you, was it?"

Maggie assured him it was not.

213

By the time they arrived in town, Maggie and Gardner had healed. Alex received treatment at an emergency room, and Maggie rented a car. She drove all day while the kids slept in the back seat. She reached Philadelphia twenty-eight hours later. Once home, they all slept, even Maggie, for another twelve hours straight.

Chapter Forty-Three

Rose had been miles from the hacienda when it blew and knew nothing of its fate. She did feel the disconnection from Mother at the moment of her death.

That's it then. I no longer have control of the wolf. Once again, I'm on my own.

She blamed Gardner for this misfortune, and if she ever had the opportunity to make him pay for her distress, she would do it gladly.

Rose remembered the days of waking up in strange places, naked and covered in blood. She remembered the vulnerability and confusion that lifestyle caused. Rose recalled the self-loathing and anger. She compared it to floating through space, not knowing where she was or where she would land.

So many times, she had ended up inside some strange barn or in someone's backyard with strange men gawking at her naked body. Dogs barked at her. She doubted the men would lust after her now. An empty eye socket showed where her left eye should have been. When she had pulled the arrow from the socket, the orb had come with it. She stared in horror at the bloody mass at the end of the shaft in her hand. She could see the stalk dangling from the back of the eye like a deflated balloon. She had cried.

The socket had since healed. There was no more pain, but there was also no more eye. She had left the eye still pierced by the arrow lying in the sand. She didn't know where she was going but wanted to get out of the desert before the sun rose. She staggered on, not even sure which direction to go. Her sense of direction went when her connection to Mother ended. She was lost and alone. But she kept moving.

As she had moved off, escaping the witch with the deadly aim, Rose had seen Bethany moving in behind the girl. She hoped Bethany had managed to do what she could not and killed the wretched girl. If nothing else, that much should have happened. She wanted to know the girl was dead, preferably stabbed with one of those stupid arrows. If the girl survived the encounter with Bethany, she hoped to have a crack at her again, too, someday. She would kill them both if she could, Gardner and the girl.

Rose walked on. She thought she could see the outskirts of a town up ahead. That gave her encouragement to continue. However, the closer she got, the more it looked less like a town and more like an abandoned warehouse or something. That was fine. Even that was better than being out in the desert when the sun came up in her present condition.

Rose quickened her steps. She was beginning to limp as her feet became sand-encrusted. Rose wanted to get into the warehouse and rest. She stumbled through the desert for a long time before removing the arrow, but when the pain had gotten too great, Rose pulled it out. None of that mattered now as she stumbled toward the warehouse. Rose would find shelter and shade and wait out the hot sun. Tomorrow night she would be on her way again.

She wondered when her change would come. Would she change tomorrow night? Would she run in the wrong direction and have to do this trek all over again? She hoped she had a few days before her transformation started.

She reached the warehouse and stopped as a stranger stepped out of the shadows.

"Good evening, Rose," said the stranger.

Disarmed and confused, Rose stared that the man. Upon closer inspection, Rose recognized him as a vampire. "How do you know my name?" she asked.

"I know many things about you. I know you are a werewolf without a pack. I know you want revenge on the ones who took your eye."

"Can you give me back my eye?" she asked.

"No, that I can't do. But you won't need it. You will learn to compensate. I can, however, give you back your ability to control the wolf inside you. You don't have to be at the mercy of the wolf. You can have everything you had with the pack returned to you."

"Why should I trust you?" she asked.

"You shouldn't. I'm a devious predator, just like you. But you and I want the same thing; we want to destroy the vampires and werewolves that destroyed your pack. I can give you what you want. Together we will form an alliance that will bring an end to Gardner and his family."

"Okay," Rose said.

And like that, Rose joined the stranger's campaign against Antony, David, Maggie, and the others.

Part Three: The Stranger

Chapter Forty-Four

When the Corpse Boy returned to the house that had belonged to his Dark Father, it pleased him to find it abandoned and overrun with bugs. There were many more cobwebs, but they were not bothersome. He investigated the basement. The broken coffins still littered the floor. He removed the pieces, not wanting anything around that reminded him of the Dark Father. Corpse Boy resumed his position in the corner and feasted on the roaches, spiders, and other crawlies that ventured near him.

It was a few days later when he heard the voices upstairs. He distinctly heard a man, a woman, and a young girl speaking in hushed tones. Were they humans investigating an abandoned building, or were they something else? He wanted to examine but knew that staying invisible was his best line of defense, so he crawled into a corner and disappeared into the shadows. He stayed there, out of sight and unseen, and watched. And he listened.

***

"I happen to know the owner of this place won't be back," the man said as he and the pretty red-haired girl came down the basement steps. "Met with a bit of an accident, or so I'm told. Our new friends can take the credit for that one, too."

The man and the girl looked around but were not in the area where the Corpse Boy crouched and did not see him.

But they did smell him. "Stinks in here," the girl said and wrinkled her nose in disgust. That woman you're with, the blind one, is she your cleaning lady?"

The man laughed but did not answer. Once the girl had seen enough, she left the basement. The man stepped over to a pile of neatly stacked metal grates. He began building something. He pounded and soldered and clamped the bars together until he had completed the task. Then the man walked away.

After the man had gone, Corpse Boy ventured out to see what the stranger had built. He turned his head first one way and then the other as he inspected the contraption in front of him. Corpse

Boy walked around the box-shaped object, knowing what it was but not why it was there.

Two cages, clamped together, stood in front of Corpse Boy. The kennel cages seemed big enough for two large dogs. Corpse Boy wondered briefly what the cells were for but decided this, too, was something he was better off not knowing. He tested their strength. They were iron and very strong. He was about to turn and leave when he heard the stranger's voice behind him.

"Who do we have here?" the man said.

Corpse Boy flinched and turned toward the voice.

"What form of creature are you?" the stranger asked as he approached. Corpse Boy staggered back, hitting the wall, and then side-stepping to the right. When pushed into the corner, the stranger came and put out his hands in a placating manner. "I'm not going to hurt you."

The stranger, a vampire Corpse Boy understood when the smile offered a flash of fang, reached out and grabbed the zombie boy's left hand. Corpse Boy then learned he had a new form of defense. When the stranger tugged on the hand, it detached, and Corpse Boy popped free. He darted liquid fast past the stranger and flew up the stairs.

The stranger looked down at the disintegrating hand in his grasp and smiled.

Chapter Forty-Five

Randal walked beside the woman he had adopted as his mother. She, and her two male companions, traveled through the Appalachian Mountains of Pennsylvania, taking their victims randomly. Even though Randal was always encouraged to take innocent victims, he still resisted the genuinely innocent, taking only men with shady intentions as his food source. They weren't all murderers and rapists, but they still had the potential to do those things. Nevertheless, his previous family viewed these men as innocent. To his new mother, they were nothing of the sort.

"To feel the intensity of the innocent victim, you have to feed on the new mother or the lost child. These are the choicest innocents. Their blood is heavenly and divine. Trust me. Once you taste a single drop, you won't want anything else."

"That's why I'm avoiding taking that next step. Have you ever considered going the other way?" Randal asked her. "Antony and David insist that drinking innocent blood corrupts the vampire's mind and spirit. They say starting down that path will ultimately destroy you."

"You spent too much time with those wimps," she said. "You need to widen your scope and start seeing how much freer you will feel when you kill without remorse for the victim. They are our prey; does the lion feel sad when he takes down a baby zebra? Does the hyena weep for the mother gazelle as he's ripping out her belly?"

For the moment, Randal stopped trying to change her mind, but he wasn't going to give up altogether. He was sure he could bring her around to his way of thinking, and eventually, she could join Antony's group. If this could happen, Randal could someday go home. He hadn't realized how much he would miss the group—Maggie, David, Antony, and especially Gardner—until he had left. Now Randal wanted to go back to them desperately. He had screwed up. He had come to this conclusion as he hunted a victim Randal believed would fit into Antony's criteria, but he was not entirely sure. He didn't realize how hard it had been to make the distinction until forced to do it alone. Randal used to hunt without any difficulty, but even then, he always had Maggie or David's seal of approval. Now, choosing a mildly corrupt victim was the best he could hope to achieve since he had left the group's safety.

His mother insisted one victim was as good as the next. Could she ever be swayed? If he returned to the others right now with her, would they want to destroy her? He couldn't allow that, and he couldn't give up the hope that he could change her mind. He wanted it all; he wanted his new vampire mother, and he wanted his immortal family. But if he couldn't get her to come around, they would most definitely kill her. The best protection for her right now was keeping her as far away from them as he could. He knew Maggie had a range her gift could reach. He was sure he and his new mother were out of that range, and as much as he loved Gardner and the others, beyond that range, they would stay until his vampire mother accepted Antony's way of life.

They trudged on through the night. He couldn't stand watching his mother kill children, young mothers, or other innocent prey. Randal had taken a man he thought was guilty of a crime, but once he started drinking his blood, he knew the truth. He was just a father of two, working two jobs to make ends meet for his family. Randal had hated the feeling of killing that the man had awoken in him. In that one instant, he had understood everything Antony had been trying to teach him. It was in that moment he had begun anew to convince his mother to give up the innocent lives for the corrupt and the guilty.

So far, he was having no luck.

When it came time to bed down before sunrise, Randal chose a nice abandoned and run-down cottage. He and his mother crawled into a closet, and the two minions took shelter in the root cellar. When morning came, he passed into death sleep with his arms wrapped around his new mother.

And he was in that position when he awoke the following evening. He yawned and sat up. It was a mystery why vampires yawned. Humans yawn when they need the extra oxygen, but vampires didn't breathe and therefore didn't need to yawn.

And yet they did all the time. Perhaps it was just some leftover human reflex vampires could not give up.

Randal stepped out of the closet and waited for his mother to awaken. He was an early riser compared to other vampires.

Randal used to wake up long before David and Antony. His mother woke a few minutes after him, but the two bums downstairs slept many more minutes longer still.

"Why do you have those clowns around?" Randal asked his mother.

"They do the heavy lifting," she replied. Randal understood that they disposed of the bodies. At least they were good for that much. Randal observed that his mother didn't mind killing innocent people; she just didn't like to touch them afterward. One of her minions had accidentally locked himself out in the sun, and she made a point to replace him right away. She gave the new minion specific instructions that she and Randal's corpses left behind were decapitated and hidden. Buried, if possible, but taken as far out of the human eye as they could manage. So far, the new guy was working out superbly.

Randal didn't talk to the minions, and he had no interest in making any of his own. That was her thing. If he could convince her to convert to Antony's way of thinking, he could protect her, but the minion had to fend for themselves. If she joined his immortal family, she wouldn't need them anyway. But Randal observed she always had them, and there were always two.

Randal's main task was getting his mother to conform to the code.

On the hunt, Randal avoided areas with schools, daycare centers, and hospitals. Instead, he led her to the seedier part of town, where the only victims were thieves and cutthroats. Perturbed, she walked away.

"No, come watch this. I want you to see what I see," Randal said.

She seemed bored and irritated, but she stood next to him. They watched from the shadows as a man with his head low approached a hooker standing against the wall at the other end of the alley. When the man was within arm's length, he reached out and grabbed the woman by the throat. She gagged and screamed, but no one tried to help her. The man pulled her into the shadows of a dumpster and punched her, ripped at her clothes.

"Give me your money," he snarled. "I know you got some. You already had three tricks tonight."

"Len is going to mess you up," the woman said.

225

"I'm not afraid of your pimp." He punched her again, knocking her unconscious.

"Now," Randal said to his mother.

"Take her?" she asked.

"No," Randal said forcefully. "Take him."

She looked at him as if he were insane. Still, she sighed and relented. She flew down the alley with a rustle of loose newsprint and a crackling whisper as she moved at the speed of sound. The man barely understood what was happening to him as she lifted him off his feet and pinned him against the wall. She held him in place with her forearm and used her razor-sharp fangs for ripping a gash in his corroded artery. She drank ravenously, draining him completely. When she finished, she called to her minions to come and dispose of the body. They did not hesitate. They decapitated the corpse and tossed him in the nearby dumpster.

The hooker came awake to her senses and ran.

"I have to admit," his mother said. "I think you're on to something here."

"And think about it, no one is going to care when they discover that monster. Every authority in the county probably wants him."

"And every pimp in the city," she added.

Randal laughed. "He has probably attacked, robbed, and murdered many hookers over the years."

"Why should we care about the hookers, though?" asked his mother.

"It's not about the hookers, Mother. It's survival. No one is going to look for that creep's killer. When you take innocent babies and young mothers, people want to know who would do such atrocities, and there is a national outcry for justice. Anonymity is a vampire's best friend."

Randal could see that his words were affecting her. He felt a warmth inside him that belied his cold skin. He had done what he thought he could never do. Randal had converted her to the Code.

Her next two victims were a rapist and a pedophile. Randal hunted a killer even as the killer hunted his next kill. In the blood, Randal learned that he had killed two previous times. The minions had pursued, but Randal didn't know or care who they took. When the hunt was over, the group headed back to the outlying rural landscape they called home.

His mother smiled, happy and content. "I never thought killing people with such hatred in their hearts could taste so good. It was *gratifying* taking evil men."

"I'm happy you approve. Is this something you could do every night?"

"Yes," she said. "I feel exhilarated with the blood of the corrupt flowing through me."

"Good," Randal said. "Because I have to go back, and I want you to come, too. But you can't take innocent victims anymore."

Her smile faded. "No," she said. "You can't. We can't."

"Yes, we can. We can —"

The ginger werewolf with the missing right eye came from the trees in the north. She moved at breakneck speed and, in a single snap of her jaws, decapitated the closer of the two minions. In her second pass, the werewolf jumped onto the second minion's chest and pushed him to the ground. The werewolf then tore out the vampire's throat. As he struggled, she chewed through the rest of his neck. Finally, with the snap of his backbone, the vampire's head came off.

Randal's mother rushed in to attack the wolf, but the stranger came out of the darkness and pinned Randal's mother in a headlock. Randal raged at the attackers. He beat against the man who had taken his mother captive, but his blows only made the man laugh.

"You would be wise to stay where you are, little man," the stranger said. "If you don't want your precious mother to get hurt, that is." Randal stopped. "Good boy."

The third member of this group approached from the same trees from where the werewolf had come. This woman was in her mid-forties. She had long wavy brown hair with a touch of gray highlighting the natural color. She wore a long flowing black dress with long sleeves covering her hands' backs, so only her slender fingers showed. She moved gracefully. When she reached Randal, he could see her eyes were such a pale blue he knew she was blind. She stopped directly in front of Randal.

"You can't see?" Randal heard himself ask her.

"I have a special sight," she said, and her voice was low and husky. She sounded like someone who had smoked for most of her life.

"You're a witch," he said then, and she smiled.

This witch woman reached behind her back and came around with an iron collar attached to a heavy chain in her hand. Randal stepped back. The stranger holding his mother stepped forward and tightened his grip on her neck.

"I can destroy her. Allow Eva to attach the collar if you don't want to see your precious mother's head come off."

Randal shook with rage. He couldn't go through this again. He had worn a leash once before, and it was the most excruciating and humiliating experience Randal had ever known. He didn't want to endure that again. But Randal didn't want his mother hurt, so he stepped forward and allowed himself to be collared. The witch-woman reached out, wrapped the collar around his neck, and clicked it in place. He was the roped boy once again.

"Good boy," the stranger said.

He released Randal's mother and took the other end of the chain attached to the collar, wrapping it around his hand.

"Why are you doing this?" Randal's mother asked.

"The boy vamp is very important to my plan," the stranger said.

"And what about me?" she asked. "Where do I fit in?"

"You, my sweet lady, do not fit into the plan at all." The stranger reached behind his back and pulled out a long-curved blade from a hidden sheath with his free hand. With a single flick of his wrist, the stranger took off the vampire woman's head.

Randal screamed and raged against his shackles. The stranger pulled on the chain attached to Randal's neck, knocking the boy vampire to the ground. The stranger placed a foot on Randal's head and pinned him to the ground. The stranger increased the pressure.

"Do not hurt your prize, my Love," the blind woman said.

The stranger seemed to realize what he was doing and released Randal's head. Randal stood but did not fight. He looked up at the stranger with eyes as red as the blood on which he had fed. Then his eyes wept crimson tears.

228

Chapter Forty-Six

Maggie arrived home with Alex and Gardner a day and a half before Antony and David. Once everyone had returned, Alex brought up the subject of her parents. Maggie offered to go with her back to Ohio. What they found there was an empty house. No one knew where Alex's parents had gone. Maggie, pretending to be a concerned relative of the Robinsons, had learned that there was a nationwide search for Tom, Amie, and Alex. All the neighbors believed Alex's parents had set off searching for their daughter and had probably met the same fate as the kids. Maggie saw the truth once she entered the Robinson house. No neighbors or family friends had not seen Alex. She grieved, and they stayed at the residence for a day or so as Alex collected a few mementos of her parents, and as they left, Maggie and Alex agreed it would be better if everyone believed Alex dead.

Once back at the house on Lansdowne Hill, Alex retreated to her room, where she stayed for days.

Gardner allowed Alex her space. But he could not sit back and wait for Randal to slip through his fingers. Gardner believed the longer he waited, the farther out of reach Randal became. "Mom," he said. "Please tell me you have been able to pick up something on Randal." Maggie's sympathetic eyes already told him what she was about to say.

"I'm sorry, Honey," she said. "He is just totally off my radar. I don't know if he is too far away or is somehow blocking me because he doesn't want us to find him, but I can't see him. Not anymore. But don't give up hope. Do you remember me telling you about the tabloid killer the papers are calling the Bath Salts Vigilante? I've been tracking the movements of this killer, and I see a definite pattern. If Randal is the Vigilante, we'll find him by following the victims he leaves behind."

"Mom, you're a genius," Gardner said and kissed her.

"The most recent victims have been found in dumpsters in small towns along the Appellations. He seems to be heading North toward New York. He is too far out of my range of sight, but once we get a more definite route, we'll plan a trip to go and collect him."

"I don't want to wait that long. The authorities might not find Randal's victims for days or weeks. We have to do something sooner." Gardner's jaw clenched. She knew that look.

"No," his mother said, maybe a little too quickly. "I don't think so. He hasn't been too concerned with hiding them. The route is coming about rather quickly. I think we'll know exactly where he is very soon."

"If we still had the Zephyr, we could have gone on a family trip. You promised me we would make him our priority when we returned from the New Mexico trip."

"I know. You just need to be patient."

"I have to find him. I can't sleep, and I can't eat. I think about Randal out there somewhere in trouble. I have to get him back. I know something is wrong."

I think so too, but if you run off, I risk losing you also. Gardner heard this and called her out when she said: "I'm sure he's fine. You can't..."

"You don't think he's fine, and I know it," Gardner said. "I'm going out to find him."

"Mind reading again?" his mother said.

"I'm going too," Alex said. Gardner looked at her with a reassuring smile.

Maggie hugged the girl, happy to have her once again showing an interest in her new life. "Someone should go with you. David or me..."

"No," Gardner said. "Alex and I are going alone."

Maggie sighed, exasperated. She didn't want him to go at all, but she knew him well enough to know he wasn't going to change his mind about this. She nodded her reluctant approval. They would leave before nightfall, so it would be her responsibility to tell David of his plan. He would blame her; he would say she should have tried harder to stop him, but in the end, he too would know that any attempt to stop this would have been futile. She kissed him and then kissed Alex. After they had gone, she had a vision: one of them would not return.

In the garage where Antony kept his massive collection of cars, Gardner grabbed the green Ford Mustang's keys from the pegboard. He pulled the Mustang out of its stall, drove the length of the warehouse's central causeway to the industrial-sized garage door, and started down the highway toward their next adventure. Gardner grew excited, knowing he would see Randal soon. He was sure of it. Alex smiled, pleased to see him happy. She would never forget her parents, but she knew that she could feel joy with Gardner at her side. She felt an urge to kiss him.

Gardner looked at her with a blush on his cheeks.

"Stop reading my mind," she said.

"Sorry."

They were quiet for a time. As the couple traveled through the Philadelphia area, Gardner played a classic rock channel. When they reached the more rural parts of Pennsylvania, he could only find classical and religious stations.

"I should have brought the iPod," he said as he played with the stereo buttons.

"We don't need a radio," Alex said. "We can entertain each other."

"You know how to sing?" he asked.

"Not with music; we can talk."

"Oh," he said, trying not to sound disappointed. "What should we talk about?"

"I want to hear about Randal. I want to get to know him as only you can describe him. You light up like a boy on Christmas day when you speak of him. Help me get to know him better so he won't hate me so much."

"He doesn't hate you," Gardner said. He wished he had said it with more conviction, but the truth was he didn't know. Gardner didn't know if Randal hated her or not and didn't know if she was the reason Randal left. These were all answers he hoped to get when he met up with Randal again.

"That doesn't matter. Just tell me about Randal."

"Randal." Gardner thought about it. "He's my best friend, has been there for days unremembered, and he has taken care of me in any situation. To you, Randal is probably a boy. He has always

231

looked like a boy, but even when I was in my teens, I knew he was older than me, and to me, he has always been a man. He is my Uncle Rand. Good old Uncle Rand, and I love him.

"Never call him Randy unless you want your neck perforated," Gardner stated flatly. Alex laughed at that last part, but it was a nervous laugh. Had it been a joke? When Gardner laughed, too, she relaxed.

"I will stick to Randal," she said.

"He helped me, and I helped him," Gardner continued. "Whenever I would have homework, he wouldn't so much help me with it as learn from it with me. Randal loves to learn. Whenever I mentioned something he knew nothing about, he would jump into an encyclopedia and look it up. By the time he finished reading, you would think he was an expert on the subject."

The car grew quiet for a while as Gardner fell into thought. Alex didn't push; she knew he would continue when he was ready. She didn't try to say something to break up the quiet, either. Alex just sat and waited.

When he was ready, he said: "Randal is a lonely soul. He rarely ever talked of his human family, and when he did, it was usually only to my Mom or me. Randal hates that he will never grow into a man. He hated the thought of never knowing the love of a woman. He came to terms with these things in his way, I guess. 'You can't miss what you never had,' he once told me. He always said he would miss the sun more than his manhood because the sun was something he had been able to enjoy and would never see again."

"I can understand that," Alex said. "I love the sun. I would rather die than face an eternity of never being able to feel it on my face again. Immortality may be something wonderful for some people, but not me. I want to grow old. I want to have children and grandchildren. I want to spend my golden years surrounded by a family I created."

Gardner glanced over at Alex as she spoke and saw the love and the happiness she expressed when she talked of this family she planned to have. Guiltily, he felt a pang of regret and sadness. Gardner suddenly wished he could be the one to give her those things, but he could not. He wanted to reach over and take her hand, pull her close to him and kiss her. Instead, he focused on the road and tightened his grip on the circle of chain link encased in clear rigid plastic that was the steering wheel. He pressed on the accelerator. When he looked back at Alex, he saw she was looking at him with concern etched on her face.

"Did I say something wrong?" she asked.

"No," Gardner assured her and sat up straighter in his seat. "Why?"

"I just thought I felt a slight change in your demeanor. You're not upset with me because I want to be mortal, are you?"

"No," he said, hoping he sounded reassuring. "I'm down with that. Did you think I would bite you on purpose or something? Don't let what my mother did to me worry you. No one in my family would ever do that to you. You are entitled to be who you are. I'm happy with who I am."

"Okay," she said. She believed Gardner but, still, she wondered what had caused him to stiffen suddenly.

A thought came to her suddenly she wished hadn't come into her head. She wished she could wipe away before he could read it there. She thought: can a human and a werewolf have a baby?

She blushed and squirmed in her chair. When she felt the heat leave her cheeks, she turned and looked at Gardner. Handsome as ever, peaceful and oblivious, he hadn't appeared to have read her mind. She sighed, relieved.

When he looked at her, he smiled, and she smiled back.

"You're nervous," he said.

"What?" she asked. She wondered if he had heard her thoughts after all.

"You're still nervous about Randal."

Then she understood. Gardner, preoccupied over finding Randal, had tuned her out. She relaxed.

"Don't be," he said. "Randal will love you as much as I do. I'm sure whatever drove him away has nothing to do with you. As soon as he sees us and he sees that we still accept him, he will come home with us, and everything will be fine."

Then it occurred to Gardner what he had said—that he loved Alex—and his face reddened.

She giggled. "Me too." Then she clarified this remark. "I believe that too."

They arrived in the Pocono area in the afternoon. Gardner paid for a room with two beds. He used a gold card Antony had offered to him for emergencies. The name read Howard Shultz.

"Do I look like a Howard?" he asked Alex. She giggled but didn't answer.

Once their room key card was in hand, they walked through the lobby and placed their overnight bags on the bed. They changed their clothes for dinner. They had approximately seven hours to investigate the dumpster where the authorities had found the latest Vigilante murder victim.

" I should have let my mother come with us. She could have made this whole process a lot easier. No matter. We can find Randal without her help."

Gardner bought a paper from a vendor in the hotel's lobby, and as they picked through their salads, Gardner scanned the news for Vigilante sightings. "There has been a rash of victims found in this area," he told Alex. "We are definitely in the right place. Now, all we have to do is scout out the same neighborhoods he has been hunting in."

"Have you considered what you will say when you find him?" Alex asked.

"What do you mean?"

She considered her words carefully. "What if Randal still refuses to come home after you've found him?"

"He won't," Gardner said sharply. "I mean, he has to come home. When he sees all the trouble we've gone through to get him home, he won't refuse."

"Okay," Alex said but wasn't convinced.

After dinner, they returned to the room and waited for nightfall. Gardner had a general idea when Randal woke from death sleep. As soon as he was sure Randal was awake, he and Alex headed out to the last place someone found a vigilante victim. He stood near the dumpster that had been cordoned off with yellow police tape and scanned the area.

Bums peaked out from doorways of abandoned buildings at the two well-dressed kids standing in the alley. Hookers walked by, eyeing Gardner with interest, and Alex with contempt. No vampires appeared.

"Something's wrong," Gardner said.

"He probably knows better than to return to the scene of a crime. We just have to find another neighborhood."

"It's not that," he said. He went silent again. He glanced around. He stared intently at the hookers and then at the bums. He frowned. "I can't hear them."

"What?"

He turned to Alex, and the worry on his face chilled her. "I can't hear their thoughts. I can't hear your thoughts. I can't hear anything. The gift is gone."

Alex fell silent. She didn't know what to say. When she started to speak, Gardner shushed her.

"I'm sorry," he said. Something is coming through. I heard something just now." He listened again.

Telling Alex what he heard, Gardner said, *"I'm blocking your gift.* It's a woman with a husky smoker's voice. *I have someone here who wishes to talk to you."*

"Hello, son. It's a man's voice now—a stranger's voice. *Randal is with us. He would very much like you to come and see him. I only ask you to come alone. If you do not come, he will have no choice but to feed on whomever I choose to place in the cage with him. He hasn't eaten tonight, so I'm sure he will have no trouble giving up the code."*

Gardner looked around, frantic and confused. He looked toward the buildings and the street, scanned the fire escapes but saw no one.

"Where are you?" Gardner shouted to the empty street. "Let me see him."

"What's happening?" Alex whispered.

"I feel they are close by."

"His need for blood must be too strong for him to hold out," Alex said. "He must be in agony."

"Don't hurt him, please."

"Who could be doing this?"

Gardner had no answer. But even before he could respond, Gardner flew back into a pile of empty boxes. Alex screamed when she saw him fly to the ground as if struck by lightning.

This witch," Gardner said as he regained his feet. "She's strong." Gardner continued to narrate the voice in his head. *"You must come to him if you wish to save him. I will tell you where he is. You have never been here, but you know where he is just the same. He's waiting for you, but if you do not come alone, I will execute him. You know where he is."*

"Do you know where he is?" Alex asked.

"No." Gardner directed his question to the alley around him. "Tell me where to go."

"Gardner." Alex's voice came out in a frightened whisper.

"He is in the place where it all started for him."

"Where did it all start for him?" Alex asked.

"I think I know now. I have to go to Randal. He needs my help."

"We have to go," Alex corrected him.

"No, you take the Mustang back to my parents. Go back to them and tell them what happened here. Tell them these people who—or whatever they are—have abilities I can't even describe. They are controlling my ability, allowing me only to hear what they want me to hear. They pushed me with an ability I've never known before."

"You can't go there. It's a trap."

Gardner set his jaw. "I can't let him suffer alone. I have to go. Get help and come back as soon as you can."

"What should I tell them?"

Gardner touched her arm and peered deeply into her eyes. "Tell them we're at the Dark Father's mansion."

Alex hugged him then and hugged him tightly. Her body shuddered as he hugged her back. "I'll be back as soon as I can."

Chapter Forty-Seven

Gardner marched up the driveway with its cracked blacktop overgrown with grass and weeds. He walked past the large white flaking pillars lining the porch like gigantic sentinels. Two big and weathered doors led into the foyer of what had once been a splendid Bed and Breakfast. The doors hung slightly open and squeaked as he pushed them aside.

As if expecting his arrival, Gardner saw a trail of red rose petals leading him through the darkened and musty rooms. He followed them through a high-ceilinged hall to a door with a note posted on it.

I'M OPEN. COME IN.

Gardner pushed the door inward, and it hit against the wall. There was a small landing and then stairs leading into darkness. Gardner took a deep breath and started down. At the bottom, a darkened bulb dangled from the ceiling to his right, and he headed toward it. Gardner pulled the chain and lit the alcove, saw the cage. It took him a moment to see what lay inside the cell.

Randal.

Randal cowered in one half of the cage, but a second section of the cell did not allow Randal access as bars separated the two halves. Separate doors led to each side of the pen. Randal sat balled up in the corner of his side of the cage. Straw littered the cell's floor. He was not alone in the cell, Gardner realized. A dead woman lay sprawled in the front of the cage. Her lifeless eyes stared out at Gardner.

"Randal," Gardner said in a whispered sob.

The boy vampire did not look.

"Randal," Gardner said more forcefully this time. He ran to the cage and collapsed against its bars. He reached in over the dead woman.

Randal looked up this time and saw Gardner kneeling at the cage, reaching toward him. Randal did not try to reach toward Gardner. Instead, the boy scooted further back in the cell.

"Randal, It's me. It's Gar." Gardner tried to pen the cage, but a padlock prevented the door from opening.

When Randal's eyes focused on Gardner, the boy climbed over the dead woman's legs and hugged Gardner through the bars. When Randal had pulled away, Gardner examined the locking mechanism. A key was required to unlock the cage. He tried to break the iron bars but could not. Whoever had built this cage knew what they were doing. Randal gaped at Gardner with sadness in his eyes and on his face. He let out a soft moan.

"Why are you here?" Randal asked.

"I have been looking for you," Gardner explained as he tried to bend the bars.

"You shouldn't have come. Now they have you, too. It's part of their plan."

Gardner stopped fussing with the bars. "Who are you talking about? Who are they? What plan?"

"I don't know who they are, and they won't tell me. All they would tell me is that they want Antony and your mom and dad. They told me you would come to rescue me. They aren't going to let you leave."

"I knew this was a trap, but I had to come. I couldn't let you go through this alone once I knew where you were."

"You still didn't tell me how you found me."

"It's a long story. I—"

"You'll have plenty of time to tell him the whole story once you are inside the cage next to him," a voice from behind them said.

Gardner turned. The stranger emerged from the shadows. Gardner tried to read his mind but could hear nothing. He tried to transform into the wolf, but that too would not come to him. He's never known a time when the wolf did not come when he called.

Then Gardner saw the woman. She was tall, slender, and wore a dark green dress that covered her from neck to heels. The hem of the dress dragged across the floor. Her hair was light brown with trails of gray throughout. When she spoke, Gardner recognized her as the voice that had brought him here. Somehow, he also knew she was the reason he could not use his abilities. She stepped forward and spoke in that gravelly smoker's voice.

"You must understand that you are but pawns in a much bigger game," she said. "The real villain in this game is Antony. Once we deal with him, the rest of you will be free to go on your way."

"My parents and I will never let anything happen to Antony. Surely you must realize that," Gardner said.

"Oh, I do, my young wolf friend," said the man from under the hood. He smiled, and Gardner saw the glint of fangs. "And I'm counting on it."

"Who are you?"

"You will know soon enough. For now, I want you to get into the other side of the cage."

The blind woman stepped forward and opened the door to the second half of the cage. Gardner turned back to the stranger. "I'm not getting in there," he said with finality. He set his feet and waited for the fight.

The stranger didn't make a move to force him into the cage. Gardner stared him down but did not make a move to leave or obey his request. The woman simply tilted her head slightly. Behind Gardner, Randal twitched. Gardner turned to see what was happening inside the cage. Randal shook and thrashed as if an electric current ran through him. The cage rattled, and chaff lifted into the air.

"Randal," Gardner screamed and gripped the bars. Randal continued to writhe. "Stop it. Stop doing that to him."

"Get into the cage, and Randal will be released. Every minute you hesitate makes his discomfort last that much longer," said the stranger.

Gardner knew that once he got into that cage, he wouldn't be getting out again. He also knew he had no other choice if he wanted Randal's torture to end. He stepped toward the open cage door but did not go in.

"Get in," the stranger said more forcefully.

Gardner lifted his leg and stepped into the cage. He ducked his head and dipped his body through the opening. The five-foot cell did not allow standing, so Gardner sat and hugged his knees. The stranger strolled casually over and closed the door. The stranger used a key tied to a rope around his neck to lock the door. Gardner noticed a second key on the lanyard. Was that Randal's key?

Once the stranger had secured Gardner's lock and stepped away, Randal stopped thrashing and lay still. Gardner reached through the bars separating the two and latched onto Randal's pant leg. He pulled Randal toward him. At first, Gardner thought Randal was unconscious, but his eyes were open and alert. He appeared paralyzed. Gardner gripped his hand and held it tightly, wanting Randal to know he was not alone.

The stranger used the second key to open Randal's cage. He deftly lifted the dead woman from the cell and hauled her into the center of the room. He produced a half-moon sword from a weapon stand, and he used it to decapitate the corpse. He exited the basement draping the body over his shoulder and the head dangling from his hand by its hair.

The mysterious woman with the white fish belly eyes stepped toward the cage, seemed to look down at Gardner, then she turned and followed the stranger up the stairs. When Gardner was alone in the basement with Randal, the vampire started to move. Gardner did what he could to help Randal to sit up.

The floor of the cages consisted of super-soft rubber. Gardner's six-foot frame could not stand, but he could lie flat comfortably. He experimented with different positions inside the cell to see how he could lie most comfortably. The straw scratched his skin.

"I'm sorry," Randal said. "This is my fault."

"It's not your fault. You had nothing to do with those maniacs catching you," Gardner assured him.

"It's my fault. I should never have left."

"No, you shouldn't have left. I missed you terribly. But this is still not your fault."

"You're here because of me."

"Stop it. Alex is on her way to get the others. Mom and Dad and Antony: they will know what to do. Once they get here, they will settle this, I promise. I haven't told you the adventure we had while you were gone. We took on a pack of werewolves and won. These two amateurs have nothing on us."

"They shouldn't come. Antony, your mom, and your dad are the final pieces of the trap."

"I'd like to see them trap my mother when she can see things coming from a mile away," Gardner said. But then he thought of the mysterious woman who can block powers. Gardner remembered his mother saying Randal had fallen off her radar completely. Suddenly he wasn't so sure his mother could see this

240

trap coming. He had no intention of letting Randal know these doubts, however.

Gardner moved closer to the bars that separated the two halves of the cage so he could touch Randal.

"I've been holding out on you," he said as he studied the back of Randal's hand.

"How do you mean?"

"I have abilities like my mother. I can read minds."

"Oh? What am I thinking?" Randal asked.

Gardner tried to read Randal's mind but could hear nothing. It was that woman. She was blocking his ability.

"I can't right now. That woman seems to control the abilities of others. But I could. You'll have to believe me."

Randal nodded. "I do."

Randal laid his head against the bars, and Gardner stroked his hair. "You used to do this for me when I was trying to sleep," Gardner said. "Do you remember?"

"Yes," Randal said.

And then Randal told Gardner the reason for leaving the group. Gardner listened to his story without interruption.

Chapter Forty-Eight

After Alex parted from Gardner with a hug and wishes of good luck, she tried not to worry about Gardner but knowing he was walking into a trap and she could do nothing to prevent it caused her severe anxiety. She knew that returning to Philadelphia and getting the support of Maggie and the others as soon as possible was his only hope. She walked to the parking garage where they had left the car. Alex hit the unlock button on the key's fob, and the parking lights flashed rhythmically in tandem with the eerie echoing beep-beep of the car's horn responding to her command. Gone were the days of fumbling with keys as the young heroine, stalked by the evil force, drops the keys as the shadow looms ever closer. The damsel in distress wasn't Alex's style anyway.

Alex dropped into the bucket seat of the car and closed the door. She jabbed the key into the ignition and twisted.

Click-click-click.

No juice.

She tried again, and the clicking just became a low whine. Alex sat back and sighed. She had no idea how to work on cars but was pretty good at thinking on her feet. Gardner had given her the gold card. She would rent a car to get her back to Maggie and the others.

She reached into the back seat for her bag and pulled it into her lap. She climbed out of the car, locked the doors, and started back toward the hotel lobby. She didn't get far before the figure came up from behind and wrapped an arm around her neck. Alex quickly reached up to put a hand between her throat and her attacker's arm, preventing the limb from crushing her windpipe. Alex squirmed, but whoever grabbed her would not let go.

"I ought to kill you right here and now for what you did to my eye," came the familiar female voice. "But he wants you alive."

"Rose—" Alex managed to choke out the one word.

A second hand came up with a cloth folded in the palm. This hand clamped over Alex's mouth and forced her to breathe in a sickly-sweet-smelling odor. After two or three inhalations, Alex's eyes rolled back in her head, and she sagged in Rose's arms. Rose dragged the semiconscious Alex back to the Mustang and collected the keys from Alex's pocket. After slumping Alex's limp form against the car and opening the doors, Rose folded Alex into the back seat and then flicked the release hatch on the engine's hood.

"Disconnected the alternator," Rose explained to Alex as the girl moaned and rolled in the back seat.

Rose slammed the hood into place and climbed into the driver's seat. She turned the key and the car hummed to life. She then left the garage and headed north to the lair of her new master and commander.

Chapter Forty-Nine

Maggie couldn't stop thinking about the vision she had had when Gardner and Alex departed. In the dream, she saw a strange man and woman standing in the road as the kids drove toward these strangers. The woman raised her hand and stopped the car with her power. The vehicle lifted from the ground and slowly floated toward the strange couple. As the car drew closer to the woman, it began to shrink in size. By the time the car reached her, it was small enough to fit in her palm. The woman closed her hand around the tiny car and placed it in the front pocket of her green dress. Maggie watched as a small figure wriggled out of the dress and dropped to the ground unseen.

She did not see who had gotten away, only that someone will come back to her, and someone was a victim. It broke her heart, but she hoped it would be Gardner who would return. She held no ill will toward Alex, but she needed her son to come back. That wasn't to say she wouldn't do everything she could to get Alex back. No, they wouldn't abandon her like that.

She hadn't mentioned this vision to David. She wasn't sure if she should. She had let him go even though the image had occurred before he had left the property. Something told her she had to let this play out. Something told her if she had tried to stop this vision from coming true, the consequences would have been even more devastating. She let him go because if she had not, these strangers would kill Randal. She believed that to be true, just as she felt one of the kids would not be returning from this excursion. She also knew no vision would have convinced Gardner to back away from his plan to save Randal.

"What's on your mind?" David asked her, and she jumped at the sound of his voice. "Are you okay?"

"I'm fine," she said.

"You don't look fine. You look preoccupied, and might I say, worried? Why do you look worried, Maggie? Where is Gardner?" She could hear the accusation in his voice.

"I had to let him go," she said. "He's gone in search of Randal."

David sighed. "I knew he would do that. I just wish he had waited until we all could go. We all want Randal back, after all."

"I'm sorry. It's my fault. Let our son go. Alex, too."

"It's not your fault," David said. "You wouldn't have been able to stop him. He'll find Randal and be home in a few days. Everything will be as it should be soon."

"There's more," Maggie said. "Randal isn't just lost. Some unseen force has taken him."

"What are you talking about?" David took a seat. "Who is this unseen force?"

Tears burned in Maggie's eyes. "I had a vision. One will return to us. The other will be held captive with Randal. I fear they are pawns in a trap. I don't know who set this trap. I only know we are the real targets. My guess is Alex will return to us, and Gardner is their prisoner."

"What can we do? How do we fix this? Tell me what you know."

Maggie explained her vision, telling him her interpretation of the image. He listened to her calmly. When she finished talking, she was near to sobbing. He leaned closer to her and wiped the moisture from her eyes.

"You did the right thing," David said. "We will figure this out and get them all back. The couple in your vision: did you recognize them at all?"

"No," she said. "I did see that this male stranger was a vampire, and I think she is a sorceress. She didn't shrink the car, but she did trap them. I don't know who they are or why they are after the kids, but I'm sure Randal is the bait."

"Do you think they took Randal from the start?"

"No. Randal left of his own free will. Whatever happened to him happened after her left. I just hope he's okay."

"How do you know the stranger didn't take him from here?"

Maggie collected her thoughts and told David what she had told Gardner about the Bath Salt Vigilante. She told him of her theory that Randal had left because he was worried about how the group would react to his mess.

"Poor kid," David said. "I hope Gardner can find him before anything happens. What can we do to help them?"

Maggie sighed. "We wait to see where this vision leads us."

Chapter Fifty

Gardner felt sick at the sight of how Randal suffered. It had been three nights since Randal had been allowed to feed. That victim had been a young boy. Randal had stroked the boy's hair, assuring the boy he would not suffer. As hard as it was for Gardner to watch that, watching as Randal starved felt much worse. Every night Randal awoke from the death sleep writhing in agony. He had suffered from tremors and muscle spasms. Now Randal lay there, barely moving. His skin looked shrink-wrapped over his bones. His eyes were sunken marbles rolling around in a sea of pain. Gardner tried to soothe Randal's agony, but nothing Gardner said could ease the small vampire's suffering.

The man came and removed the dead boy, but blood stains from Randal's clumsy efforts remained. Randal crawled slowly to the small dark spot and licked at the dried blood.

Gardner cried tears of frustration and rage as he watched his dear friend suffer in such horrible agony. Gardner worried about Randal's fragile mind. Was this destroying who he was? Who he is? Was there anything left of the Uncle Rand he loved and missed so much? His mind raced with thoughts of escape, but nothing seemed feasible. If the blind witch would leave, he could transform and force his way out of the basement. But, although only the stranger came into the cellar, the blind witch was still there somewhere, blocking his ability to transform. The milky-eyed woman stopped his powers since the day Gardner had entered this hell. He had been trying every day to get the wolf to come, but his efforts proved useless. His ability to read minds was gone as well. Hearing others' thoughts had been as easy as flexing a muscle, but now that muscle was as lifeless as a sleeping vampire.

Gardner glanced into the adjacent cell at the skeletal being that had once been Randal. The vampire gave up trying to divine any nourishment from the bloodstain and slowly crawled toward the back of the cage. Gardner caught the haunted look in the vampire's eyes as he used whatever last bit of strength he had to crawl to the rear. At one point, those sunken orbs passed over Gardner's face, and there was no look of recognition in his eyes.

Gardner shuttered at the thought that Randal saw him as just another object in the room. Maybe he even saw Gardner as part of the thing that was causing his pain.

When Randal reached his destination, he collapsed against the bars and slid to the floor. Gardner was relieved when Randal closed his eyes.

At first, Gardner just needed to count the times Randal woke from death sleep to keep track of the days, but lately, the vampire barely moved, and Gardner had no way of knowing if he had passed into sleep or was just incapable of moving.

Gardner knew that he had spent at least five days in his cell, and he had diligently stayed awake watching over Randal with a constant vigil. But now, his endurance was waning, and his eyes tried to close. He may even have dozed off when the sound from the basement entrance caused him to wake up. Stairs creaked as someone approached.

Please bring Randal someone to feed on.

Gardner peered into the dim lighting, letting his eyes adjust until he could make out the stranger standing there. He was alone; no victim for Randal trailed him.

"It's time for a little test," said the stranger.

"What kind of test?" Gardner asked. His voice cracked, and it struck him suddenly that he had been going without food or water about as long as Randal had been without blood. His vision swam in and out of focus. Gardner searched for a second guest, but no one came forward. Gardner turned his attention back to the stranger.

"You will know soon enough," the stranger said when he saw that he had Gardner's attention once again.

"Will you please let Randal feed," Gardner begged.

"That's part of the test. I will let your friend feed. I will also give you water if you want it. Do you want it?"

"I'll drink after Randal does," Gardner said.

"Very well then." The stranger turned toward the stairs: "Bring her down, please." He turned back and watched Gardner with a smile etched across his handsome face. Gardner suddenly felt fear creep through the bars and grip him by the throat.

247

Gardner forced his eyes to focus on the shadowy movement near the stairs. He watched in horror as Randal's latest victim came into view.

Alex.

She seemed unchanged, but she looked haggard, and someone had tied her hands behind her back. Gardner saw red-rimmed and bloodshot eyes filled with tears as if she had been crying a long time.

Gardner turned his gaze to Randal. She didn't have a chance against the blood-starved vampire in the cell next to him.

As the captor forcibly shoved Alex into the cage with Randal, Gardner realized who escorted her. He met Rose's one eye, and he pleaded with her. "Please, Rose, don't do this."

Rose smiled and shoved Alex inside the cage, removed the gag on Alex's mouth even as Alex struggled. After Rose cut zip ties on Alex's wrists, she locked the cage door and stepped back.

Randal became invigorated by the smell of new blood and moved with renewed strength. The vampire's eyes opened, and his lips peeled back, exposing fangs. Alex cried but made no effort to protect herself from the approaching vampire. Her eyes grew wide and filled with terror as she watched the hungry, tortured creature crawl toward her. She cringed when the hand, as cold and hard as a chicken claw, touched her leg.

"Remember," Alex whispered to Gardner. "I would rather be dead. Please make sure they destroy me after."

"Randal, listen to me. Listen to my voice. It's Gardner, you know me, buddy. Listen to me. You cannot drink from her. It's Alex, and she's my friend, so you cannot drink her blood. Do you hear me? You can't take her." Gardner's voice boomed, firm and healthy but filled with hurt. How could he expect Randal to choose Alex over his ravenous hunger? His voice cracked. "Randal, please."

Randal gave no indication he heard or cared about what Gardner said. Gardner desperately reached through the bars and barely managed to catch a piece of Randal's pant leg. He wound the fabric around his finger and pulled the pant leg into his fist. Once he had a firm grip, Gardner pulled with all his strength and dragged Randal away from Alex. The skeletal figure grunted when his prey came free from his fingers. Gardner pulled him to the bars that separated the two halves of the cage and wrapped an arm around Randal's neck. Randal raged against the arm pinning him. He wailed, sounding so much like an agonized, wounded, and frightened animal that Gardner's heart sank.

But then the wail turned bitter and angry. Randal growled and latched onto Gardner's wrist. He tore a ragged gash into the soft flesh.

Randal drank. He sucked and sucked at the flowing blood. Gardner watched as Randal's flesh returned to its original shape like air blowing into a deflated tire. Randal continued to drink. He drank until he had had more than he could hold. Gardner tried to pull his arm away from Randal's teeth, but his strength had left him. Gardner stopped struggling and let his friend finish drinking from him. Randal dropped the arm. Gardner collapsed against the bars, exhausted. Within seconds Gardner's wrist wound healed.

"Gardner," Randal muttered, realizing now what he had done. He reached through the bars and clutched Gardner's shirt.

"I'll be...okay..." Gardner panted as if he had just run a marathon. He closed his eyes, but Randal shook him awake.

"What have I done?" Randal asked.

"You did what you had to," Gardner said in a barely audible whisper.

"Is that fair?" Rose asked the stranger. "I don't think that's fair."

"It is what it is," the stranger said tiredly. "It's all part of the test."

"But I wanted the little vampire to kill the dumb girl."

Randal ignored the voices outside the cage. He tried to keep Gardner from falling asleep. He was afraid that if Gardner went to sleep, he would never wake up again.

"I have to sleep," Gardner said as he slid to the floor. "Let me sleep now."

Gardner closed his eyes. Randal fell back. He stared at Gardner, watching the rise and fall of his friend's chest as he breathed. Gardner's breathed shallowly, but he lived. Randal sighed, relieved. After a moment, Gardner started to snore.

Randal turned to Alex. He looked at her with shameful eyes. He wanted to say something to her—apologize or something—but

249

no words came. Randal turned away from her and continued watching Gardner sleep.

"Thank you," she said eventually.

"Thank him," Randal said and crawled to the back of the cage.

***

Rose huffed, stomped her foot, and stormed away, disappointed. The stranger smiled. The events in the cage did not go as expected, but still, the outcome pleased him. He had expected the vampire to kill the girl. He had been hoping to see how the vampire-werewolf alliance would have fared if that had happened. Vampires drinking from Werewolves? That was a new one to the stranger. Now he would see how well the werewolf regenerated. And there were many more tests planned. He would see how long the werewolf could feed the vampire. If he could survive more feedings, he would have Eva force the change on the young wolf. In wolf coat, the werewolf was not a viable food source for the little vampire.

And what about the girl?

I'll leave her in there for now, but I have other uses for her. The stranger's worried that Rose would kill the girl before he could figure out how to use her next.

***

Randal watched the vampire stranger leave the basement then stared at Alex. She tried not to meet his disturbing gaze. But she turned to him watch him with frightened rabbit eyes every time Randal moved.

"I'm not going to hurt you," Randal said. "When I need to drink again, I'll take it from Gardner. I'm not the one you need to worry about anymore."

He searched the cage, scrutinized the bars, looking for a weakness.

"What are you doing?" she asked.

250

"We have to get you out of here," Randal said. "You are useless to that vampire now. He will probably kill you or leave you to that red-haired girl. If we don't get you out of here, you'll die."

Alex helped him attempt to pry the bars apart. They weren't moving.

"It's no use," he said. "We don't have the right leverage. We need a tool of some kind. I felt a rush of power drinking Gardner's blood, but it's still not enough." Thinking of Gardner made Randal glance over to see that he was still okay. Still sleeping, even snoring. He was fine. But could he regenerate fast enough to prevent Randal from suffering from hunger again?

He could either kill Gardner slowly or kill Alex unintentionally. Were there no other choices?

Gardner woke just before morning when Randal had about a half-hour before the death sleep would take him.

"I was right," Randal said as Gardner rubbed the sleep from his eyes.

"About what?" Gardner asked.

"I told you werewolf blood is probably the worst tasting thing I've ever had."

Gardner laughed.

"How do you feel?" Randal asked with concern deepening his voice.

"I feel better, almost finished regenerating. We can do this."

"I don't feel good about it. Even if you feel strong enough to let me drink from you again, what's not to say I'm slowly siphoning the blood out of you. What if, eventually, you reach a point where I kill you."

"Don't drink so much the next time, pig," Gardner said.

"I'm serious," Randal said with an authoritative tone.

"Look, right now, we don't have a choice. Our situation is what it is until something else presents itself."

"Like what?"

Gardner didn't have an answer, and Randal slipped into the death sleep before he could come up with something.

***

Gardner watched Randal fall into a vampire's slumber. Having seen it happen so many times before, it wasn't as scary as Randal watching Gardner pass out from lack of blood. But the death sleep did signify the coming of a new day and the survival of another night.

Alex crawled to Gardner, and they hugged.

"What is there to do all day?" Alex asked. "Apparently, all the excitement happens at night."

"Now we wait and hope they come to give us food and water," Gardner said.

At midday, someone did come with food and water. It was the blind witch, Eva. She placed the rations inside the bars and stepped back. She seemed to be studying them with her stone-cold opaque eyes.

Gardner noticed him first, and he stopped with his bit of bread mid-bite. Alex saw Gardner's confused expression, and she turned to look as well.

She almost gasped, but she kept the sound in her throat.

"What is it?" the witch asked.

The two in the cage turned back to the witch.

"What is what?" Gardner asked and finished chewing his bread.

"You see something that I cannot. Tell me what it is.

"There's nothing to see," Gardner said.

Eva turned to the left and right. "I sense that something is in the room, but it is not visible in my mind's eye." She reached out but was able to touch nothing.

After she darted up the stairs, Gardner dared to look at that which the blind woman could not see. Alex stared, too.

Timidly, the corpse boy stepped into the light.

Chapter Fifty-One

Randal woke at dusk and looked around. Alex was still there in the cell with him. Gardner was already leaning through the bars with his wrist exposed. Randal rolled his eyes.

"Let me wrap my head around this first, why don't you?" Randal crawled through the straw to the bars where Gardner's two wrists jutted out at him. He squatted down and took the left wrist in both his hands. Randal opened his mouth and pulled back his lips, exposing his fangs. Just before touching the skin, he turned to Gardner. "Are you sure you're okay?"

Gardner nodded.

Randal resumed his approach. Just before biting down, he muttered: "disgusting."

Gardner did not feel as weak this time and did not pass out. He leaned against the bars feeling light-headed but not tired. He wasn't sure, but he believed blood regenerated faster than he had the last time. Their new plan was going to work. Gardner smiled dreamily, which Randal took as feebleness. He moved quickly to catch Gardner if he fell.

"I'm okay," Gardner said.

Gardner felt no ill effects from losing so much blood. He could *feel* the blood filling up inside him as his cells regenerated exponentially. He recovered in minutes. It was another half hour after that when all hell broke loose.

***

The stranger entered the basement at vampire speed. He opened the cage and pulled Alex free, then relocked the cage and handed the lanyard with the cells' keys to the blind woman as she approached.

"Where are you taking her?" Gardner asked as he pushed himself tightly against the bars. "Leave her alone."

"Her time here is over. I have other uses for her," the stranger said as he examined her slender neck.

Alex went rigid in his grasp and refused to cry.

"Why do you want to die, child?" the blind woman said.

253

Alex looked at her, startled. Alex then looked at Gardner. "She read my mind."

Gardner stared fixedly at the woman and her milky white orbs. The woman smiled.

"Yes," the woman said in her raspy voice. "That gift no longer belongs to you. I control it now." She turned and headed for the exit.

The stranger took Alex from the basement. Randal and Gardner raged at the bars.

Alex stumbled up the steps. Occasionally the stranger nudged her to make her continue. She entered the reception area and stared around at the cobweb-infested room, with its old-fashioned furniture covered with heavy sheets that had turned gray with age. Above her, the cathedral ceilings loomed with ornate wooden carvings. Heavy drapes, dusty and torn, adorned the four floor-to-ceiling windows.

Once she had grown accustomed to the enormity of the room, she glanced around for Rose. Somehow, she thought it would be the ginger wolf leading her toward death.

The stranger said nothing as he led Alex from the mansion and directed her to get into the Mustang. She climbed into the driver's seat, and the stranger took the passenger side. She stared over at the stranger waiting for him to provide her with some direction. He sat quietly. He didn't even look at her. Alex turned to the ignition and saw that the fob in its slot. She turned the key, and the engine started. She didn't know where she was taking the stranger. He would have to tell her something now.

"Just drive," he said. "I'll let you know if you're going the right way or not."

Alex shifted the car into drive and pulled away from the house.

Chapter Fifty-Two

Corpse boy walked through the dark and dusty halls of the mansion as silent as a ghost. He knew every inch of this house and could move unseen from room to room. He walked past the red-haired girl's room and heard her complaining about the dust, the smell, and the comfort level. He laughed at her when she cringed away from a spider crawling out from under her dresser. He considered rushing in there and rescuing her from the spider by eating it.

He didn't. He continued to the room at the end of the hallway, a room bigger and more ornately designed than any other in the house. The blind woman had taken this room as hers. He liked toying with her because, for some reason, she could see others but not him. Corpse Boy made this woman crazy, and he enjoyed watching her try to figure out who and what he was. But making the blind witch crazy was not the goal this time. He had another reason for entering the room.

The woman was there. She glided across the room on slipper-clad feet that barely seemed to touch the floor. She stood in the center of the room as he entered. She tilted her head slightly as if listening. She then lifted her face, sniffing the air. She knew he was there, but that was okay.

Corpse Boy crept through the room, making no sound. "Who is there?" she asked. She reached out to him, but Corpse Boy stepped back. He quietly skirted past her and hurried to the wall where the two keys dangled from their assigned hook. Corpse Boy carefully removed the lanyard by gripping it in his palm and muffling any noise the keys might make by hitting together. Then he deftly removed the leather strap from the hook.

The woman moved toward him, and he had to back away. She reached out for him again. She seemed to have a rudimentary sense of where he was, but not his actual location.

Corpse Boy attempted to dart past her, but she blocked his path to the door.

"Rose," said the blind woman. "Rose, come here, girl."

The corpse boy glanced frantically at the door.

Corpse Boy squatted and brushed past the woman, causing her to turn and reach out to him. She missed.

Corpse Boy glanced into the hall. The red-haired girl was not there, so he slipped down the hall and hid just out of sight.

Moments later, Rose entered the room. "Did you just call me like a dog, woman?" Rose asked angrily.

"Who is in the room with us?" Eva asked, ignoring Rose's complaint.

"No one," Rose stated flatly.

"Do you smell something? Is there something rotting and putrid here with us?" Eva asked.

The whole place smells rotten," Rose said.

The woman turned red. "You are a bold little child. My breath? I'll have your other eye — and your tongue — if you insult me again in such a manner."

Chapter Fifty-Three

Corpse Boy entered the basement slowly. He crept up to the cages and showed the captives inside the keys.

"Who are you?" Gardner asked.

Instead of answering, Corpse Boy used the first key to open the vampire's cage.

Randal climbed out and studied Corpse boy. "The Dark Father created you, didn't he?"

Corpse boy nodded.

"Do you have the other key?" Gardner asked.

Corpse Boy nodded and reached down for the lock. Before he could use the key to open Gardner's cage, the door at the top of the stairs opened. Corpse Boy heard the sound of footsteps on the stairs. The key slipped from his grip, and as he reached down to pick it up, the red-haired girl came to the bottom step.

"What the bloody hell is this?" Rose rushed at Corpse boy, but he managed to slip away. Gardner and Rose lunged for the key simultaneously, but Rose got to it first and snatched it away.

Randal hesitated, but when Rose looked at him, he gave Gardner one last glance.

"I'll be fine," Gardner said. "Go and get help. I'll be okay. Go."

Randal disappeared in a crackling wind.

Corpse Boy pulled himself into the shadows where the red-haired girl couldn't see him.

"No matter," Rose said. "The boss didn't want the little freak anyway. You are the main prize, and I think he'll reward me for keeping you from escaping."

"Whatever you're all planning, you won't get away with it, Rose. We slaughtered your entire pack. Do you genuinely think we won't do the same to you three?"

Gardner rattled his cage, and Rose flinched. Gardner laughed.

Rose shrugged. "Maybe you will, maybe not. The pack didn't have the witch to help them. Now we do. She'll decimate your meager group."

"You forget, Rose. My mother is a witch, too. Who do you think is more powerful?"

Rose and Gardner stared at each other for a time. Then the girl answered.

"I'm betting on the blind bitch."

Chapter Fifty-Four

Alex stopped the Mustang when the vampire told her to stop. She looked at where they had stopped and then looked at the stranger seated next to her. She waited for him to direct her. Her heart thundered in her chest. He didn't speak; he simply handed her an envelope and continued to stare blankly out the windshield. She waited another few seconds and then opened the door.

"Give that to Antony," he said as she started to get out.

"I will," she said. There was a flavor of anger in her words because the stranger told her several times what he wanted her to do. She understood and didn't need reminding. She closed the door to the Mustang and glanced across the street at the Lansdowne house. When she looked back at the mustang, she found it empty.

She crossed the street and mounted the steps to the front porch. A floorboard creaked under her feet. She reached for the doorknob, but the door opened before she could touch it, and Maggie burst from the open door. She hugged Alex with tears streaming in torrents from her eyes. Instead of hugging Maggie back, she dropped into the woman's arms, sobbing. Maggie helped her into the house.

David helped the shivering and exhausted girl into a chair. He had questions—lots of them—but he refrained from asking them right away.

"He's safe for now," she said. David wondered if she had acquired Gardner's ability to read minds. "A vampire is holding Gardner and Randal, assisted by a gifted blind woman with the ability to dampen abilities, and—" She lifted her head to meet Maggie's gaze. "Rose is there, too."

David glanced at Maggie. "Rose?"

"Who is this strange vampire?" Antony asked.

Alex shook her head, defeated. "I don't know, and he wouldn't identify himself."

Maggie said: "This woman with the gift to 'dampen' abilities: explain this to me," Maggie said.

"She could control Gardner's abilities, stifle them. She took away his ability to read minds, as well as his ability to transform."

"Do you know where he's keeping the boys?" Maggie asked.

"And why did he let you go?" David asked.

"I can answer both of those questions with the same answer." Alex pulled the envelope out of her pocket and handed it to Antony. He took it from her and ripped it open. Antony glanced down at the paper briefly and then crumpled it up. He let the paper drop to the floor.

The air in the room crackled as if someone had ignited a string of firecrackers. As Antony exited the house in a burst of speed, David realized he had gone and followed him. Maggie had a vision of where they were going, and in the image, she saw the vampire who was holding her son captive.

She noted that his black aura pulsated, just as Minerva's brown aura had pulsated. She pondered the two auras' meaning and wondered how many more she would see in the coming days.

Chapter Fifty-Five

The parking lot of the nursing home was alive with activity. The night sparkled red and blue from the line of emergency vehicles and police cruisers, forming a perimeter of safety for evacuated staff, patients, and other onlookers. Some people cried as others spoke in excited gasps. Still, others stumbled about, numb and confused. Antony and David brushed past all of them. They forced their way past protesting officials and entered the building.

Antony led David to the fifth floor, taking the stairs at vampire speed, to where Grace resided. The first corpse they came across was an orderly, drained of blood and not yet decapitated. They took note of him but left him where he was and continued.

The next victim was the aide Antony knew from previous visits. She had chosen not to or had not been able to get Grace's name right. She lay sprawled against the wall, drained and also still bearing her head.

Antony stopped when they entered the main living area, where the residents congregated to play games and watch television or visit. David stood next to him. At the other end of the room, the two newcomers observed a slumped figure with his back to them.

The stranger stood and turned, still clutching his prize in his arms. Blood dripped from his smiling lips. "It's so good to see you again, my long-lost friend," the vampire said. David glanced at Antony and knew that this vampire was no stranger. Antony knew him and knew him well.

The vampire let Grace's corpse drop from his arms and roll like a life-sized doll to the floor.

"Looks like you have a dilemma," the vampire said. "You can come after me, or you can clean up this mess I left for you. Just like old times, eh?"

Then the vampire crashing through the window and into the night. Antony did not follow. He directed David to dispose of the two corpses in the hallway as he walked slowly and deliberately over to Grace's corpse.

David took off the head of the aide and the orderly and then returned to the lounge. Antony kneeled over the body of the elderly woman, touching her pallid face lovingly. Then, as if the corpse had meant nothing to him, Antony removed his dagger and took off Grace's head.

"We'll leave the bodies here so the grieving families will have closure," Antony said flatly.

"Who was that?" David asked.

"David." Red tears glistened in Antony's eyes. "That was my previous sire, Bane."

David gulped. "I thought he was dead?"

Antony closed his eyes. "As did I."

Epilogue

After returning to the house, Antony informed the others that the authorities would probably figure out they were involved. Cameras at the nursing home would have observed Antony entering the crime scene. They would eventually trace him back to the house on Lansdowne Drive. "We must go," he said. He owned other homes, but they, too, were not safe. He would find them a safe place to reside, but their stay in Philadelphia was over.

Maggie packed a bag and then helped Alex gather her few belongings. She and Alex then met David and Antony in the living room. David had gassed up the Mustang and pulled it up to the front door with the trunk open. They took only essential belongings. They could probably return for more later, but first, they needed to find Gardner. Alex did not know the mansion where the stranger kept them prisoner had been the same place Maggie described as the place where Dylan died, but she was confident she could find it again.

Maggie opened the door to lead everyone out to the Mustang. Instead of stepping out into the night, she stepped aside and allowed Randal into the house.

"We're not all going to fit in the Mustang," Randal said.

Maggie dropped to her knees and hugged him. Hugged him tightly and cried. He hugged her back.

"I'm sorry for going away. I've messed everything up."

"You didn't do anything," Antony said.

"How did you escape?" Alex asked. "Where is—?" She looked past Randal to the darkness outside.

"Gardner couldn't get away; we came here to help you get him out."

"We?" David said.

Corpse Boy stepped around the doorframe into the house's lighted interior. He moved slowly, cautiously, and waved to the group gathered around him, staring at him.

"You," David said with a broad smile. "I remember you. You helped us destroy that vampire."

Corpse Boy pulled himself up as straight as he could and nodded vigorously.

"Great," David said. "Welcome to the group."

265

David glanced around, doing a headcount.

"We need the Zephyr right about now," he said.

"The Caravan will be fine. Take the Mustang back and retrieve that," Antony said.

They arrived at the mansion and found it completely abandoned. Maggie and Alex raced to the basement to find Gardner, but the cages were empty. When they returned to the front room, David stood with a piece of paper in his hand. Maggie took it from him and read it. Alex took it from her when Maggie looked as though she might drop it.

Alex read it. It said: *Find us if you can.*

Maggie clapped her hands together. The sound echoed through the massive room like a gunshot. "Look around you," she said. When everyone had looked around but was still unsure of what they were looking for, she clarified. "Get cleaning. This place is going to be our home until I get my son back."

Thank you for reading book two of the Immortal trilogy. The story concludes in Immortal Conquest.

Excerpt from Immortal Conquest

The tall man with the slicked-back hair adjusted his black leather jacket and pushed the gun shop door open, causing a bell to jingle somewhere. He stepped through the threshold and moved slowly through the store, glancing at displays lined up on both sides of the central aisle. He made a mental note of the different types of guns presented in many different positions throughout the exhibitions. The man was not interested in buying any of them. The tall stranger turned his attention to the last two customers the man behind the counter was assisting. The gun shop was nearing its closing time, and the tall man was excited to get his business here out of the way.

When the young men talking to the proprietor stepped away from the counter and headed for the exit, the proprietor followed them.

"I'll be right with you, sir," the proprietor said to the tall man with the leather jacket. "Let me see these fine young men out, and I'll be right back."

"Take your time," the man in the leather jacket said.

Abruptly, the tall man with the slicked-back hair and leather jacket grabbed the taller of the two customers by the shoulder and pulled him back. The strange tall man spun the younger man until they were face to face. The tall man held him in place and peered into his eyes.

"Hey, man. Leave me alone. What's your problem?" The young man scowled.

The tall man stared deeply—intensely—into the other man's eyes before letting him go with a look of satisfaction on his face as if he had seen in that man's eyes what he had wanted to see. The young man muttered unintelligibly. "Fag," he said after giving the tall man a look of disgust mingled with a slight touch of fear and then continued on his way to the exit.

The proprietor glanced at the tall stranger warily. *Is this one going to be a trouble-maker?* He thought this but said nothing. Thugs like this one had robbed him too many times, and that had made him more jumpy than cautious.

When the two customers were on their way down the street, the proprietor locked the door and turned back to the man with the leather jacket. "Is there something I can help you with?" the proprietor asked. "I'm closing, and you're the last customer of the day."

The proprietor walked back to the counter and stood on the other side, not liking the idea of being so close to this stranger without something like the counter (or even better would be some bulletproof glass) between them.

The stranger stepped up to the counter, stared at the store owner with a look of mild interest, and then reached into his leather jacket. The stranger reached into his coat and held up the gun that had been in the lining. He studied the gun for a moment, turning it at different angles, and then set it down on the counter.

The proprietor stared down at the gun as though he had no idea what it was. He was afraid to touch it or look away from it.

The weapon was a Glock 17c third-generation semi-automatic pistol. It was very familiar to the proprietor because it had been displayed in his store only a month ago.

"I...I d...don't b...buy guns here." His nervous stutter caused his head to shake as he spoke. "I only sell."

The stranger pulled out another gun and laid it next to the Glock. He pulled out another and then a fourth. The proprietor stared at all four guns, knowing beyond a shadow of a doubt they had once adorned his store.

"Do you know what these guns have in common?" the stranger in the leather jacket asked calmly. The proprietor's vision swam, and he had to grip the counter to keep from falling over.

"They were all sold by me?" he asked as if he didn't know if that was the correct answer. Tears streamed down his face.

"That is correct, but that's not the answer I was looking for." The stranger smiled, but instead of feeling comforted, the proprietor's knees buckled. He caught himself before he hit the floor. The stranger gave the store owner a moment to compose himself.

When the proprietor had locked his legs securely underneath him, the stranger continued. The stranger pointed to the Glock.

"This one killed a little girl walking home from the park with her brother," he said.

Then he pointed to the next gun.

"This gun killed a liquor store owner in a hold-up. Said owner never returned home to his family.

"This one was used by two in a bank robbery in which people lost their lives, and this one on the end here, this one, I saved for last. This last gun you sold to a man who had just lost custody of his kids in a messy divorce. He used it to kill his ex-wife and two children."

The proprietor leaned over the counter, using it for support. His hands clasped together as if praying, and he cried openly now.

"They were legal sales," he said defensively. "They were all legal sales. I have no control over who uses the guns once they leave here. I am clean of these murders." He said this as if he were attempting to convince himself of the fact. The stranger did not seem in the least persuaded of his innocence, however.

The store owner collected himself, stopped crying, and straightened out.

"You should be going after the men who committed these crimes, not me," he said sternly.

The stranger smiled, and the store owner noticed the gleaming fangs. The momentary resolve the store owner had managed to build up collapsed like a house of cards when he saw the man's eyes turn from bright blue to fiery red.

"I have already dealt with them. Last night I took the drive-by shooter and his driver. Then I killed the liquor store attacker. Earlier this morning, I killed the bank robber — who unfortunately had already killed his partner. As for the distraught husband…" The stranger trailed off. He looked around the store and then back at the store owner. "I took him so recently that I'm still feeling the flush from his blood washing over me.

"But the dead bank robber left me one victim short. I needed one more infusion to complete my nightly feeding. Then I got the idea of going after the man who sold all these guns to those killers. As far as I'm concerned, you might as well have pulled those triggers yourself."

"No." The proprietor shook his head violently.

But the vampire was through talking. In an instant, he held the proprietor by the collar, pulling him toward his open mouth, toward those gleaming fangs. The proprietor winced, closing his eyes and waiting for his imminent death.

The vampire had not yet broken the skin when the sound of shattering glass drew his attention away from the food source. There was a moment of confusion when the food was falling away from him rather than toward him. As the vampire's mind cleared, he saw that there was now a third person in the store. It was another vampire.

"This is not right," the second vampire said. "This man was only running a business and had no hand in the deaths you described. You have the right idea, and I commend you on your previous selections, but this one does not fit the code."

The vampire in the leather jacket was furious. Who was this bloodsucker to interfere with his third transfusion?

"He is guilty of —"

"He is guilty of bad judgment, that is all." The second vampire pulled the taller man away from the counter by the shoulder.

"But..." The vampire in the leather jacket hesitated and was interrupted by a loud blast. When he looked down, he saw that his leather jacket was in tatters, and a nine-inch red hole had appeared in the center of his chest.

The second vampire rushed to the store owner, yanked the shotgun from his grasp, and threw it across the room.

"This was my favorite jacket," the leather-clad vampire said. "Can I kill him now?"

The store owner turned pale.

"No." The second vampire removed his hand from the other's jacket. Then he turned to the store owner and said: "You must scrutinize your customers more carefully, be more selective. If you do not improve your customer base, my new friend here will return, and I will not stop him the next time." The vampire placed his index finger on the store owner's forehead and pushed. The store owner fell and landed with a loud thump flat on his back. He was out cold.

The second vampire turned back to the other, who continued to examine the leather jacket's damage. The hole in his chest had already begun to heal. He shoved his fingers through the holes, wiggled them for effect. "I loved this jacket," he said.

"We will find you a new one. And I have prey for you. What is your name?"

"I'm Jarod," said the vampire. "And I'm hungry." This last came with childlike innocence, but the words carried an ominous warning.

"My name is Antony Grayson, and I am happy to meet you. Come with me, Jarod, and never again worry where you will get your next meal."